WELCOME TO
THE
HAMILTON

A HOTEL HAMILTON NOVEL

TANYA E WILLIAMS

For Justin,
"Family is not an important thing. It's everything."
~ Michael J. Fox

CHAPTER 1

*N*ewbury Apartment Building
Vancouver, BC, Canada
Saturday, May 7, 1927

I lie awake in the early morning hour, the view through the bedroom curtains still far removed from the day's promise of illumination. The rhythmic breaths emerging from my older sister's slumber keep time like a grandfather clock. In our small shared bedroom, Louisa's bed is a short arm's length away from mine. A sigh slips past my lips. Another night's sleep lost to restlessness and worry.

The apartment door's lock clicks, drawing my attention before the hinges yawn in response to being opened then closed. I hold my breath and listen, imagining Father shuffling through the compact kitchen and bumping down the narrow hall toward his bedroom.

I slide my legs from under the covers and place my feet on the cool, hard floor. After ensuring Louisa is still asleep, I tiptoe from the room, gently pulling the bedroom door closed behind me. I slip into the hall like a shadow and feel the corners of my mouth curve downward. A sad state envelops me as my eyes, already adjusted to the darkness, take in his defeated silhouette.

"Come, Papa. I'll help you." My voice is low and soft, but it startles him all the same. He's either too lost in his own thoughts or too liquored to implore even a basic level of awareness.

"Clara, girl, I didn't mean to wake you." Papa's downcast eyes do little to hide his embarrassment at needing help from his youngest daughter.

A plain expression accompanies my honest words. "You didn't, Papa. I was already awake."

He seems to consider this for a moment before leaning against the wall for support. "I imagine the market won't be open for several more hours." Papa pats his jacket pocket with his free hand. "But don't you worry yourself one bit. I've got your market money, safe and sound."

Stepping forward, I hook his arm over my shoulders and guide him toward the light of the bedside lamp in his bedroom. "Thank you. I will put it away for safekeeping."

Arm in arm, we shimmy through the narrow bedroom door before I release his six-foot, two-inch frame onto the edge of the bed. A shame, I think to myself as an image of the man he used to be flits through my memory. I kneel to untie his shoes.

"Your mother used to be able to untie my double knots. Just like you, Clara. You remind me so much of her." Papa exhales an alcohol-laced breath that no amount of ducking can save me from. "Just like you, Clara."

"Yes. I remember," I whisper, rising to stand as his chin droops to his chest in what I assume is regret, drunken or otherwise. Taking advantage of his brief steadied position, I walk around the bed, drawing the curtains closed before pulling the top quilt back from the pillow.

"Let's get you out of your jacket." My words remain slow and calming. "There you go. Now the other arm."

I place the jacket at the foot of his bed before guiding his feet and legs under the quilt. I support his head as he lowers it to the pillow. A deep sigh releases from his lips as his body relaxes into the soft bedding. "There you are. Are you comfortable now?"

A faint "mm-hmm" is his only response.

"Okay then. Sleep well, Papa." I turn off the lamp and slide the jacket from the bed. His deep, steady breath is an unspoken comfort as I soundlessly close the bedroom door.

As I walk with muffled steps toward the kitchen, my head swivels away from the smoke-infused jacket. I hope it airs out before the scent permeates every soft surface in our little apartment.

I retrieve a wooden hanger from the entryway closet and ease open the sole kitchen window before hanging the offensive jacket on the curtain rod, hoping it will catch the cool morning breeze. The fresh air from last night's rain is a welcome relief from the stale smell of tobacco, and I wonder how a man who hasn't smoked a cigarette in the seventeen years of my life comes home reeking of the stuff.

I envision the establishment he frequents as a cavernous room filled with low tables and solemn men, lost in their own thoughts, unable to see one another through a haze of smoke. Having never ventured into such a place myself, I let my imagination fill in the gaps of what I suspect is a dismal display. I could blame British Columbia's repeal of prohibition five years ago for Papa's frequent outings. But in my heart, I know his grief over losing Mama leads to both his overconsumption and our shrinking grocery funds.

Remembering the market money Papa mentioned, I search the jacket's pockets. The weekly grocery allowance has been dwindling these past few months. Each week brings a little less money, which has more than once arrived in my hands far later than the agreed upon day of Monday. Stretching the allotment for seven days is one thing, but this week I've made do for thirteen. Not knowing when or if another infusion of funds will arrive is the primary cause of my growing unease and frequent sleepless nights.

Papa's slim wallet is buried in its usual place within a deep outer pocket. I wrap my fingers around the smooth folded leather and tug. A jagged piece of paper bites at my skin, and my hand retreats in response to the sting. My fingers lose their grip, the wallet falling to the deepest part of the pocket.

I hold my hand toward the dim light from the window, searching for the source of pain. "Ow," I mutter as the cool air hits the invisible injury. "How can something so small cause such pain?" I suck on the paper-cut finger to soothe its discomfort and then flip the light switch. Muted light creates a shadowy glow. Turning my attention back to the jacket, I retrieve Papa's wallet and place it on the counter. Then I reach into the pocket once more. Peering into the dark opening, I grasp an envelope and lift it to the light. The hastily torn edges coax me to investigate the envelope's contents. Though I know I should respect Papa's privacy, I have too many questions running through my mind.

On the back of the envelope, a logo stamped in the top left-hand corner is familiar but not fully remembered in my sleep-deprived state. A quick glance over my shoulder confirms the bedrooms are quiet and filled with slumber. Sliding my fingers into the open envelope, I extract a single sheet and unfold the stationery, flattening it against the kitchen counter.

The red ink stamped at the top of the page in large bold letters floods my body with trepidation. The words *FINAL NOTICE* bring a hand to my open mouth while my eyes dart across the typed words.

DEAR MR. WILSON,

This is to inform you of the amount outstanding for rent on apartment number 3D at The Newbury apartment building.

This is your third and final notice. If payment for the rent in arrears is not received by May 31, 1927, you will be evicted.

Please remit your past due payments immediately to the building manager, Mr. Ralph Watkins.

Sincerely,

Robert J. Mitchell

Management for The Newbury

I STUMBLE TOWARD THE KITCHEN TABLE, BARELY PULLING A chair back fast enough before sinking into its wooden frame with a thud. The room spins, forcing my head into my hands. "But we've only just arrived. Surely Papa can't be behind on the rent this soon." My voice wavers as I attempt to talk sense into a situation I am now forced to see. I count on my fingers. "Four months. It has taken me the better part of four months to make this hovel of an apartment feel like a home Mama would have been proud of, and now . . ." My head shakes defiantly with the knowledge of this new reality. "Now, we may have nowhere to go."

A strangled groan forces its way past my lips as I accept the dismal feeling that life could quickly become much worse. "Oh, Mama, whatever am I going to do?" I say her name out loud, as if summoning her spirit will set us straight again.

Missing Mama is a constant state of existence for each of us, though Papa, Louisa, and I express our grief differently. Five years after her passing, her presence remains in all that I do. She is the reason I put every effort into keeping our house a home. Though I am the youngest in the family, she taught me to cook, clean, and mend. Mama taught me how best to live my life.

I gather my strength, along with the eviction notice, stand, and travel the few steps to the kitchen. After returning the letter to its envelope and then to the jacket's pocket, I open Papa's wallet and count the coins he has left for the weekly shopping. "Coins," I say with a frown. "Paper money seems in short supply in the Wilson household. No wonder he is late with the rent."

CHAPTER 2

*S*aturday, May 7, 1927
The crowd moves as one at the corner of
Georgia and Howe, in front of the roped-off Hotel
Georgia. Anticipation radiates from the group like a cloud
of noxious fumes. The fanfare of the hotel's opening, set to
include more than two hundred of the city's most
distinguished guests, is scheduled for later this evening and
is the reason, I assume, for the frenzied gathering.

With their claims staked, the throng pays no heed to
their surroundings, spilling over the recently added sidewalk
and into a lane of afternoon traffic. I crane my neck from
the opposite side of the street, searching for an alternate
route so I can skirt the commotion. My heels lift as I inch
upward on tiptoe, an unladylike dampness dotting my
upper lip in apprehension. My annoyance at having
forgotten today is The Hotel Georgia's opening gala event
has me muttering scolding words under my breath.

The twitter on the street, in the shops, and plastered on
the front pages of this week's newspapers should have

reminded me to avoid the block where the hotel stands. Alas, I find myself jockeying for a position to cross the street to the other side of the hotel's entrance. Foresight must have eluded me this morning when I chose the location to meet Louisa upon the completion of our individual errands. Having trekked several blocks further than usual, hoping to extend the grocery money at a market on the outskirts of the city, my patience is marred by exhaustion. Checking my wristwatch, I note my tardiness.

Newspapermen with their oversized flashbulbs mingle at the edges of the crowd, cigarettes dangling from barely closed lips. Even the courthouse lawns across the street from the hotel's grand entrance are littered with curious onlookers. Seeing no other solution, I grit my teeth and move forward with the throng. The image of a twig being snapped in two dashes across my mind as I enter the fray of the excited crowd and am swept into the wave of people, no longer able to determine my own destination.

The mob of onlookers concentrates on nothing except maintaining their position within the fervent crowd. They jostle my slight frame back and forth like a rag doll tossed between a group of children. A muted yelp emerges from my throat as I tumble off the curb and into the lanes of traffic.

I duck my head to dodge flailing arms and, in a flash of recognition, see the chaos for what it is: the physical manifestation of my internal struggle to keep my head above water these past several months. Like a fish swimming against the current, I clutch the small paper bag of groceries to my chest with one hand and cover my head with the other, my pocketbook gripped between white-knuckled fingers atop my cloche hat.

A motorized jitney horn trumpets behind me, startling

me into a stilted and short-lived sprint. With nowhere to turn, I dodge a man on a bicycle and dive back into the crush. Concentration burns into my back as I strain to steady every step while advancing through the crowd. Fresh concrete, a mere three weeks old, is barely visible between the brown polished oxfords and the blue and red heeled shoes. Body odour permeates the space and mixes with perfume more expensive than anything I've ever known, causing my stomach to churn.

Spotting a break in the swarm, I angle myself low and weave forward. I am careful not to step on the toes within a navy brocade T-strap, its wearer hoisted onto tiptoes and wobbling unsteadily with excitement. Snaking my way toward fresh air and freedom, the jumble of well-dressed spectators mingles with that of newspaper corner boys, shopkeepers, and residents. The usual separation in class and social standing, though a polite subtlety on the surface, creates an undercurrent like the electric tram that travels through the city.

A trickle of sweat slides down the side of my face, highlighting my dishevelled presence among the city's upper crust. Desperate for stability in physical and societal standing, my survival instinct pushes me forward. As I regain my balance, Mama's remembered voice cuts through the noise, as clear as glass. *Everyone is on the outside of something, at one time or another.* Her words, originally intended to console a small child left out of play, have today reminded me that all of those in this crowded gathering, eager for a glimpse, have found themselves on the outside, desperate to get in.

Mama's ability to put my struggles into perspective was one of her greatest traits. I snatch a glance inside the elaborate hotel's glass doors while I skirt the fringe of the crowd. A wide red ribbon stretches across the lobby, just beyond the closed doors. My gaze shifts to the line of staff, with smiles as white and wide as the snow-capped North Shore Mountains. They prepare to welcome guests and the city into what is being touted as the most state-of-the-art hotel Vancouver has ever seen.

Though the afternoon sky holds no breeze, my face rejoices at the feeling of fresh air as I step free from the throng. Out of sorts and exhausted, I stop at the edge of the hotel's smooth stone exterior. The bag of groceries slips from my arms as I check the time. Brushing sweat-soaked hair from my forehead, I scan the many faces in the crowd, searching for Louisa.

Standing almost a full head above the gentlemen in the crowd, Louisa waves to me. Her face is aglow with excitement. I marvel at her ability to find enthusiasm in a moment where I've located only discontent.

HOME AND BEDRAGGLED FROM THE AFTERNOON'S EVENTS, I put the groceries away before taking a moment to wash my face with a cool cloth. Needing words of comfort, I reach behind the breadbox for Mama's recipe book and flip through its pages until I find what I seek: her parting words to me, written in her delicate hand.

Despite the strength the cancer stole from her, she was graceful and stoic until the final breath left her lips. Over the past four months, I have moved my treasured letter more times than I can count. I hid it beneath my pillow and then in the clothes cupboard I share with Louisa. After it was nearly discovered, I decided the one place Louisa would never look was in the cookbook. Should she ever take an interest in a domestic task, I will rethink the letter's hiding spot. Until then, the letter is quite safe in our kitchen.

Seldom does an opportunity to read Mama's letter in full present itself in our close quarters. My eyes follow the curves of her handwriting, searching for the wisdom my heart so desperately craves.

TAKE CARE OF YOUR SISTER, CLARA. I WOULD NOT ASK THIS OF you if I did not believe you were capable of such a task. She may be the eldest in terms of age, albeit by months rather than years, but she is a fragile soul, my love, and you were born with both feet planted firmly on the ground. Your resourcefulness will serve you well in all things, Clara. This I am certain of. Believe in yourself and let your heart guide you.

 All my love,
 Mother

MY FINGER TRACES HER WORDS. THROUGH TEAR-BLURRED eyes, the word "resourcefulness" leaps from the page. A solution to all of our problems is forming, and I know what I must do. I pluck the few remaining coins from my pocketbook, slide on my sweater, and stuff my feet into shoes. I slip out the apartment door and down the three flights of stairs without a word.

The idea has been percolating in the quiet of my mind for the past month and a half, but today's tardy distribution of market money combined with the awareness that employment suitable for a girl like me was available in the city ignited a spark within me. As I ducked through the crowd outside the hotel, the staff caught my attention. They didn't appear to be much older than my seventeen years. Given their age, I surmised they must not be any more experienced than I am, either.

Since Papa has neglected to register me for classes after our relocation into the city, I have contemplated finding summer employment, if only to help fund Louisa's theatre classes. She clearly misses them desperately, as she hasn't stopped moping.

The newsstand on the corner isn't much to look at. It's a mere step up from a derelict shack, but today, it has exactly what I am looking for: the Saturday paper.

With the paper tucked under my arm, I return to the apartment and make a cup of weak tea by reconstituting yesterday's steeped and re-dried leaves. Settling myself at the table, I open the paper and flip pages in search of the Help Wanted section. Bold letters and a quarter-page ad catch my attention.

THE HOTEL HAMILTON IS LOOKING FOR YOU!

Seeking capable and pleasant kitchen staff, bellboys, and maids. Located in the heart of the city, our new stately hotel will outshine the others with its upscale design and attention to detail.

I CAN HARDLY CONTAIN MY EXCITEMENT. NEVER WOULD I have guessed another hotel was due to open so soon after the fanfare at The Hotel Georgia. I read the brief description, noting the time and location. Given this morning's discovery of the eviction notice, a job in a stately hotel could be the answer to all of our worries. I feel my cheeks lift, a slight smile gracing my lips as I imagine myself in the working world, wearing a uniform and earning a way out of our money troubles.

I have always thought I would obtain further education. Mama never shied away from telling me how clever I was, giving me the confidence to learn new things. She championed all of my and Louisa's efforts, no matter how insignificant they might have seemed. She seemed able to summon a book on any topic we dared show an inclination toward, passing on her love of books and libraries to us both. If I had to guess, I would say Mama's support of Louisa's drive for theatre life still fuels my sister, even after so much time without Mama's words of encouragement.

My finger traces the face of my wristwatch, the one Papa gave Mama the last Christmas we shared together. Upon opening the gift, her surprise was evident as her emotions battled with her frugal nature. The love she felt at being given such a gift edged out the concern over the money required to purchase it. A few weeks before her passing, she pressed the watch into my palm, telling me all time was precious. *Both the good and the challenging, Clara. Promise me you will look for the beauty in each day. The smallest moments are often the ones that make up a life well lived.*

I dab at the tear threatening to fall and contemplate what Mama would do. My finger taps the edge of my teacup as I consider the options. Apprehensive or not, Mama asked me to take care of this family, and that is what I must do. Papa is out of time. It is now up to me to ensure our family is safe. Mama said my resourcefulness would serve me well. I have to believe she knew what she was talking about.

I scan the announcement for further details, delighted to learn the hotel will open by the end of June. That is good news for someone who is seeking paid employment as soon as possible. I bite my lip, a nervous bubble rising in my chest as I think ahead to my next steps. I take another sip of tea. The advert said to come at two o'clock on Monday. I stow my wary thoughts and decide The Hotel Hamilton is exactly where I plan to be Monday afternoon.

CHAPTER 3

*M*onday, May 9, 1927

A quick glance at my wristwatch tells me it is one thirty-five. A flush of nervous energy warms me as the thought of what I am about to do runs like an electric charge down the length of my spine. I stare at my reflection in the hall mirror, tucking my cropped brunette hair underneath my nicest cloche hat. My hair is far from Louisa's exotic soft curls yet miles away from being straight, a continuously unruly mess I seldom bother to tame. I contemplate asking Louisa for help, but without a convincing reason, I am left to my own devices.

My palms smooth the front of my Sunday dress, the hemline and design a few years out of season, but tidy all the same. Precisely what a responsible girl would wear when seeking employment, I think as I catch Louisa inspecting me questioningly in the mirror's reflection. Flipping through a magazine while reclining on the sofa, Louisa's posture remains relaxed while her stare narrows in suspicion, propelling me to stop fiddling with the limp sailor knot at my dress's neckline and hurry myself along before my all too clever sister gives voice to the questions simmering behind her eyes.

A trip to the market is the cover story for my afternoon outing. The story itself is not untrue, I've convinced myself, but guilt still wraps around my words like the tangled string in a misplayed game of cat's cradle. I do plan to visit the market with the infusion of coins Papa produced earlier this morning, Saturday's grocery purchase barely filling the cupboards. The market just happens to be an additional stop on the way home, after I tend to the real reason for my absence from the apartment. I spot the frown forming on my reflected image. With only a few coins transferred into my pocketbook, the shopping list is meagre yet again.

Sensing my deviation from the truth has not been as readily believed as I hoped, I hustle myself out the door, grabbing my jacket and pocketbook without another word. My feet grace the treads lightly as I descend the stairs, bolstered by my determination and purpose. As I step onto the sidewalk, the sun is bright, cheering me on my way.

Checking my watch again, I contemplate taking the streetcar but decide to avoid both the additional cost and the crush of people. Turning my attention toward my destination, I opt for a brisk walk to the hotel. A warm breeze sneaks between rows of buildings as I cross the street. The crisp ocean air travels from the water's edge all the way through the city, bringing with it a freshness and rebirth after the long, dark, rainy winter days. Springtime in Vancouver always delights, never failing to make me feel as if all things are possible, and today I cling to that notion with every fibre of my being.

The sidewalks are busy this afternoon. I manoeuvre through streams of businessmen in suits and hats, coming or going at a clipped pace, the seriousness of their day etched into the lines on their faces. I try to picture Papa in a crisp suit with an air of importance about him, but the image sweeps by me as quickly as the businessmen do. The thought of Papa brings a smile to my lips. He is meant for outdoor work. If only he could overcome his grief long enough to find solid footing in the gardens he so dearly loves to tend. The gardens at the Murray estate were his favourite. For years they provided him immense joy along with an income and a home for our family. Though the details regarding the termination of his role as head groundskeeper remain unclear, I am certain his entanglement with alcohol has something to do with it. My steps quicken. I must secure a position at The Hotel Hamilton. With a steady income and the resulting alleviation of stresses, perhaps Papa will quit the drink, return to us, and be the father he was before Mama passed. Yes, a job at the hotel is the answer to all of my worries.

Tumbling through my mind, Papa's arrival home in the wee hours a few days ago troubles me. I am uncertain enough of his reaction to the idea of me working to keep my endeavour a secret. Mama always cautioned me to make up my own mind first and then go about informing others of my intentions. She said that was the only way to ensure I would be ready to stand behind that which I believed in. *Don't dig your heels in unless you are willing to be buried up to your knees in muck. If you are willing, then stand strong. If you are not, then there is no reason to cause a fuss.*

There is no point in initiating either a delighted or displeased reaction from Papa until I have secured employment and am positioned on firmer ground. If I am being honest, I am more than a little concerned about whether he will be pleased or ready to scold me for pursuing employment without his knowledge. Under normal circumstances, my worry over his reaction would have already halted me. With the eviction from our home looming, the possibility of Papa's displeasure doesn't feel nearly as critical.

A mother clasping her small child's hand strides purposefully several paces ahead of me, catching my attention when the little girl drops her doll to the sidewalk. Her mother, unaware of the fallen doll, tugs her along. The little girl's face contorts with panic. I dash forward, snatching the doll from the sidewalk before catching the mother's attention with a tap on her shoulder.

Bending at the waist, I return the girl's doll with a smile and a pat on the head. I wave goodbye and peek over my shoulder so as not to step in someone else's path. A woman, whose form at first glance appears familiar, catches my eye. She turns into a shop's darkened alcove before I can gain a better view, but something about her reminds me of Louisa. With time dwindling until the two o'clock hour, I dismiss the thought. Louisa is most likely still in her nightclothes, lounging on the sofa as she was when I left the apartment. I turn my attention back to the street. Looking both ways for traffic, I cross over, another block closer to my destination.

The Hotel Georgia stands tall and proud on the corner. Thankfully, the sidewalk is less of an obstacle course than it was during last Saturday's gamut. Walking with a brisk stride, I am eager to arrive with a few moments to spare before the appointed time. I manage a sideways glance past the glass revolving doors of the new hotel before crossing Georgia and Howe Streets.

The immense stature of The Hotel Vancouver on the opposite corner is the reason I was unaware of the new Hotel Hamilton. The new hotel has been lost within the other's shadow during its construction. The Hotel Vancouver's looming structure is both tall and wide and, in my opinion, a tad unwelcoming. But then again, I remind myself, those in my social class are not the intended guests of the great Canadian Pacific Railway-owned hotel.

The Hotel Hamilton's front entrance comes into view as I pass the final bricked corner of The Hotel Vancouver. I inhale slowly, sucking air past my teeth as I observe the deep blue awning embossed with the hotel's name in gold. Plush red carpet covers the four stairs leading to wide glass doors trimmed in gold, as if they expect royalty to arrive at any moment. Understated but elegant is my first impression of the hotel, and I nod in approval.

Pulling myself away from the welcoming entrance, I make my way past the hotel's cornerstones to the far less opulent back entrance. I take another deep breath to steady my nerves, then reach for the handle and pull on the heavy door.

"This doesn't look like the market." Louisa's voice spins me around so fast that dizziness sets in with a rush.

A smug *I caught you* expression lines her lips. Louisa taps a toe impatiently and crosses her arms haughtily over her chest. She has found me out, and every muscle in my body is on high alert. My sister is unlikely to let this go.

"What are you doing here?" I force my best impression of indignation. "Are you following me?"

Amusement sparkles in her wide brown eyes as her housedress and spring jacket billow in the light, back-alley breeze. "I think perhaps you are the one who needs to do some explaining, Clara."

"This has nothing to do with you," I say, my nerve crumbling more by the second. "Just go home, Lou."

"Come on, Clara. You've never been able to hide

anything from me. You couldn't lie to save your own life." Louisa cocks her head as her eyes scan the height of the building. "This place doesn't even look finished yet. What could you possibly want with it?"

My mind fills with unkind words, desperate to be unleashed on Louisa. Backed into this corner, resentment of her ability to always get precisely what she desires bubbles within me. A lifetime with my sister has taught me that few things stand in Louisa's way. Her ability to turn on the charm and bulldoze her way through life is a trait I both covet and despise. Her bold nature unsettles me, especially when paired with the importance of my acquiring a position at this hotel. Louisa's involvement is sure to ruin my chances of becoming employed, not to mention forcing me to burden her with our family's precarious financial situation. I simply don't have the luxury of allowing that to happen. I force a stern stare while my brain searches for a solution.

"Is it a boy?" Louisa asks, a mischievous grin melting her pretend displeasure like ice cream on a hot summer day. "I thought so. You were acting all strange, fussing with your hair and dress. I knew straight away you were not heading to the market. What choice did I have but to follow you? Don't you see, Clara, I had to know what you were up to. So, tell me. He will of course want to meet me."

I am unsure whether her words stem from her God-given status of older sister or pure self-serving stubbornness. "Not everything revolves around you, Louisa." I will the sting of my words to at least scratch the surface of her awareness.

"Who is he?" Louisa, undaunted by my clear displeasure, presses on. "You won't be able to keep this a secret for long, so you might as well tell me."

My lips twist in contemplation as my mind chases every option available to me. And then defeat sets in. Louisa is unlikely to yield so easily, and the minutes are ticking by with speed. Lifting my wrist, I check the time again and let out a huff. "If you must know, I am not meeting a boy."

Louisa's delight vanishes, replaced by a perplexed expression.

"The building isn't open yet either. I am here to apply for a job." I turn my back to her, hoping to indicate a close to our conversation.

"Well now, aren't you full of surprises?" Louisa's delight lifts again, with a touch of playfulness.

"Let me be, Louisa. Just let me be." Down to my last option, I plead with Louisa and wonder how she will ever see me as anything but her little sister. "This is something I need to do. I will feel more settled, more in control, if I can only . . ." My words trail off.

Reaching out a hand, Louisa squeezes my shoulder, her expression subdued. "If there is anyone who should worry about being more settled, it is Papa. Not you." Her voice lightens, shrugging off what I interpret as disapproval toward our father and once again donning her magical cape of effervescence. "Maybe you should try to let loose a little. Have more fun."

I feel myself turning inward, like a turtle retreating into its shell to protect its soft and exposed underbelly.

"I know. Why don't we apply together? That would be fun." Louisa's enthusiasm shifts into full speed with the idea.

The frown I deliver does little to stall her forward momentum. "Come on, Clara. It will give us both something to do. Who would ever have thought living in the city would be so dull?"

I incline my head to the side, the thought of two wages causing me to pause before regaining my senses. "I am applying for a maid's position. Lou, you haven't even made your own bed in months." I deliver my words with more of a scoff than I intend and see the hurt settle across her face, clear as morning light. My regret is immediate.

Cringing at my own words, I soften my delivery. "I think it would be better if you went home, Louisa." I straighten my posture and meet her eyes. "We can talk about this later. Right now, I have somewhere to be." My backbone reinserted, I am once more about to pull on the door handle when a stern-looking woman emerges, eyeing us both with the scrutiny of a microscope.

"In or out, ladies? We will begin momentarily, and I need to lock this door." She stands to the side of the door, holding it open.

I seize the opportunity and turn to Louisa, whispering through clenched teeth. "Go home, Lou. I will see you there." Stepping past the woman, I offer a polite smile and enter the darkened entrance alone, leaving Louisa with no other option but to return home. My eyes adjust to the darkness as I move through the entranceway, and I hesitate a moment, making certain Louisa has not accompanied me.

I follow the posted signs down a hallway. A door is propped open at the end of the corridor, guiding my steps with a subdued stream of light. The cavernous hall feels as if it might go on forever. The unadorned walls and dimly lit interior might feel spooky without the aroma from a fresh coat of paint.

Midway down the hall, I look over my shoulder once more. The sight of the empty hall helps settle my nerves. Louisa has apparently heeded my wishes and returned home. A first, I think to myself before continuing down the hallway. I take a left turn, then a right, and finally the long corridor ends with another propped-open door. Stepping onto plush carpet deep enough to sink into, my eyes wash over the dark wood-panelled walls. The smell of fresh paint is replaced by that of wood polish, the panels gleaming under strategically placed wall sconces. Understanding dawns on me. The drab hall is a passageway for employees, while the stunning, expansive space before me is the only view guests will see.

The chatter of young women spills past a set of wide-open double doors, guiding me toward an oversized banquet room. I catch my breath as I see hundreds of women, all waiting for the opportunity to apply for a maid's position at the hotel. My heart feels as though it has broken free from my chest and landed near my feet. I didn't realize a maid's position would be so sought after. This being my first experience with applying for a job, I hadn't thought to consider how many others would also seek employment at the hotel.

My foot catches on the thick carpet between the hall and the banquet room, causing me to stumble forward a little. I steady myself and do my best to hide my surprise and my gaped open mouth. My eyes search the room. A few empty chairs remain. I look for a spot where I will cause the least possible disturbance to those already seated.

My gaze lifts to the ceiling. The banquet room is impressive, with an intricately painted textured motif. Several sparkling chandeliers cast light and shadows around the room, adding a touch of elegance and artistic design to the ceiling and walls. Like toy soldiers, rows of chairs form a line facing the front of the room and the small, elevated stage.

Reminding myself to breathe, I hold my pocketbook tighter to my body as I make my way toward an empty chair near the back of the room. I offer a polite smile as an apology, and I sit beside a young woman, neat in her attire, with a swipe of colour on her lips. My own lips are dry and chapped. I admonish myself for not thinking of applying a bit of rouge or lipstick.

Aiming to calm my nervous energy, I remind myself of the reason for my presence here today: to secure employment as a maid and, along with it, a steady income. This is what my family needs to remain in our home and keep food on our table. This is what Papa needs to stop the drink and return to us. I all but pinch these realities into my being as I hold tight to my midsection, tumbling nerves swirling within my stomach.

The buzzing of anxious voices echoes through the room, rising by the minute and undermining my hopes as the clock ticks closer to two. I check my wristwatch and release a slow breath, convincing myself that I can do this. I will succeed. When I do, everything in my life will simply fall into place. This, I am certain of.

CHAPTER 4

*M*onday, May 9, 1927

After we've been waiting in the banquet room for several more minutes, the stern-looking woman I encountered at the back door brushes up the centre aisle, past the rows of chairs. The swish of her calf-length suit skirt moves with a cadence that commands attention and respect. As she steps onto the raised platform, her straight-backed posture and scrutinizing stare silences the chatter, and all eyes turn to her. "Welcome to The Hotel Hamilton," she says with a confident air before introducing herself as the hotel's matron, Ms. Thompson.

Movement to my right catches my attention, begging me to sneak a glimpse behind me. I feel my eyes widen in disbelief as Louisa slides her tall, delicate frame into a seat in the back row, across the aisle from me. She must have come in with Ms. Thompson. Snapping my head forward in a hurry, my mouth grows dry while my palms perspire. A suffocating clamminess takes over, leaving me uncomfortable in my skin.

An impossible situation this is. I covet a true sisterly relationship with Louisa but her desire to push in where she hasn't been invited unsettles me to the core. I suppose I could seek employment elsewhere, but this opportunity within the hotel is right here, and the need for additional household income is imminent. My mind spins with the dilemma of wanting a kinship with Lou while ensuring our family's basic needs are met. I have no option but to choose our family's well-being over everything else, including my desire to be wrapped within the fold of Louisa's affections.

Thoughts of my sister's presence quickly sour my mood. Everything Louisa is—confident, beautiful, daring, carefree, and impulsive—threatens me in this moment. She has always been the girl who seems capable of having it all. Only I know the truth, and nobody would believe me if I ever uttered a word, which of course, I would never do. A weighted sigh escapes my lips. Whether it is a dress in a shop window or a new friend, Louisa picks out anything I show interest in before moving forward to claim it as her own. Challenging or not, Louisa is my sister, and with that bond, sisters must stick together, come what may. At least that is the idea Mama did her best to instill in me.

The familiar sense of defeat tips my chin toward my chest. My downcast eyes take in my small pale hands, mottled and trembling. Louisa's mere presence here may very well eliminate my own chance at being awarded a maid's position. Through the years, I have learned that Louisa not only prefers coming out ahead in any given situation but almost requires it to sustain herself. Sometimes it feels as though winning is as essential to her as air. She could secure a maid's position, taking it right out from under me, only to decide shortly thereafter that the job isn't for her.

I am unsure whether her desire to shine the brightest among a crowd or her deeply camouflaged insecurities propel her to be recognized. Even if we were both granted positions at the hotel, I am wary of the tightrope I may have to navigate to ensure Louisa doesn't ruin things for me. I cringe at my selfish and ill-mannered thoughts about my sister, but with our family's stability on the line, I am not comfortable leaving my endeavour's success to Louisa's unpredictable whims.

A trickle of sweat meanders the length of my spine and pools. I angle a hand discreetly between the chair and my body, brushing the moisture collecting at the back of my floral print dress. I am attempting to ease the tickle of apprehension coursing through me when the young woman seated next to me leans in and nudges my shoulder. She inclines her head in Louisa's direction and whispers, "You would think if someone really wanted a job, they would be a little more inclined to show up on time. Wouldn't you, now?"

I offer a weak smile, aware of how my association with Louisa and her tardy entrance has already cast an unflattering light in another's eyes. I shift uncomfortably in my seat before returning my attention to Ms. Thompson's commanding voice. As the hotel's matron delivers a brief description of Hamilton maids' duties, my thoughts shift gears. The stranger's words have ignited thoughts of the family bond I share with Lou. My sister isn't a bad person. She is impulsive, yes, but that nature has frequently led to memorable and laugh-out-loud moments together.

My cheeks lift as a smile steals some of my anger toward Louisa. She did say we should apply for the maid's positions together. I admonish myself for allowing my fear to get in the way of my relationship with Louisa. Perhaps another solution exists. I pull my shoulders back and tilt my chin to watch Ms. Thompson from beneath the brim of my hat. I refocus my attention once more, reminding myself that I am here for a reason and that, if I desire a positive outcome, I should certainly pay better attention to the details involved.

Ms. Thompson clasps her hands in front of her as she speaks. Her posture is erect, and her hair is pulled tightly into a headache-inducing bun at the nape of her neck. She isn't old necessarily—I estimate twenty-six—but her take-charge demeanour exudes a feeling of age and wisdom that is both comforting and foreboding.

"Today, our focus will be on completing an application form." Ms. Thompson takes a few steps toward a table, retrieving a stack of papers. "We will go through the form together first, and then you will fill in your personal details."

Stepping from the platform, Ms. Thompson distributes a handful of papers to the young ladies seated near the aisle, each girl taking one before passing the rest along to the others in her row. "The application form is the first step in our hiring process," Ms. Thompson says as she inches toward the rear of the room. "Please take a few moments to read through the questions."

I pass the last application form to the young woman to my left before turning my attention to the questions typed on the page. A bubble of excitement rises within me. My first job application. This is an occasion to stow in my memory, as the moment I took a determined step toward something important. Yes, this is precisely what Mother was referring to when she wrote that my resourcefulness would serve me well.

I think of Mama's other words. *Take care of your sister. She is a fragile soul.* Shame for my ugly thoughts toward Louisa rises like a heat rash up my neck and face. I pivot in my chair to find Louisa's eyes watching me, bright with excitement. Her wide smile is sincere, making it almost impossible to suppress one of my own. She shoots me a little wave, the application form fluttering in her hand, as Ms. Thompson clears her throat, redirecting my attention forward.

"The top half of the application form is fairly self-explanatory." Ms. Thompson reads from her own copy, "Name, address, birthdate, et cetera."

The young woman seated to my left leans toward me. "Silly me, I have forgotten to bring a pencil. Do you suppose they have some on hand for our use?"

I dip my chin to ensure a quiet delivery of my whispered response. "I have one. We can share if there aren't pencils available."

The young woman squeezes my hand in thanks, and I am uplifted once more. Camaraderie among women is a good occurrence. Mama always said that you never know where your next dear friend will come from, so you should be the best version of yourself at all times.

"Further down the page, you will note a space for listing previous employment experience." Ms. Thompson eyes the room, and a few heads nod. "If you have previous experience, please fill out this section as completely as possible, citing previous duties and responsibilities. However, should this be your first employment opportunity outside of the home, we will not penalize you for not having such experience."

Ms. Thompson takes a step closer to the platform's edge. Her features soften into a faint smile as her head inclines. "We here at The Hotel Hamilton believe in the virtue of hard work, and we are quite aware that keeping a home is far from easy. Please do not undervalue your contribution to your family or your community. If you have life experience, you have employment experience."

A sigh of relief rushes past my lips, relaxing my shoulders, which I hadn't noticed were ascending toward my ears. I exchange a smile with the young woman to my left, a kinship forming between us.

Ms. Thompson pivots on the temporary stage. "We will train the most suitable applicants fully. However, I will caution you. If you are looking for easy work, this isn't the job for you. Being a maid in any hotel is demanding." Ms. Thompson pauses while she connects with every face in the room. "Being a Hotel Hamilton maid is much more than just hard work.

"The Hotel Hamilton is about splendor, convenience, courtesy, and understanding. We aim to offer our guests a luxurious environment, a home away from home. We strive to make their stay as unruffled as possible, with the conveniences of a larger hotel in a quaint and cozy environment. Our guests are to be treated with the utmost courtesy, and our employees will strive to anticipate each guest's needs and wishes, understanding them as individuals while treating them like royalty." Ms. Thompson opens her arms wide as if she intends to gather all of the young women within them. "This is a tall order, I realize, but it is one we strive to achieve for each guest who enters The Hamilton. Do not fret, ladies. We believe we can train you to this level of excellence, and once we have, you can proudly call yourself Hotel Hamilton maids."

Sounds of lighthearted remarks and a few clapping hands bounce around the room. My eyes take in the many exuberant faces alight with wide smiles, and I find myself caught up in the moment of excitement. Ms. Thompson's gesturing hands direct our return to quiet.

"Thank you, ladies, for your enthusiasm." Ms. Thompson turns her head, addressing all corners of the banquet room. "We too are excited to showcase the excellence The Hamilton will provide visitors to Vancouver."

Ms. Thompson pauses another moment, I assume waiting for our giddiness to subside. "The hotel manager and I will go through your applications this afternoon and, given the abundant number of you in attendance today, likely most of tomorrow morning as well. We will select our top applicants to be interviewed first. Others who show promise will be interviewed after them."

The room is silent. Her words emphasize the reality of the limited number of employment opportunities. "Once we have completed the interviews, we will decide which of you will move forward into our training program. For training, we expect you to be available Monday through Friday over a two- or three-week period."

Ms. Thompson resumes her short pacing atop the platform. "During the training, you will learn all that is required to be a Hamilton maid." The hotel matron's discerning glance slices through the crowd. "During those weeks, should we find one or all of you to be unsuitable candidates, we will dismiss you immediately from the training program. It is best to think of the training as a trial period, during which you should showcase your absolute best at all times."

My heart feels as if it is being tossed around like a kite on a windy day. The bit of elation I experienced only moments ago has plummeted to the ground. The knowledge that I will leave today without a permanent place of employment held firmly within my grasp, as I so dearly hoped, is one thing. But a two-week training period, should I move forward, is not at all what I envisioned for myself as I read and reread the newspaper advert.

Finding a job may not be as simple as I expected. My head aches and I feel myself tuning out Ms. Thompson's words as I tumble backwards in my mind, flailing as my control over the situation unravels. Images of the eviction notice filter through my mind. It could be weeks before I learn whether I am to be awarded employment at the hotel —weeks which, given the red *FINAL NOTICE* stamped atop the letter, I am certain I do not have.

I am instantly uncomfortable in my seat. The room feels warm, and the mingling of perfumes worn on the necks of far too many women seems smothering. If I do not get a paying job soon, I will not be able to afford the overdue rent. "No, this won't do." The words, muffled under my breath, earn me a questioning look from the young woman to my left.

I imagined returning home this afternoon with good news, a freshly pressed maid's uniform, and a celebratory chicken to roast for dinner. How am I to tell Papa that I don't actually have a job but may have one several weeks from now, if I can prove myself? No, he is sure to put a stop to my working before it's even begun. I convinced myself that he could not argue if I were to arrive home with a job in hand. If he did, I was prepared to battle his words with logic. Now, though, hope seems to be slipping through my fingers like sand.

Ms. Thompson's voice cuts through my panic. "Rest assured, the training will be thorough and we will compensate you for your time. The training wage is slightly lower than a regular maid's weekly salary, but we will value your time and effort as you train for your new position."

Training wage? A light glimmers in the dark tunnel of my thoughts. I may be able to work things out, even with a lower salary. Instinctively, I peek over my shoulder in Lou's direction. She is nodding as she listens to Ms. Thompson. Even in a situation where Louisa certainly did not expect to find herself, she is fitting in, morphing into a delightful and attentive applicant.

Panic, not far from reach, settles within my chest once more. How does she do it? I wonder. Louisa simply falls into step, no matter her surroundings or whether she has an invitation. I look around the room at the sheer volume of competition. Without knowing how many positions are available, my confidence dwindles. I find Louisa to be an easy target for my blame.

Louisa is the complete package. This I've known for years. Capable of lighting up any room she enters while always appearing easygoing and amusing. My worry over Lou's presence has little to do with her charisma, though that could cast her as the preferred choice. Instead, I worry at her inability to recognize when she should back down and let someone else be centre stage, if only for a moment.

Ms. Thompson's words draw my awareness back to the front of the room. Her tone softens as a gentle expression relaxes her features. "Each of you has something special to offer the world. I see it as part of my job as hotel matron to help you nurture that aspect of yourself. Women in British Columbia have been voting for the past ten years, and it is my belief that when we each confidently step into the person we are meant to be, the world becomes a better place."

I sit a little taller in my chair. Ms. Thompson's words

strike a chord within me, as if she has pulled out a piece of my soul I should examine more closely. My motivation to secure employment with The Hotel Hamilton is reignited, and I find myself eager to move forward with the lengthy process, training and all. What began as a solution to a financial challenge may prove to be an answer to more than I imagined. I was right to think The Hamilton would be the place to find the stability I seek.

"If there aren't any questions, you may begin filling in your application forms." Ms. Thompson steps from the platform and positions herself in the front corner of the room, available but unobtrusive.

CHAPTER 5

*M*onday, May 9, 1927

My heart is thrumming in my chest, alighted like a racehorse before the gun at Exhibition Park, eager to fly down the straightaway.

The young woman sitting next to me turns and extends her hand. "I am Jane. Jane Morgan."

"Clara Wilson." I briefly squeeze Jane's slender hand before digging into my pocketbook for the stubby pencil.

"Isn't this exciting?" Without a pencil of her own, Jane waits for mine to become available. Her voice carries a shrill of enthusiasm mixed with what I imagine is a tinge of nerves. Though, upon consideration, I recognize I may be noting my own nerves instead of hers.

My fingers wrap around the slender bit of wood at the bottom of my pocketbook. "Success." I smile at Jane as I lift the pencil into the air.

The pencil has resided in my pocketbook for several weeks. When I noticed the weekly market allowance dwindling, I became an even more careful shopper. I made lists of necessary items and planned our meals days in advance, all the while discovering new ways to stretch both the ingredients and the funds.

I turn my awareness to the application form. Placing my pocketbook on my lap, I arrange the top line of the page on its flat surface. With a gentle hand, careful not to puncture the paper, I print my first and last name in clear block letters. I acknowledge the rush of exhilaration and then nudge it aside with a few deep breaths.

The top section of the form is basic information requiring little thought, so my attention goes toward a steady and neat hand. I doubt they will grade me on the tidiness of my penmanship, but one cannot evaluate that which one cannot read.

Beside me, Jane prattles on with nary a breath between words, thoughts, or sentences. I listen absentmindedly. Living with Louisa has prepared me to maintain focus on a task amid idle chatter.

"When I learned The Hotel Georgia had completed its hiring and I was too late to be considered, I must have moped about the house for days." Jane laughs quietly and waves a hand before adding, "I am desperate for this position."

"Isn't it fortunate that we both saw the advert in time?" I slide the application form up and begin answering questions related to my work experience.

"Oh, yes. Indeed." Jane's shoulders drop as she sighs. I wonder whether she is exasperated with my purposeful approach toward the application form or her own musings. "I hope we will see celebrities here, don't you? I mean, The Hamilton is just around the corner from The Hotel Georgia, after all."

My head swivels toward Jane, a question lining my

expression. I am about to reply with what I deem to be an agreeable answer when Jane, clearly unconcerned about the polite back-and-forth of our conversation, continues her monologue.

"I can see myself now, hair gathered neatly into a bun." Jane presses a hand to the back of her head, pumping her shiny dark curls with a flourish. "Freshly pressed uniform. Polished Oxford tie shoes." She leans in with a wink, nudging me with her shoulder. "Nothing too stylish, but just a hint of design to show my keen sense of fashion."

I smile politely before returning my attention to the last question on the application form: *Why do you wish to be a Hotel Hamilton employee?*

Aside from the obvious and likely unrefined answer that I need a job to help my family pay the rent and put food on our table? Dipping my chin, I concentrate and search for a more suitable response. I turn the question around a few times, letting it tumble through my mind before I see it from an alternate point of view. A pleased expression lifts the corner of my mouth, and I begin writing.

"Anyway." Jane lets out another exasperated sigh, either coming up for air or attempting to hurry me along. "So, what brings you to The Hotel Hamilton on this fine May day, Miss Wilson?" Jane pauses, and a quick glance at her tells me she isn't truly awaiting a response but is once again lost in her own thoughts—thoughts I am happy to let her wade through as I put the finishing touches on my application.

Jane breaks her own silence. "I mean, well, I know why I am here. My life depends on getting this job."

I am midway through rereading my answer to the last question. My head snaps up and my heart lurches. Moisture gathers in my eyes and I tilt my head away from her, not wishing to give away my predicament.

I hand the pencil to Jane, with a stab of knifelike understanding. I struggle against the awareness that I may not be alone in seeking salvation for my family. Here sits another young woman in a similar position. I search Jane's eyes for recognition, but I find them lacking both emotion and concern.

Jane thanks me as she takes the pencil from my hand and sets to work. I respect the silence between us and contemplate how many maid's positions are available. Perhaps we can help one another. There must be opportunities for many of us to succeed, after all.

I let my eyes move about the banquet room, taking in row after row of young ladies with a fresh perspective. I remind myself that I do not know what brought each of them here today. Their hopes, dreams, and needs are mysteries to me. What first overwhelmed me when I entered the room, I now find compassion for.

I swivel my head for a quick look at Louisa. She leans over, focused on the application form. Compassion begins at home, I remind myself, scolding my earlier displeasure with my sister. For all of her high spirits and gaiety, I am well aware of Louisa's deep-rooted insecurities.

Mama did her best to cajole from me an understanding of Louisa, but I must admit, I didn't believe her. Instead, I spent most of our childhood viewing my sister from the perspective of someone her impulsive nature had wounded. The truth of the matter dawned on me only after our move into the city. Being uprooted from the comfort of her life and familiar surroundings, not to mention being separated from friends who perceived her favourably, sank her into a melancholic and subdued state for weeks. Then I understood the depths of what Louisa needs in order to thrive.

What may appear to be a facade is, in truth, the line Louisa follows to ensure she remains on stable ground. It saddens me to know that my sister is compelled to wear a mask, hiding her nature to protect herself. At her core, Louisa is a seeker of joy, avoiding all but the pleasant aspects of life. To many, I am sure, this is a delightful way to live. But it is the polar opposite of my practical nature.

How two sisters, born barely a year apart, can be so different from each other confounds me regularly. We have shared the same parents, experiences, and bedroom for our entire lives. Yet we have little in common. Where I go inward with self-doubt and worry, she projects exuberance and a tendency to grandstand. I care for our family, while she excels at being cared for.

When mother died, I picked up the role of homemaker like I was picking up her well-worn apron, intent on carrying on as she taught me to do. Louisa hid behind her grief and even more elaborate masks. She took on more roles at the theatre, working on every new production like her life depended on it. An uneasy sigh sneaks past my lips. Perhaps it did.

I shake my head to rattle loose my spiralling thoughts. Being a sister is equal to being trapped in a lifelong complicated relationship. Regardless of the world's constant evolution, the rules set in place at birth remain the same throughout life.

Jane looks up from her paper. "Well, that about does it."

"All finished? You must have far more credentials than I if you could jot them down with such speed." I hide my admission behind a bashful smile. Jane beams confidently, handing back my pencil. "Life experience. Isn't that what

Ms. Thompson said was of value?" She shrugs indifferently. "I've plenty of that. Besides, all I can offer are the skills and knowledge I've arrived here with today."

I sit a little straighter in my chair. "You are right, Jane. Ms. Thompson said the training program was quite involved. If we are prepared to work hard, we are certainly more than qualified to become the best maids this hotel will ever see."

Jane takes my hand in hers and squeezes, infusing solidarity between us. "That's the spirit, Clara."

Ms. Thompson stands on the platform once more and claps her hands to gain our attention. "Ladies, I can tell by the chatter that many of you have completed the application forms." The circulating voices grow quiet.

"If you will, please place your application forms in the box at the front of the room." Ms. Thompson points to a shallow box at the edge of the platform. "Should you remain interested in a maid's position at The Hamilton when you wake tomorrow morning, we ask that you reconvene here at two o'clock. Those selected from the applications will be interviewed by myself and the hotel manager."

A hand goes up, and Ms. Thompson indicates for the young woman to speak. "What about the girls who are not chosen for an interview?"

Jane leans over and whispers in my ear. "I do hope there will be positions available to both of us, Clara. Just think, we could become lifelong friends simply because you sat next to me when applying for a job." Jane hesitates slightly. "Of course, even if you don't get a position, we could still be friends."

I am mid-smile when Jane's words stop me, my face contorting from delighted to confused. Ms. Thompson's reply halts my ability to think further on Jane's comment, though it has unsettled me.

"All applicants who do not move forward will be informed tomorrow. We will call out the names of those we wish to interview, and the others will be free to go. At this time, we are looking for fulltime maids for the fifth floor. All other fulltime maid positions have been filled, though we are still sorting out the part-time opportunities." Ms. Thompson attempts to lessen the disappointment by adding, "We will keep the remaining applications on file. Should a position become available, we will notify those applicants immediately."

Ms. Thompson scans the room. "Thank you again for coming, ladies. Please place your application in the box, and I will meet you by the doors to offer you a quick look around the hotel before guiding you out."

The shuffling of chairs and papers raises the volume in the cavernous room. We make our way to the front, Jane linking her arm through mine. I've missed the familiarity of close friends since we moved to The Newbury several months ago, but I can't quite dismiss the niggling suspicion that Jane's intentions may not be as honourable as I originally assumed.

"Ready?" A broad smile spreads across Jane's face as she extends her application toward the box

"Ready," I say, unable to hide my excitement. Together, we place our applications into the box before walking arm in arm down the centre aisle. Our mutual enthusiasm nudges Jane's overconfident demeanour from my thoughts. Certainly, my anxiety must be the root of my unease.

We follow the crowd, sharing our observations about the hotel as Ms. Thompson takes us on a brief tour of the completed sections. The ornate woodwork remains consistent throughout the halls' panelling. Pieces of artwork showing grand estates and elegant countrysides create focal points at the hall's end. Long, slender tables are set neatly into alcoves, their polished surfaces gleaming under tall table lamps.

At my first glimpse into the lobby, I exclaim a little more loudly than I intend, drawing a few amused glances. A two-story ceiling arches high above, making me feel as though I have entered a fairy-tale castle. Large chandeliers trimmed with gold anchor the vast room and watch over us. Plush furnishings and glossy low tables invite guests to relax, while the expansive, dark wood reception area stands ready for inquiries.

Ms. Thompson pauses occasionally to ensure the group is close on her heels, detailing a few items of note as we make our way toward the exit. "You may not be able to tell from within these walls, but the hotel is built in the shape of an H." Ms. Thompson points to the corridors above, outlining the H as she explains the overall layout of the space. Before turning to guide us further, a knowing smile graces her lips. "*H*, of course, is for Hamilton. Mr. Hamilton, the hotel's owner."

Jane and I giggle, chatting animatedly at the thought of having a hotel's shape determined by our last name's first letter. Neither of us think the *W* of Wilson nor the *M* of Morgan would be a suitable option.

We file through a set of double doors into a well-lit hallway. Unadorned and clearly meant for staff use, the hall provides a clear view into the kitchen. With crisp white walls, tiles, and countertops, the expansive kitchen is larger than anything I've ever seen. Even the Murrays' estate kitchen would be a thimble compared to The Hamilton's.

An angular-featured man with a tall white hat is

ushering a young Asian boy through the kitchen door. Members of our group bump into one another as our group's forward movement comes to a standstill. I crane my neck to take in the commotion.

"This is not a soup kitchen. This is a hotel." The flustered man gives the boy a direct push, causing him to stumble slightly as he makes his way through the crush of maid applicants.

I catch the boy's eye as he pockets an apple. He grins cheekily and raises his eyebrows at me before lowering himself closer to the floor to weave toward the back door.

The man from the kitchen pushes past us, politeness foregone in favour of his intention to see the child out. As the back door closes with a thump, he calls out in a heavily accented voice. "This is a hotel. We have nothing for you here!"

I dip my chin to stifle a chuckle. The man retreats to the kitchen and shouts orders at an unfortunate soul beyond the kitchen door.

"Pleasant individual, isn't he?" Jane tilts her head in question, and her hand covers a creeping smile.

Ms. Thompson reaches the end of the hall first and pushes open the heavy door. Sunlight filters into the space and she guides us through, saying farewell and commenting that she will see us tomorrow.

As we step away from the luxury of The Hamilton and into the brightness of the day, the disparity between the young Asian boy seeking a piece of fruit and the hotel's elaborate existence seems to slap me in the face. I need this job, I think to myself, the joy I felt in the hotel leaking from me like rainwater down a gutter. Who knows how close my family is to being turned out onto the street, begging for food—or worse, stealing it?

Jane, who seems to enjoy hearing herself talk, chatters beside me as we walk from the alley toward Howe Street. I am still thinking about the boy, my family, and the eviction notice when we pause near The Hamilton's red-carpeted entrance.

Jane exclaims, her voice rising with glee, "Oh, there is my ride. Got to go. It was so nice meeting you, Clara. See you tomorrow."

My eyes follow Jane as she takes a few hurried steps toward an expensive-looking automobile parked close to the curb near the hotel's entrance. A chauffeur exits the driver's side before dashing around the front of the car. He tips his hat to Jane and pulls on the back door handle, offering her his hand as she slides inside.

Puzzlement morphs into disbelief. My jaw drops as I watch Jane and her upper-class life merge slowly into the busy traffic on Howe Street. "In desperate need of a job, my foot." The words fly from my scowling lips before I can think to reel them in.

My mood shifts like Vancouver weather in springtime, transitioning in seconds from delighted to distraught and then to shocked and outraged.

Jane's chauffeured car navigates toward the more luxurious Vancouver homes. I can't believe Jane would be so bold as to say her life depends on getting a job at the hotel when, clearly, her life is afforded by some other, much more affluent means.

"New friend?" Louisa saunters up beside me.

"Just another girl looking for a place of employment." The familiar echo of disappointment fills a void in my chest. I shake my head lightly, taking slow steps away from The Hamilton's front entrance.

CHAPTER 6

*M*onday, May 9, 1927

Not being hired immediately, as I naively expected I would be, has put a damper on my mood. Louisa catches up with me, looping her arm into the crook of mine, eager to dissect all that transpired at the meeting. I sense her excitement growing and anticipate the explosion of boisterous jubilation before she utters a word.

"Wasn't it just to die for, Clara?" Louisa continues without waiting for a response, like a terrier let loose in a park full of pigeons. "I met the sweetest girl. Tabatha is her name. Anyway, she said we've got a solid chance at getting a position."

Raising an arm toward the hotel across the street, Louisa continues without taking a breath. "Seems the Hotel Georgia snagged every formally trained maid in all of Vancouver. Isn't that great? Clearly, we are more than capable of learning new skills. I mean, with my ability to play any role and with your—" Louisa's eyebrows furrow for an almost imperceptible moment. "Your industriousness and work ethic. Surely, we are shoo-ins." Louisa's voice rises another excited octave. "Won't this be just wonderful? It will be the best summer ever, Clara. You and I, out on the town together." As we cross Georgia Street, Louisa tugs me closer with her entwined arm, causing me to stumble slightly.

"Out on the town?" I lift my head in question, failing to hide my incredulousness. As we step onto the opposite curb, The Hotel Georgia beside us, I weigh my words. "You aren't planning to continue with the application process, are you?"

"Why, of course I am." Louisa stops her long-legged stride, halting both of us. "Why wouldn't I?"

A man in a dark suit bumps into my shoulder before skirting around our abrupt stop. A noticeably perturbed attitude laces his words. "Excuse me, ladies."

I nudge us forward, guiding Louisa past the glass doors of The Hotel Georgia's front entrance. "Well, I just thought you'd be more interested in having the summer to yourself." I lighten my tone, attempting to remove the edge from my voice. "You know, days at the beach, meeting up with friends. I thought you'd been looking forward to it since we moved into the city."

Louisa extracts her arm from mine, leveraging her height. She coats her words with condescension but delivers them with a flurry of lightheartedness. "Don't be silly. I will have plenty of time for the beach and friends. They can't possibly expect us to work seven days a week."

I press on, determined to convince her otherwise. "Yes, but you've never worked at a job before. Do you really think you are up for it?"

"Neither have you." A flash of anger cuts through Louisa's words.

"This is true. But I keep the house and do the shopping, mending, and cooking." My voice squeaks as I detail my list of chores. I recognize the worrying sensation of having stepped too close to the cliff's edge where Louisa's joy races time itself before plunging out of sight, replaced by a sharp-edged tongue and a fiery temper.

"Clara Wilson, are you telling me that, simply because I don't find fulfilment in the same domestic tasks you do, I am"—Louisa's indignation steals her words for a beat—"unsuitable and unlikely to gain employment as a maid? Theatre acting is hard work, I'll have you know. Long hours, fiery lights, singing, and dancing, not to mention all the memorization of lines that go into a production."

Louisa's toe taps the sidewalk as a scowl etches onto her usually pleasant and delighted face. I am aware that our disagreement has ventured beyond a private exchange of words. Those passing us by shoot second glances and raised eyebrows over their shoulders.

My cheeks feel as though a flame has struck them as my annoyance leans toward outrage. I have no desire to be penniless on the street, begging for food. This time, it isn't about what Louisa wants. This is far too important to allow my adventure-seeking, single-minded sister to pout and get her way. No, my gaining employment at the hotel is far more important than any long face Louisa can produce. She will not manipulate me this time.

The cutting words I so often swallow churn like bile in my stomach. In our family, the status quo revolves around Louisa's state. *If Lou is happy,* Mama used to tease, *then everyone is happy.* Mama's laugh swirls through my memory like the rustle of autumn leaves in an alleyway, no longer full of vibrant life but present all the same. She was the steadier of quarrels and the drier of tears. She was the glue

47

that held us all together. Now, that task lies with me, whether or not Louisa realizes it.

A haughty huff sneaks past my pursed lips as I remind myself that I did not invite Louisa along today. She simply showed up and inserted herself into my plans. Childlike resentment builds within me, and before I can think better of it, I lower my voice and meet Louisa's eyes. "You've shown no inclination to tidy our own home. What makes you think you are remotely capable of holding down a job that will require you to clean up after others?"

"You know, being the perfect little homemaker isn't the only way to gain employment, Clara. I may not be as skilled as you in the home, but I have personality and am confident I can accomplish anything I set my mind to." Louisa's chin inches upward with an air of arrogance. "Besides, I have more than enough acting ability to muddle through until I get the hang of things."

An unladylike snort is my only reply as my eyes scan the sidewalk, the courthouse, and the bustle of people moving about the city.

"You're always cleaning, planning, cooking, taking care of the laundry," she says. "Don't you tire of it? Don't you get tired of handling everything?" Louisa yanks on my sleeve. "I'm talking to you, Clara."

Without meeting her eyes, I play the card that has the best chance of ending our discussion. "Mama always said there is much value in a job well done. Even if that job is making a house into a home."

"An orderly house does not equal a happy life, Clara." Louisa's eyes mist. "And don't think you can use Mama's words to shut me up this time."

For a fleeting moment, I feel a thread of guilt braided through the impatience, before the impatience wins out.

"Easy for you to say when your house is clean because of my effort."

Louisa sighs, crossing her arms over her chest. "I've let it go before because taking control of the household seemed to soothe you. But Clara, don't you see that you can't solve the world's problems by keeping a tidy house? Heck, that doesn't even solve your own problems." Louisa's words falter to a whisper. "Mama was exceptionally skilled at caring for our home, and the cancer still took her. Control is an illusion, Clara, and a disappointing one at that."

I suck in my trembling lip, determined to prove I am stronger than Louisa thinks I am. "There is no harm in trying, at least. Besides, this isn't about keeping a home. This is about me applying for a job and you stepping in and ruining things for me. I am quite certain you have already put me at a disadvantage for a position. Ms. Thompson witnessed your uninvited appearance and our exchange of words. Both of us are clearly too unruly to employ."

I am growing weary of being a spectacle. The most luxurious hotel Vancouver has ever seen, at least according to the newspapers, looms in my periphery while I argue with my sister. My shoulders slump as the intensity of the late-afternoon sun wears me down. "I didn't even think you wanted a job. In fact, I am sure I heard the stage calling you." I twirl one arm in the air with a flourish. Despite its lacklustre effect, my strangled attempt at striking a pose garners an amused smile from Lou.

"You are right," Louisa concedes with a single nod. "I wasn't looking for a job. But when I saw the determination in your eyes, I knew something was up." Louisa nudges my shoulder with her own in an attempt at sisterly camaraderie. "Our world has been turned upside down these past few years, I know." With a weary sigh and a subdued expression, she says, "You might not realize this, but I worry too." Louisa tugs at her jacket's belt. "Papa isn't exactly making things easy on us."

Her words tell me she is aware of the slim nature of our family's finances. How could she not be? Her precious theatre classes were cancelled midway through a session with an abruptness that must have felt akin to a slap in the face. I am certain, though, that news of the eviction letter has yet to reach her. If it had, she would surely be spitting nails.

I'd like nothing more than to produce a quick-witted comment that would put us on equal footing, but words escape me, as they so often do when Louisa has her teeth into something she desires.

"Seriously, though, you should try to stop obsessing about things, Clara. Trying to force situations to bend your way will cause more hassle than not."

My lack of a response only adds fuel to the fire behind Louisa's eyes. I can read my sister's motives like a newspaper headline. As she changes tactics, the hair against my collar rises. Louisa's eyes conveniently find the sidewalk, her demeanour filling with self-pity as she shuffles toward home. She shrugs in a put-upon display of disappointment. "Besides, I don't even know what my friends have planned. So many of them will be busy with the summer theatre program—working the stage, following their dreams, and such."

Louisa walks mournfully a step ahead of me, and I shake my head at her antics. I catch up and match her stride to ensure she will hear me. "Lou, I wish you would let me do this. Without you." My words are quiet but far from downtrodden. I consider confiding in Louisa my reasons for applying at the hotel, but I am unable to add to her disappointment toward Papa with news of the eviction notice. In this moment, I'm not sure whether I am protecting him from Louisa or Louisa from herself.

Understanding that her attempt to convince me by tugging on my heart has been unsuccessful, Louisa picks up her pace. She raises her head, enlisting her full height once more. "Sorry. I can't do that, Clara."

"Louisa, please. I hardly ever ask you for anything." I try but cannot keep the begging tone from my voice. "Just this once." I know all too well that I have already lost this battle.

"Come on, Clara, don't be so down in the mouth." Louisa grabs my hand, swinging it back and forth as her victory radiates through her. "I want to do this together. It will be fun."

The whine in her voice grates on my nerves as her swinging arm pulls me faster than my short legs can comfortably walk.

"Besides, a job at the hotel will give me something to do. You've been suggesting for weeks that I get out of the apartment and find some way to occupy myself. Now I have." Louisa's smile fills with confidence as she prattles on. "I mean, who would have thought moving into the city would be more boring than living in its shadows on the estate? Papa promised me an adventure, but so far . . . Well, this will be an adventure for both of us, Clara. Just think of it. The two of us working together, meeting glamorous travellers and perhaps even a few Hollywood stars."

Louisa's eyes seem to take in a future complete with bright lights and movie stars, when all mine can see are hard work and long hours. But work will secure the roof over our heads. I can't deny that two paycheques may be beneficial, as long as Louisa doesn't let her enthusiasm for all things that glitter ruin our chances of working at the hotel.

Louisa steps all over my thoughts, just as she did my plans. "Trust me, Clara, this will be an adventure."

Louisa's and my ideas of fun are worlds apart, but I submit to her current excitement and decide to keep my unsavoury thoughts to myself. I know that her struggle with our relocation to the city lies just beneath the surface, like a blue vein beneath alabaster skin. Mama's death and the loss of everything Louisa held dear have tested her bright worldview. Mama tasked me with taking care of the family, and that is precisely what I intend to do, even if it means swallowing my own disappointment.

CHAPTER 7

*M*onday, May 9, 1927
          Delighted by the excitement of today's
application process, Louisa talks incessantly during the walk
toward home. I pass the time worrying over what tomorrow
might bring and considering whether the churning in my
stomach is the result of a courageous plan or an impending
calamity.

Two blocks from our apartment, I stop with a jolt,
remembering my intended trip to the grocer three blocks
back. Telling Louisa I won't be long, I dig through my
pocketbook for the scrap of paper containing the grocery
list. In the top right-hand corner of the paper, I have
scrawled *$3.05* as a reminder of the funds available to me. I
scold myself for not paying better attention. I know all too
well that the list is longer than those funds will allow. I must
choose wisely, I think as I enter the butcher shop, already
bustling with afternoon shoppers.

My decision to visit the butcher first is based on
previous experience. The cost and availability of meat will

determine my ability to purchase the rest of the items on my list. I select a small mound of ground beef, complete my purchase, and move next door to the grocer. I am quite aware that I will need to prepare more than one meal of beans and vegetables this week if I am to have any hope of replenishing necessary staples.

Carefully weighing each item, I select a variety of dried beans, a basket of potatoes, a small bunch of carrots, one turnip, and a bag of white rice, all the while keeping an eye on the prices. I forego fresh-baked bread from the bakery and decide instead to restock our cupboard with flour, eggs, lard, and milk. With a little extra work on my end, the individual ingredients will yield more loaves. Rolled oats, though not one of Louisa's favourites, are a filling and sturdy breakfast option, so I place them in the shopping basket.

Although Roger's Sugar Refinery is local, I choose yellow sugar over the pristine white granulated variety. To save a few pennies, I select a quarter pound of tea instead of the full pound. It won't be the first time I've resorted to reusing leaves for my morning tea. Two weeks ago, I began stretching the tea by first making Papa's cup, then Louisa's, and finally my own, squeezing all that I could out of the water-soaked leaves by pressing a spoon against the mesh strainer.

I add a pound of butter, hard cheese, and a dozen eggs to the basket. I decide milk will have to do for Louisa's tea this week, abandoning any thought of the more expensive cream. The lonely section containing a handful of milk bottles gives me a moment's pause, and a cold sweat dots my upper lip. I swipe at the moisture and regain my composure, concealing my humiliation at having to purchase dairy items from the grocer.

Most homes are in good standing with the dairy driver and receive regular deliveries of milk, cream, butter, and eggs. At the Murray estate, the horse-drawn milk delivery was an anticipated part of our week during the summer months. The Murrays' cook, Tildy, would usher us kids out to meet the friendly man and his even friendlier mare. She would have a fresh carrot for the horse and a few extra coins at the ready in her apron pocket. When I think of summer, I think of eating ice cream while sprawled on the lush green front lawns of the estate.

I add the bottle to my basket with a discreet hand, positioning it to the side, a little further away from the prying eyes of other shoppers. With a subtle shake of my head, I refocus and begin mentally tallying my humble collection of provisions. I decide to splurge when a display of canned peaches catches my eye. The colourful label, along with the sale price, calls out to me. The display at the end of the aisle promises happy times and joyful remembrances. Given that peach season remains a few months away, the sweet treat would be a welcome accompaniment to Sunday's dinner.

I cross the missing loaf of bread from my list with my stubby pencil and move toward the checkout. I allow a pinprick of gaiety to lighten my mood. The can of peaches filled to the brim with sweet nectar elicit a tinge of hope for good tidings for me and my family.

The woman in front of me in line is juggling a small child on one hip while chatting politely with the clerk, who is placing her groceries into brown paper bags. I glance about the shop as I wait my turn, letting my eyes wander over neatly stacked pyramids of apples and a precariously erected corner display of tomato juice tins.

The cash register chimes and the little boy clamours for

a piece of stick candy. I place my groceries on the counter and smile at the clerk, who offers to add my ground beef from the butcher to the bag with the other items. The clerk places the heavy sack of flour in the bottom of the brown paper bag and nestles my coveted can of peaches amid the other groceries. Though my purchase is small compared to what other shoppers must buy for a week's worth of meals, a wave of relief runs through me at having successfully acquired enough staples to feed our family for another week.

"That will be three dollars and nine cents," the clerk announces as he places the eggs carefully on top of the other items.

My heart feels as though it has dropped and taken up residence in my shoes. "Pardon?" My voice quivers as the word falls from my lips and sweat prickles, threatening to bead across my forehead.

"The total is three dollars and nine cents." The clerk stares at me expectantly.

Trying to comprehend where I went wrong in my calculations, I stammer, "But the peaches, they are on sale." My voice resembles that of a child.

The clerk scans the line forming behind me before delivering a smile cloaked in weariness. "When you buy two cans, they are fifteen cents each. Buy one and the price is twenty-five cents."

My head bows as I pick the coins from my pocketbook with clammy hands. "I see." My disappointment over the peaches cripples my ability to think straight.

A man behind me shuffles his feet. A child cries out over the bustle of late afternoon shoppers. Minutes seem to pass before I gather my words, along with what remains of my dignity. "I will leave the peaches, then."

The clerk makes no attempt to cover his sigh as he removes all the items from the grocery bag to extract the offending can of peaches before adjusting my total and repacking the bag.

I pay my bill and rush from the shop as fast as my legs will carry me. My face burns with heat. Embarrassment courses through my veins as I attempt to put as much distance as possible between me and the grocer. I make it as far as the street corner before my body revolts.

With nowhere else to go, I dash around to the back of a brick building. The grocery bag drops to the ground, and I brace one hand against the cool, shaded brick while this morning's piece of toast and tea empty from my stomach.

My mind spins with disappointment and self-doubt, standing like a gatekeeper against any potential for easier times. I can't even pay for a week's worth of groceries, let alone the rent. A shiver runs the length of my spine, doom settling in as I wipe my mouth with the back of my hand. A few moments later, I straighten my dress, swallow hard, and pick up the grocery bag once more. Time is running out for my family, and the only other option I know looms before me, lurking like a childhood monster in a nighttime cupboard.

CHAPTER 8

M onday, May 9, 1927
        Despite the ill, hollow feeling in my
wrung-out stomach, all I desire right now is enough money
in my pocketbook to afford a decent meal. I amble toward
home as the groceries, heavy in my arms, mimic the weight
of the responsibility lying heavy on my heart.

I must do everything I can to earn a maid's position at
the hotel. After today's information session, I realize the
task before me is far from easy. It's become more
challenging still with Louisa intent on accompanying me.
The thought of her doggedness forces a scoff from my lips
as I shift the grocery bag within my arms.

The situation, as it is, has forced my previous
excitement over the job at the hotel to wane. Dread now
fills the space where hope lived, albeit briefly, this
afternoon. With the prospect of employment, I had
afforded myself the luxury of delaying one thing I have no
inclination to pursue. A block away from the apartment, I
resign myself to what I must do, and it pleases me none.

I must go behind Papa's back and speak with Mr. Watkins, The Newbury's building manager. Perhaps he will allow me to work out an arrangement for paying the overdue rent. Surely, Papa is aware of how close to ruin we are. His actions tell me he either isn't concerned or doesn't care, and neither sits well within my heart.

I must show Mr. Watkins I am taking the necessary steps to secure employment in order to remain in our apartment. As a young woman, with little negotiating power, I will have to appeal to his kindly side. Surely, he will find it in his heart to help a family in need.

As I climb the steps to the apartment, I consider other options. If human compassion isn't enough, I will appeal to his practical nature. After all, if he can remain patient until I secure a job, he will receive not only the past due amount but also future rental income for several more years.

The key slides into the lock of our apartment's door. I pause a moment, hiding my discontent behind a forced smile. "I'm home," I call out as I place the grocery bag on the kitchen counter. I am turning each egg in the carton, praying none cracked during their rapid descent to the ground, when Louisa walks in.

"What is that stench?" Louisa's nose bunches in displeasure as she peeks into the half-empty grocery bag.

"What smell? I don't smell anything." As the words roll off my tongue, my eyes glimpse my splattered shoes. Barely able to conceal a gasp, I dash toward the bathroom. I seal the door behind me, determined not to elicit a litany of questions from Louisa and hoping to skirt another round of humiliation.

A few moments later, a soft knock at the door startles me. I wipe the toes of my shoes clean, tears of frustration streaming down my face. "Clara?" Louisa's voice is gentle, concern wrapped around each word. "Are you all right in there?"

"Yes. Yes, I am fine." As I reach for my toothbrush, I search for a believable cover story. "I stepped in something on the way home. It will just take a moment for me to clean up. I am fine. Nothing to worry about. I will be out in a minute."

I return to the kitchen, with my face washed and shoes scrubbed clean, ready to unpack the groceries. As I place the oats jar, satisfyingly full to the brim, in the tall cupboard, Papa wanders into the kitchen. He is fresh from a day's long slumber, a habit he has taken to more often in recent weeks.

"Clara, let me help." He steps behind me, easily placing the jar on the top shelf. "How was the market?"

I demurely avoid his eyes. "Fine."

I may be imagining what I'd like to hear, but Papa's words sound cloaked in shame. "You were able to get everything you needed, then?"

"Yes, Papa, I have everything we need." Before pulling the sack of flour from the brown paper bag, I pat his arm, confirming all is well.

"I was thinking I might take a walk to the water's edge, if you'd like to join me? Louisa too, if she can tear herself away from the magazine she is reading." Papa chuckles softly, his head dipping toward the table where Louisa is pretending to read as she listens to our conversation.

I smile at his attempt to make things right between us after his drunken return home the other night. "You go on ahead. I want to get dinner started. The fresh air will do you well. It is a beautiful day out. I am sure the water will glisten in that mesmerizing way you so enjoy."

"Louisa, how about you, love?" Papa's expression

softens. "We can see how the rhododendrons are blooming. Should almost be ready to burst with colour by now."

"You go ahead. I'll stay and help Clara with dinner."

I sneak a glance in Louisa's direction, quite certain I could count on one hand the number of times she has helped me with dinner. My stomach clenches as I think of the inquisition that is sure to descend upon me once we are alone.

"Another time, then." Papa squeezes my shoulder with a warm hand before leaving the kitchen to ready himself for the walk.

I am folding the brown paper bag to store in the cupboard beneath the kitchen sink as Papa bids us farewell, closing the apartment door behind him. Louisa waits less than a minute before cornering me in the kitchen with an inquiring look and a raised eyebrow.

"Is everything all right with you?" Perching a hip against the counter's edge, Lou folds her arms across her chest. Her face takes on the best concerned-older-sister expression I have seen in a while. "You know how pitiful you are at lying, especially to me." Her exaggerated eye roll sends a flush of colour to my cheeks.

"I'm fine. You could have gone for the walk with Papa. I don't need a babysitter, you know." My words come out sharper than I intend. I pivot away, busying myself with the removal of carrot tops and shielding my face from Louisa's view.

"Oh, how I miss the cottage." Louisa's voice sings, and her deep sigh settles over the room, shifting the tension like a warm breeze after a thunderstorm.

I glance in her direction, still wary of her motives. "Me too."

"Remember the tea parties? It was all so *Alice in*

Wonderland-like. Don't you agree?" Louisa's face is aglow with fond memories of our life on the Murray estate.

"I loved it there. I miss them still—Sophie and the others and Mr. and Mrs. Murray." Our gazes meet as we share smiles and teary eyes. "The cottage is the only home I knew until here." My free arm gestures about the small apartment, one sweep encompassing its entire space.

"Do you think we'll ever go back?" Lou's childlike shrug does little to hide her wish for life to return to how it was.

I am sure my sister already knows the answer to her question. All I can think is that she is looking for reassurance that everything will be well once again.

"I don't know." I take a moment to search for words that are true but less harsh than the reality of our situation. "Mr. Murray is a kind and decent man."

Louisa's head bobs in agreement, moisture gathering in her eyes.

"But Papa could no longer manage the grounds of the estate like he used to"—I brace myself with a sharp inhale before ushering the words—"before Mama died."

"I just don't understand why he couldn't have stayed on as a junior grounds worker, and then we could have kept living in the cottage." Louisa dabs her eye with a finger, transforming into the wounded and insecure little girl that lives at the core of her being. Few ever see this side of her, but I know what lurks behind the confident facade my sister shows the world.

"I know it is hard to understand, but the cottage is for the head landscaper and his family. When Papa could no longer maintain the role of head landscaper, we had no other option but to move." I step toward Louisa, placing a hand on her arm and meeting her eyes. "Mr. Murray was more than patient with Papa, but the situation just wasn't working out any longer. Don't you worry though. We'll be all right."

I fold Louisa into a tight hug and murmur into her hair, "We will be all right. I promise we will."

Louisa smiles sheepishly as I take a step back. "So, what's for dinner?" She changes tracks like a locomotive moving in a new direction, one that is sure to take her far from uncomfortable thoughts and feelings.

"Rice, bean, and vegetable stew." I turn my attention to the ingredients waiting for me on the counter.

"Again?" Louisa's scrunched-up expression requires no translation. Her disappointment is clear.

"Yes, again." I hide my annoyance as I remind her, "Beans are a healthy source of protein, and besides, Papa enjoys a hearty stew."

"I know money is tight, but at this rate, I'm going to sprout bean shoots instead of hair." With her voice barely above a whine, Louisa's disappointment in tonight's dinner pushes her away from the kitchen. Snatching her magazine from the table, she flops onto the sofa, burying her nose in the four-month-old edition of *Motion Picture Classic*.

"Sure you are," I mutter as I reach for Mama's cookbook.

My mind fills with memories of the Murray estate as I chop vegetables and soak the beans over a slight heat, hoping to soften them before mixing them into the stew. The estate's lush gardens stretch the entire expanse of the Murray property, and I was never able to visit all their nooks and crannies.

When we weren't living the charmed life, playing make-believe and hosting tea parties, Papa used to take my hand and guide me through a magic green canopy. His smile was always warm and wide, his hand sturdy in my little one. A sigh breezes past my lips. Most of my favourite moments took place on the Murray estate. Even when Louisa's enthusiasm would take over and begin directing our play, things were always more manageable on the estate. Back then, it was easier to let Louisa be Louisa. When Louisa is happy, my world is simply a better place to be.

My thoughts return to the beginning of my day, and I wonder if every day will feel as long as this one has. I peek into the living room to ensure Louisa remains engrossed in her magazine before pulling Mama's letter from within the pages of the cookbook. As the beans simmer, I reread her last letter to me, the same one I've reached for again and again when life becomes overwhelming.

My Dearest Clara,

If anyone understands my time is short, it is you. You are my brave and thoughtful child, and I so wish I could see you grow into the wonderful woman I already know you are going to be. Stay true to yourself, Clara, dear, and stay your course. Others may have ideas about how you should live and what you should do, but I must insist upon you to remain true to your nature. Your own internal compass knows exactly how to lead you. Listen to it and you will always find happiness.

This is difficult for me to write, as my intention is not to be one of burden. I know, however, that I would be remiss if I did not tell you everything that is in my heart. Your Papa has yet to grasp the finality of my life's existence. I fear I am weeks, if not days, away from leaving all those whom I love so dearly. As I write this letter to you, your dear Papa is not in a position to believe that our time together is short.

My passing will be hard for all of you. This I know and I am deeply sorry to have caused you suffering. Please understand, I fought

*as hard as I possibly could to remain with you all. Clara, I fear your
father will not be ready to accept my passing when the time comes. I
worry for Louisa and you, as I will not be there to pull the family
together as I have done in the past, and I am uncertain of how he will
move forward without my presence in his life. He's said it himself a
thousand times. I am his sail and his anchor. But alas, I fear I can no
longer be either.*

*This, I must ask of you. Please do all that you can to keep our
family together. I am deeply sorry to ask such a task of you. You have
already done so much, taking on the cooking and cleaning while I have
been unable. Clara, you are strong. You are brave.*

THE APARTMENT DOOR OPENS AND I HASTILY SWIPE A TEAR
from my eye and shove Mama's letter back between the
pages of the cookbook. I am at the stove, stirring the beans,
before Papa's tall frame enters the room.

"How was the walk?" My voice fills the air, pushed out
with the help of a manufactured smile.

"Ah, Clara, love, springtime is the most beautiful season
in Vancouver."

I stifle a giggle. "Papa, you say that about every season."

A sheepish grin emerges. "I suppose that is true enough,
but today, springtime is the most beautiful one of all." He
plants a kiss atop my head. "Do I have time to clean up
before dinner?"

"Dinner will be ready in an hour. You have plenty of
time." I mix the chopped vegetables with the beans and rice
before turning down the heat and covering the pot.

I check the time on my wristwatch before settling into
the sole chair in the compact living room. With the memory
of my experience at the market still shadowing my every
move, I let out a slow, weary breath as I reach for the basket

of socks. Our mismatched and threadbare socks have been in the basket since we moved in. Now, with the lack of funds weighing more heavily on my mind, I find myself more compelled than ever to darn the socks I can.

Louisa's eyebrows furrow in question, but a word never leaves her lips.

"Darning socks is a pleasant way to spend some time." I reach for Mama's sewing kit and thread a needle.

Louisa's eye roll does not go unnoticed, but I decide I would rather spend an hour in comfortable silence than acknowledge it. I contemplate what I must do tomorrow morning. Seeking Mr. Watkins' help will certainly require an added depth of courage.

Forty minutes later, I am deep in thought, practicing a speech in my head, when Papa joins us in the living room. A wash and a shave have done him well. A glimmer of the man I know him to be descends into the room like an ocean breeze, and his presence lightens my mood.

Louisa scoots over and sits up to make room for Papa to join her on the sofa. I check my watch, noting the time, then put the sock and needle aside and stand to check on the stew.

"So, Lou," Papa says, "what did you get up to today?"

Papa is indeed in good spirits, I think as I move toward the kitchen. He only uses Louisa's nickname when he's in a delighted mood.

"Well, Clara and I—" Louisa's animated voice plunges a hot iron of fear into my heart. I realize she is about to tell Papa about The Hotel Hamilton.

Admonishing myself for not thinking to inform Louisa that we should not mention the maid's position to Papa, I turn abruptly and narrow my eyes in her direction.

The subtle shift in Louisa's expression conveys that she

has received the message. "We went for a walk through the city streets today. We popped into a few shops, but mostly we enjoyed wandering around the city." Louisa's hand goes to Papa's arm, exaggerating her delight of our afternoon adventure. "We even walked by The Hotel Georgia again. We weren't daring enough to go in, but someday, Papa, I will have plenty of reasons to visit the new hotel."

Papa beams at Louisa as I make a beeline for the kitchen and the stew that will boil dry if not tended. With the lid off the pot, I cannot determine whether the steam rising from the bubbling stew or my sheer panic is causing my body to warm. Pressure mounts behind my eyes as the tasks that lie ahead of me swirl through my mind. I busy both my hands and my thoughts by ladling steaming stew into bowls before slicing and buttering bread.

The conversation over dinner becomes tense when Louisa mentions her desire to re-enroll in acting classes. Papa listens quietly as he chews. I hold my tongue, already aware that the cost of classes is further from our reach than even I realized.

Louisa scoffs at Papa's suggestion that she inquire about a volunteer position at the school. She could then be involved with the theatre, even if it is not in the capacity that she wishes to be.

I marvel at Louisa's ability to go from an awareness that money is in short supply to an all-out tantrum. I keep my head down to remain out of the line of Louisa's fire.

"And what about Clara?" Louisa's voice shrills an octave higher, and my head bolts up in response. "Shouldn't she still be in school? She must finish her education, Papa, if she is to go on to something else." Louisa tilts her head in my direction. "What would you like to be, Clara? A teacher? A secretary? There are many positions available for young women these days, but I think you would make an exceptional teacher, Clara. Really, I do."

Swivelling her attention back toward Papa, she says, "Are we waiting on something in particular, Papa? We all know the luxury of being unemployed has overstayed its welcome. I know you can do better." Louisa's voice softens, but her words cut through all the same. "Mama would want you to do better."

Pushing his chair away from the table, Papa stands and places a firm hand on my shoulder. "Thank you for dinner, Clara. A lovely stew it was."

Without another word, he walks to the hall, reaches for his jacket, and steps out of the apartment.

Louisa hangs her head, a dejected expression contorting her face. "Well, I guess he isn't going to talk about it."

"Really, Lou? You didn't realize that until he walked out the door?" The dishes clatter as I force them on top of one another and clear them to the kitchen sink. My heartbeat keeps pace with my frenzied worry over Papa's brisk departure.

"Don't blame me, Clara. This isn't my fault." Louisa folds her arms across her chest. "If he would go out and look for a job instead of sleeping the day away, I am quite sure we could afford more than just beans for dinner."

I cannot argue with Louisa's logic, and guilt over my harsh words creeps in as she quietly excuses herself from the table. She wraps herself in her favoured blanket, the one Mama stitched the year before she fell ill. I watch with downcast eyes as she lies down and curls into a fetal position on the sofa before fixing her stare on the blank wall. A shiver runs down my spine as Louisa's mood filters through my heart.

CHAPTER 9

*M*onday, May 9, 1927

The months I busied myself with organizing and sorting out the apartment, Louisa spent in a trancelike state, barely rising to dress most days. At first, annoyance with her tendency toward laziness fuelled my constant desire to interrupt her quiet. Soon though, I came to understand she felt despondency, not only for Mama but also for something else. I'd become accustomed to Louisa's grief over Mama, pulsing constantly and steadily beneath the surface of her skin. Like the golden hue of a sunrise, Mama's death still colours everything the light touches.

When the relocation from our cottage on the Murray estate into the tiny two-bedroom apartment became an unavoidable reality, all Louisa knew was yanked from beneath her. Louisa's inclination to avoid the uncomfortable aspects of life caused her to withdraw. For weeks, I cajoled, insisted, and propped her up as she re-entered her life. I watched in utter disbelief as she snatched pieces of delight like a thief who hadn't eaten in days, hoarding rare bits of joy with a survivalist instinct I hadn't seen before. Time and courage were the only things that got us through, both of us requiring more than was available.

I clear the table before washing and drying the dishes, my thoughts competing over Louisa's current anger toward Papa and my worry over Papa's destinations outside our home. By the time I am finished in the kitchen, Louisa is asleep on the sofa and I desperately need some time and space to think.

I wrap my jacket around my shoulders and quietly let myself out of the apartment. The ocean air promises to clear my head, so I turn right and walk toward the ocean's steady tide. So often, these days, it seems the sun and the moon and the ocean's tides are all that I can count on. Between the buildings, the evening air is crisp with a salty flavour, and I relish knowing that the tide is coming in to greet me.

Louisa's impassioned words to Papa during dinner echo in the further reaches of my mind as I stroll the downward sloped streets toward the water's edge. Though I often find reason to be annoyed with my sister, I cannot ignore how she bravely stands her ground, not only for herself but for me and our family as well. Two months have passed since I came to terms with the awareness that I would not be returning to school for my final year of education with my peers. With more than half of the school year complete, returning a year late seems like a waste of my time. When I consider our current financial situation, the opportunity to earn a living outweighs the need for further education.

Louisa wasn't wrong though. Finishing my education and earning a proper career was a dream I once believed in with my whole heart. At one time, I thought becoming a teacher would be nice, but I suspect I would have preferred to see what other options were available for a girl like me. My shoulders rise toward my ears as the tension of my life engulfs me. I push back just to keep my head above water. I force my shoulders down and nudge a smile into place as I pass a well-dressed couple out for an evening stroll.

I cross the street, leaving nothing else between me and the salty waves. The ocean breeze cleanses me of my incessant mental chatter, and I inhale deeply, desperate to be soaked through by the Pacific's magical breath. I still my mind and turn my attention toward the horizon. No matter how harried the rest of my life may be, in this moment I give thanks for the serenity of the water's edge.

Picking my way closer to the waves lapping the sand, I allow the wind to tussle my hair, unbridled from the constraints that otherwise suffocate my every move. My eyes scan the long stretch of sand as a smile lifts the corners of my mouth. I relish being alone at the beach. Save for a gaggle of squawking gulls, only a lone figure in the distance falls within a hundred feet of me.

I follow the horizon, the sun's light igniting the world with a magical paintbrush. I ignore the needling of my rampant thoughts as they poke at me, waiting to hook me into their darkened lair. A whoosh of air rushes past my lips as the events of my endless day unfold behind my eyes.

The incoming tide threatens to dampen the toes of my shoes as I bend down and extract a smooth, round pebble from its nest of grainy brown sand. Rinsing the pebble in cool water, I step back, gently fingering the rounded stone. A memory creeps in to keep me company. Mama adored the ocean. We spent hours tossing pebbles into the water, seeing who could skip one the furthest. I remember a picnic lunch and an afternoon spent reading out loud with our backs pressed up against a water-tossed log, the rest of its life to be spent nestled in the sand. Though she never said, I always knew the ocean made her feel whole. I could read it on her face and see it in her posture. Moisture tickles the edges of my eyes. If only the ocean's healing power had been enough to keep her well.

I examine the stone again. Mama's words, softened by her English lilt, come back to whisper in my ear. *You see, Clara, everything can be smoothed out when given enough time and encouragement.* I dab at the tear leaking from the corner of my eye, certain Mama was referring to a disagreement I'd had with Louisa over some nonsensical complaint only an eight-year-old would worry about.

We wasted so much time on silly arguments. My arm arcs back and I toss the stone with a low-angled throw, watching it skip along the water's surface. I count six jumps before it sinks from sight. Desperate to escape the disgruntled nature of my runaway mind, I stroll the wet-packed edge of the sandy beach, leaving my footsteps and, with any luck, my disappointment behind me.

As I meander closer, a woman sitting on a beached log comes into view. Her wide-brimmed picture hat, its crown wrapped in a delicate rose-coloured silk sash, dips and shields her face as I edge closer. The woman is bent over something, her head bobbing with the movement of her right arm. The woman doesn't look my way as I step into her line of sight. I notice she is writing, her pen moving with speed across pages balanced atop her lap. A sturdy hardback book peeks out from beneath the pages, offering a stable platform.

Wandering past, I smile to myself. The woman is still unaware of another in her presence. My imagination turns with make-believe guesses. Perhaps she is writing a novel or a letter to a beau across the ocean. Or she could simply be jotting down her weekly shopping list. I stifle a giggle.

As I turn toward the street, electric lamps cast a soft yellow glow onto the sidewalk. I bid one last farewell to the ocean with a glimpse over my shoulder, taking in a sweeping view of the water, the beach, and the woman. She is still hunched forward, writing furiously, as if time is running out. Crossing at the corner, I begin the uphill climb toward Robson Street. As I catch my breath, a memory washes over me like an ocean wave, eliciting a full-body shiver.

"Mama's letters!" The words tumble out. I produce a sheepish smile at the questioning glance from a man walking the opposite direction. "Good evening," I say with pinked cheeks before picking up my cadence, now in a hurry to return home.

I climb the stairs to our third-floor apartment. Aunt Vivian, Mama's sister, has been a hotel maid in London for as long as I can remember. Excitement courses through me as I consider the gold mine of information I am sure to find on how to become the most suitable maid The Hotel Hamilton will ever see. Mama and Aunt Vivian were in constant communication through letters. Sometimes two or three letters a week would arrive in the post, with Mama always sending immediate replies. Mama often laughed out loud at Aunt Vivian's stories about her job at the hotel. Occasionally, Mama would detail a funny story or a helpful bit of cleaning advice from my infamous aunt at our dinner table.

Pausing at the apartment door, I take a few deep breaths to steady myself before sliding my key into the lock. I remove my jacket and toss it onto an empty hook. Without a backward glance, I tiptoe into the living room.

No Louisa. Turning back down the hallway, I gently press the bedroom door open and see Louisa settled in bed, breathing deeply, a rhythm of sleep holding her in its care.

Closing the door as quietly as possible, I return to the living room and the oversized trunk beneath the window. Mama brought the trunk when she journeyed from England to Vancouver. I drag it forward to gain clearance and open the lid. A bubble of relief rises within me as the musky smell fills the room. Inside the trunk, I spot Mama's carved wooden letter box.

I carefully lift the box from the trunk, its weight requiring both my hands, and place it on the floor. My fingers run across the smooth wood, and dust floats upward in the dim light of the living room lamp. I lift the box's lid, and a gasp spills from my lips. The sheer number of letters sends chill bumps up my arms. My lips purse in concentration and my enthusiasm dips a notch at the expansive task ahead of me.

I settle myself at the kitchen table with a weak cup of tea and the box of letters. My hand graces a blue-tinted envelope. The letter slides from the envelope with ease. A fleeting thought of consideration toward Mama's and Aunt Vivian's privacy niggles at me. The notion lingers for less than a moment before being replaced by thoughts of the more immediate need to secure employment and gain control over our family's downward spiral. I reason, admittedly suspect of my rationale, that Mama is guiding me. With her assistance, of sorts, I can establish solid ground within our lives. I believe in my heart of hearts that is what Mama would want for all of us.

FEBRUARY 3, 1921

My Dearest Elizabeth,

Words cannot convey how deeply my heart is breaking for you and your family. Your letter with news of the diagnosis arrived in this morning's post. I feel as though I may lose you all over again, and I am uncertain whether I can survive in this world without you. I do not say this lightly, nor do I intend to cause further pain in such dire times, but you must know, dear sister, how I mourned your leaving all those years ago.

I realize you have made a life, and a happy one at that, in Canada, but not a day goes by when I don't wish that you had remained here in London with me. Of course, dear sister, I would never begrudge you the happiness you have lived, nor would I ever entertain the thought of a life without your beloved husband and children.

My LIP QUIVERS AS EMOTIONS BUILD IN MY EYES. I straighten my posture, willing myself to remain strong as I return the letter to its envelope and set it aside. I sip my hot tea, staring with glassy eyes at the box of letters. Collecting my emotions, I reposition them into a dark corner of my mind and plunge my hand into the depths of the box. Desperate for a letter filled with lighthearted humour and hotel maid stories—anything other than a reminder of my mother's final months—I rummage through the box like a stray dog frantically digging for a lost bone. Having originally set a plan to examine the letters in an orderly fashion, the rash nature with which I press forward unsettles me. Logic, though, encourages my efforts. The older letters must be nestled deeper within the box. My fingers grasp a corner of paper. A quick tug frees the envelope from the weight of decades of letters piled atop it. I peel up the brown-edged flap and remove a crisp, white folded letter, perfectly preserved in its original state.

. . .

APRIL 21, 1908

 Dearest Elizabeth,

 I was quite excited to receive your letter. I must have read it twenty times over. Thank you for your February telegram informing us you had arrived safely in Halifax. Mother and Father were quite relieved at the news. Though, I must say, the two months without word from you has been quite the topic of conversation at the dinner table. Between Mother's fussing and Father's grunts, I could hardly get a word in edgewise.

 A proper congratulations on your marriage to Joseph is in order. Shall I address you as Mrs. Wilson now? You know I am only teasing you, dear sister, but it came as a bit of a shock to learn you married so quickly after having arrived in Vancouver. I suppose the heart knows best, and I believe you knew Joseph's heart through his letters before you stepped foot on that ship.

 Well, I have a bit of news of my own to share with you. I have been eager to tell you and desperately missing you all at the same time. It will please you to know I am now a maid in full employ at The Grosvenor Hotel. The convenience of the location near Victoria station, along with the hotel's fine history, helped me cajole Father into allowing me to accept the position. While I know it is not The Ritz, I am happy nonetheless. As you well know, Father would prefer I marry, and when news of your marriage arrived, he all but pushed me into Paul's arms, exclaiming that I will be a spinster, unlike you, my younger and clearly much more astute sister. But for now, I am quite pleased with myself and my position at The Grosvenor. As for Paul, well, he will have to wait, at least until I can make my mind up about him.

 Before I sign off, I simply must share a funny story from the hotel. I swear, Elizabeth, there is never a dull moment to be had. One morning, after a guest had departed, we discovered the dark wood furniture in the room had been scratched so terribly that garish white streaks glared from the piece. A frenzy ensued as the matron of the hotel called for hot cloths, damp cloths, and polish as she tried desperately to salvage the ruined piece of furniture.

It was then I remembered reading in a magazine or newspaper clipping of some sort that a Brazil nut was a creative fix for scratched furniture. I told the matron I had an idea and, with her permission, dashed from the hotel in search of a Brazil nut. Oh, what a sight I must have been. There I was, running from shop to shop, my maid's cap barely attached to my head while my apron swivelled around me like a disobedient toddler.

I visited more than seven shops until a grocer of fine goods finally rescued me. After I explained my story, he took one look at me and asked, "You want a nut for what?" I laughed out loud before purchasing the entire bag of nuts, since he was not keen to sell me just one. Upon my return to the hotel, I sliced off one end of the nut and used its oily juice to fill in the scratches, rubbing the nut against every slight the poor piece of furniture had endured.

My cleverness pleased the matron, and she said she would be sure to detail my positively helpful solution to the hotel's manager. With a bag full of Brazil nuts at the ready, I handed one to each maid in the hotel to keep it in her apron pocket, just in case.

Well, dear Elizabeth, I am so pleased we will correspond with regularity now that you are settling into your new home. Please give my love to Joseph. I eagerly await your next letter.

All my love,
Vivian

PAUL. THE NAME ROLLS AROUND IN MY HEAD. YES, AUNT Vivian married him after all and had a daughter, who is my cousin, though I've never met her. Mama referred to him as Uncle Paul, and I remember now that his life was lost to the Great War, like so many were.

I read on for several more hours, losing myself in the entertaining and informative banter, doing my best to skip the years surrounding the war and Aunt Vivian's deep grief, in the interest of keeping myself from the pit of despair. By the time I look up from the letters, my tea is cold and the sky beyond the curtain is black. Checking my watch, I stifle a yawn before realizing the night has almost passed me by, the hour edging into morning. Gathering the letters, I tidy them into a bundle and return them and their box to the trunk before turning toward the bedroom.

Beneath the covers, I let the events of the day unfold in my mind. Armed with a few tidbits about what it takes to be an upstanding maid, I am emboldened by the prospect of being hired. Louisa means well, I concede, despite having stepped all over my toes this afternoon. And Jane— A small exasperated sigh leaves my lips. I expect I will be better prepared than she has even thought to be. I will be friendly, of course. How could I not be? I simply must be the better applicant is all. This endeavour may be more challenging than I originally considered, given the obstacles still before me. The idea of going up against both Louisa and Jane is daunting, but I am determined to do what is required to secure my family's position.

I roll over and snuggle deeper into the mattress. Ms. Thompson didn't mention how many positions were available, but I am quite confident the hotel will require more than one maid. Perhaps all is not as dire as I imagine it to be. My eyes flutter closed as awareness that Papa has not returned home presses forward in my mind. With exhaustion taking over, I console myself with the fact that worry over Papa's whereabouts will blessedly evade me tonight. With few hours of darkness left, the best I can do for our family now is to succumb to sleep.

The world narrows. As sleep tries to take hold, my mind whirs with the many tasks requiring my attention. First, I will write to Aunt Vivian. I am confident she will be more than pleased to hear from the daughter of her own dear sister. Next, I will speak with Mr. Watkins. In the morning, I will locate him in his basement office and work out an arrangement. All I can hope is that he will respond well to a young lady with the possibility of employment on the horizon.

CHAPTER 10

*T*uesday, May 10, 1927

The morning light pierces my eyes as the sound of curtains being pushed back on their rod awakens me.

"Come on, lazybones." Louisa presses a hand to my shoulder before shuffling about the room.

The cupboard door closes with a thud, and my sleep-crusted eyes attempt to adjust to the brightness, filtered through half-closed eyelids.

"You are the last person I expected to be dawdling this morning." Louisa's teasing voice sings her enthusiasm for the day ahead.

I stifle a yawn and stretch my arms above my head in an effort to clear the cobwebs of sleep from my body. "We aren't due back at the hotel until two o'clock this afternoon. Surely, one can sleep in a bit and still be ready in time." My disgruntled tone goes unnoticed as Louisa lifts a rose-coloured dress and tucks the hanger beneath her chin as she spins.

"What do you think?" Louisa sways back and forth, making the skirt swivel and twine around her long legs, her melancholy from last evening erased by a day's fresh start. "Isn't it just the bee's knees?" Without waiting for my reply, gale-force Louisa pushes on. "This shade of rose has always complemented my skin tone. With a bit of rouge and a dab of lipstick, I think I will make a memorable impression."

I avoid meeting her eyes, running my fingers through my bed-flattened hair. "You always do."

"Come now, Clara, you can't still be sore about yesterday?" Louisa slumps beside me onto the narrow bed, forcing our bodies toward one another. Bumping my shoulder with her own, Louisa's voice dips to a conspiratorial level. "I'll help you find the perfect dress." At my lack of enthusiastic reply, she ups the ante, continuing in a breezy tone, "Borrow one of mine, if you like. What were you planning to wear?"

Given my naivety, I had thought I would wear a freshly starched maid's uniform this morning. I hold back the sigh that is determined to escape my lips. "I suppose I was thinking I would wear the same dress I wore yesterday. It is the best dress I own, after all." A nonchalant shrug offers little support to my words, and the disappointment on Louisa's face needs no interpretation.

"Clara, if I had known where you were heading yesterday, I wouldn't have let you walk out that door." Louisa's pointed finger emphasizes her displeasure as it lingers in the air, pointed toward the closed bedroom door. "That dress is barely suitable for the market, let alone an establishment as fine as The Hotel Hamilton. No, that won't do at all." Louisa's displeasure propels her from the bed and into action. She riffles through my section of the clothes cupboard and then her own, tossing a few options onto the bed, murmuring to herself the entire time.

Thirty minutes later, with my stomach rumbling and my patience wearing thin, Louisa reluctantly releases me to make breakfast while she continues. With a plan hatching behind her eyes, Louisa's creativity is on fire. As I turn to watch her from the doorway, I find myself in awe of my sister. Her tenacity and flair for fashion are on full display, highlighting everything I adore about her. My heart swells in my chest as I head to the kitchen to prepare a light breakfast.

AFTER BREAKFAST, WITH THE DISHES CLEARED AND WASHED, Louisa's head is bent over one of her dresses, several seasons old. Unable to see her vision for the tired garment, I put on a plain day dress and brush my hair into submission before grabbing a sweater and heading for the door. With a needle and thread in hand, Louisa barely glances up when I inform her I am going for a walk.

"Don't be too long," Louisa's warns. "I want you to try this on once I've hemmed the skirt and added a few pleats to the waistline."

I poke my head into Papa's room, ensuring he found his way back. He apparently made it home after I fell into a short but deep sleep. He removed his shoes and crawled under the covers. Though his jacket remains stretched tight across his shoulders this morning, he is home safe and sleeping.

A sliver of guilt creeps in as I close the apartment door with a braced hand, intent on drawing as little attention to my leaving as possible. Papa would be furious. No, not furious, I correct myself. Embarrassed. He would be embarrassed and ashamed if he knew what I was up to this morning.

It can't be helped, I tell myself as I move past the sunlit lobby, toward the musty basement of The Newbury. I pick my way down the cement stairs. My hand grips the wobbly rail as I descend into the bowels of the building.

My eyes are slow to adjust to the dim light. A bare bulb in the centre of a narrow hallway casts an eerie glow. The shadows against the walls elicit a shiver and a thread of imaginative thought that could send me running in the opposite direction.

I gather my courage—all two cents of it—and cock my ear, desperate for the presence of another in this less than hospitable space. I check behind me before stepping forward once more. Two strides later, I hug the grimy, whitewashed wall in a panic as a rat scurries past.

Sweat pools in the small of my back and adrenaline courses through my body. I push away the thought that I'll soon need to retrace my steps out of the basement, same as the rat. Brushing the hair from my face, I peer down the shadowy hallway, certain a door or an office must be closer than my eyes can determine.

As my vision clears, the meagre light forcing my eyes to work harder, I notice the wide pipes lining the ceiling above me. Cobwebs weave between the rows of pipe, and I consider the likelihood that anyone, save perhaps a spider or a rat, would find this basement an ideal place to spend any time at all. I wonder what kind of hardened individual would seek employment in such an environment. At this thought, a deeper level of worry embeds itself under my skin like a tick. What if Mr. Watkins isn't a kind man at all? Perhaps he is the sort of man who enjoys spending his days in such a dreadful place? All of my what ifs rise to the surface like cream.

"Can I help you?" The soft voice of an older gentleman startles me from my spiralling thoughts. I look up and find a face that appears scruffy around the edges but kind.

"Mr. Watkins?" My voice wavers as I question whether this is indeed the man who helped Papa move some of the larger pieces of furniture into our third-floor apartment several months ago. It was a dreadful day in so many ways, the weather matching our forlorn moods as the wind howled. An unexpected dumping of snow hindered the process, causing the task to take several hours more than originally expected.

"Yes, I am Mr. Watkins." His warm smile reaches all the way to his eyes, crinkling them and bringing to mind an image of Santa Claus. In his smile, I remember the man with the generous spirit. After hefting a table, a trunk, and a sofa into our sparse quarters, he returned only minutes later with cups of hot cocoa for all of us.

"I—I don't know if you remember me, but I am Clara. Clara Wilson." I stammer as though I've forgotten how to speak.

"Ah, yes, Miss Wilson." His smile fades, and I imagine his mind entertaining troubling thoughts. "Is everything all right with your father?"

"Oh, yes, Mr. Watkins. My Papa is well enough." I feel my cheeks redden, and I am grateful for the dim light in the hall. "Thank you."

"Is there something needing repair in your apartment? The water is working?" Mr. Watkins scratches his scruffy beard.

"Actually, sir." I bow my head a moment, trying to clear my thoughts. "Well, you see . . ." My mouth twists, not wishing to admit the reason for my visit.

"Come, child, it can't be all that bad." With a wave of his hand, Mr. Watkins guides me toward a room that escaped my notice in the gloomy light.

He opens the door and I step, to my surprise, into a brightly lit, warm office. Complete with a desk, filing cabinet, and coat rack, the room offers a reprieve from the harsh basement hall.

"Please have a seat, Miss Wilson." He gestures to a chair opposite his own and rests his elbows atop the desk. "Now, what seems to be the trouble?"

"I found the eviction notice, sir." Tears attempt to spill from the corners of my eyes. I gather my resolve and watch as the tears retreat like a scolded child.

"I see." Mr. Watkins' smile holds no delight.

"My father doesn't know I am here, sir. He does not know I have seen the letter." I straighten my posture, shoulders back, spine stiff. "I have come to speak with you, to see if we can come to an agreement, sir."

"An agreement?" Mr. Watkins leans back in his chair, causing it to groan. "What kind of agreement?"

"You see, sir, I have applied for a position as a full-time maid at The Hotel Hamilton. I am on my way there today to continue the process, and I expect to be awarded a position soon."

"A maid?" Mr. Watkins' bushy eyebrows gather, meeting at the centre of his forehead. "Aren't you just a child, with school and whatnot?"

I flinch at the notion and press forward. "No, sir. I am a reliable and responsible member of the Wilson family, and I am determined to seek employment in order to support our household."

"Miss Wilson, to be honest, I am not sure this is a discussion we should be having." He scratches the back of his head, which I interpret as a means to buy a moment's pause. "The rental agreement is really between your father and The Newbury. I don't think"—Mr. Watkins allows another brief silence—"a young woman such as yourself should be involved in a disagreement between a resident and the owners of the apartment building."

"But I am a resident, sir. My sister and I both are, and if they evict my father, we will be evicted as well."

Mr. Watkins' head bobs with slow understanding, a solemn expression straining his face.

"Please, sir." I stifle a tear-laced gasp. "Please. We can't handle another devastation. My sister is fragile when it comes to change, and further instability will only cause her more harm. I know you must think my Papa is . . ." My words hang in the air like a fly caught in a spider's web. "Well, to be honest, I don't know what you think of my family, but he is a good man. I swear he is. It is just that we have lost so much these past few years." I catch my shoulders slumping in defeat and force my back to straighten, a fabricated attempt to deliver with strength the words that pierce my beating heart like shards of ice. "We have no family, no distant relatives with a farm to move to. There is only the three of us, sir." My chin juts upwards in defiance of the ramshackle existence where I find myself suspended. "I can't allow us to become homeless. Apologies for my frankness, sir, but I—I can't."

Mr. Watkins' chin droops toward his chest as my biggest worry, the fear that has prodded at me day and night, fills the room with its looming silence. There is no backup plan, no alternative. The next stop on this train leaves my family destitute and living on the street. My lip trembles as the weight of my words hangs heavy, like the damp air that consumes the dank basement room. I suck in my lower lip, clasping it between my teeth in an effort to still its quiver. The fleeting image of Louisa dressed in rags and begging for food on a street corner plays in my mind's eye.

"Tell me about this job, Miss Wilson." Mr. Watkins regains his composure with a deep sigh.

"Yes, sir." I take in a breath and clutch it to my chest. Then I clear my throat and detail the hiring process for the hotel maid's position.

Mr. Watkins nods his head, listening to my every word. "You are a determined young lady, aren't you?"

A weak smile lifts my cheeks as I try to maintain a polite and well-mannered disposition, despite the unease spreading through my body with every passing moment. I understand Mr. Watkins means to compliment me, but I can't help thinking that being determined seems the only option available to me. "I promise you, sir, our rent will be my priority. Now and always." I try to etch the despair from my voice, but I hear in the words falling from my lips that I am unsuccessful. I scold myself silently as I wait for his response.

"Miss Wilson, I would be remiss if I didn't inform you that there are others, individual apartment owners within the building, who would be more than happy to send your family and all of the building's renters packing. They were never keen on the idea of rental apartments, fearing the building would go into disrepair and their investments would lose value. If they get so much as a whiff of this, it will not be good for either of us." Mr. Watkins' eyebrows converge on his forehead once more. "Do you understand what I am saying?"

"Yes, sir. The arrangement we agree to will remain between you and me." I give a single nod. "No one else is to know."

"Good." Rubbing his chin, Mr. Watkins says, "Now, you mentioned you may be eligible for a training salary. You could then pay the overdue rent for March?"

"Yes, sir. I expect to begin earning a training wage within the next two weeks." I infuse my message with a false sense of confidence. The sliver of courage and the inflation of my assuredness are present only because of Aunt Vivian's letters. In a few short phrases, Aunt Vivian showed the necessity for such a deft manoeuvre in situations beyond her scope. A bluff is a necessary tactic in this situation, as much for me as for Mr. Watkins. "I will deliver March's overdue payment the moment I receive my wages."

"Yes, Miss Wilson, but what about April?"

I suck in stale air. "I—ah, well . . ." Coherent words escape me as I grapple with the reality of our debt.

"We are well into May already, Miss Wilson. Come the first of June, you will be three months behind in rent again."

I think of Louisa. What would she do? What would she say? I lift my hands nonchalantly, palms up. "Well . . ." I hesitate, wondering if my words will play in the intended lighthearted manner. "I suppose, Mr. Watkins, it is better to be three months behind than four." I feel my cheeks warm as I blush from my boldness.

Mr. Watkins laughs heartily before nodding in agreement.

"With full-time employment, sir, I am positive I can get us caught up and back on schedule by August." The seriousness of my delivery must somehow convince the kind man.

"Well then, Miss Wilson, I suppose we have nothing to lose." He shuffles some papers on his desk. "I will see what I can do regarding The Newbury building owners. Please know I will have to tell them the situation if they come asking. I can't lose my job or my apartment over this, I'm afraid." Another sigh passes through his pursed lips before he offers a soft smile. "You just focus on getting yourself that job, and we will see what we can do."

"Thank you, sir." I stand abruptly and grasp his hand in a tight grip. "Mr. Watkins, I won't let you down."

"I don't expect you will, Miss Wilson. I don't expect you will."

Mr. Watkins walks me from the basement to the light of the lobby before bidding me farewell and good luck.

The breath I've been holding for what seems like hours releases from my chest in a rush of air. I lower myself onto the top step of the lobby stairs, gathering my thoughts while attempting to pick up my remaining nerve from the floor. Contentment with the current situation is but a flash in the pan. The unpredictable nature of the job I have yet to secure still looms before me.

After a few deep breaths and a prayer of thanks to the heavens above, I brace myself against the railing and climb the three floors to our apartment. I force myself to think ahead. There is little time to bask in the knowledge that I have made an agreement with Mr. Watkins. The Hotel Hamilton must hire me. Agreement or not, we cannot afford our rent without a salary. The sooner I can start paying down the overdue rent, the sooner my family will be on solid footing. And the sooner Papa will have to face the fact that his grief has steered us into dangerous waters. My only hope is that he will do so willingly. His drinking has cost us so much already.

As I approach the door to our apartment, I pray for the strength to give everything in pursuit of a maid's position. I must do so as quickly as possible. The clock is ticking.

CHAPTER 11

*T*uesday, May 10, 1927

"There you are." Louisa is standing in the living room, a dress draped over her forearm. "I was about to send a search party for you." Her teasing tone kisses my soul like a breath of fresh air.

"Sorry, I didn't mean to keep you waiting." I hang my sweater and meet her as she holds the dress at arm's length for my examination. Louisa beams in delight at her own handiwork.

"What do you think? I must admit, this might be one of my better alterations. I'd forgotten how fulfilling it can be to take something old and turn it new again." Louisa hands the dress to me. With a gentle hand on my back, she pushes me toward the bedroom. "Try it on. If there is anything more to adjust, we must get to it straight away if we have any hope of taming that hair of yours."

Slipping the dress over my shoulders, I am buoyed by the silkiness of the pale blue fabric. The petal-like layered skirt falls about my legs. Louisa has outdone herself indeed.

Bringing up the hem so it sits just past my knees has done wonders for the skirt's swish, elevating the garment from a 1923 fashion faux pas to a 1927 delight.

Louisa exclaims as I enter the living room. "Oh, how lovely! You are a vision in blue, Clara, and that hemline does wonders for those sturdy legs of yours."

I swivel my hips from side to side to show both my appreciation and my skirt's fanciful swish. "You have done an exceptional job, Louisa. Really, you have."

"Don't sound so surprised." Louisa says, her eyes smiling in jest. "I spent years creating theatre costumes from little more than scraps, you know."

"I didn't know." My embarrassment at not knowing this about my sister rests heavy on my heart. "Really, I didn't know you had such talents." I hold my tongue rather than asking why she hasn't put them to use until now.

"Well, it is no secret that I prefer to shop for the latest fashions." Louisa's downcast eyes give away her realization that she has wasted her talent for sewing, instead coveting things she can't afford. "But, well, I suppose I could spend a little more time and thought on transforming our current wardrobes into something more appropriate for outings."

"It is a lovely dress. Thank you, Lou." I wrap my sister in a warm embrace and vow to give her the benefit of the doubt more often.

TWO HOURS LATER, WE ARE DRESSED, PRESSED, AND powdered. With my nervous stomach curtailing any desire for lunch, I grab an apple for later and slip the novel I am currently reading under my arm before taking one last glance in the hall mirror. Louisa has applied a dab of rouge, along with a delicate pink lip colour, enhancing my eyes and helping them sparkle. She even smoothed my hair before tilting my hat at a fashionable angle and securing it with a pin. My delight tingles all the way to my toes as I bask in my sister's care. I did not know a little extra effort could make me feel as though I've stepped from the pages of one of Louisa's movie magazines.

Louisa is stunning in her rose-coloured dress. Everything about her glows, ensuring all will notice her as we pass en route to the hotel. A full, bright smile completes her ensemble, and the carefree Louisa I know and love lights up the room as she twirls and laughs.

Sliding a small matching purse over her arm, Louisa gestures to the door. "Shall we? It is a beautiful day for"— she leans in conspiratorially and lowers her voice, as Papa has yet to emerge from his bedroom—"a job interview." With a wink, she exits through the door and starts down the three flights of stairs.

I lock the apartment door and follow her into the sunlit day. For Louisa, it seems, an adventure has begun. She seems eager to get on board and leave her worries behind. In contrast, my insides twist in apprehension. The importance of today's tasks marches through my mind.

THE BACK DOOR TO THE HOTEL IS OPEN, AND WE FOLLOW the unadorned hall until we are once again deposited into the hotel's guest corridor, with its ornate wood panelling. Stepping onto the plush carpet, I once again feel the hotel's quiet luxury wrap around me. Mr. Hamilton clearly spared no expense while designing the understated yet exquisite hotel that bears his family name. The expression "simple yet expensive" comes to mind as my eyes roam over the details that help make the corridor a masterpiece.

Cutting short my time admiring the passageway's refined elegance, chatter from the meeting room spills over its tall wooden doors. The voices accost us as we step into the room. There seem to be more girls here today than there were yesterday. The chairs have been removed, and as I contemplate why that may be, I realize that bringing a book to fill the afternoon was likely unnecessary.

Louisa leans close to my ear. "Why do you suppose the chairs are gone?"

My eyes scan the crowd. "Perhaps they were expecting more applicants today." I slide my novel under my arm and lace my fingers together as my nerves take over, causing my hands to shake. "Or perhaps they want those not chosen for an interview to be able to exit more discreetly."

"You don't think so, do you?" Louisa arches one eyebrow, questioning either my comment or my state of mind.

"I know I would rather slink away unnoticed if the unfortunate situation presented itself."

Louisa squeezes my hands in support. "Chin up, Clara. Chin up."

I find myself unable to force a smile as Ms. Thompson steps onto the raised platform, clearing her throat to gain everyone's attention.

"Ladies. Ladies, please." Ms. Thompson dips her chin as she speaks to the gathering of young women. "Thank you again for your interest in employment at The Hotel Hamilton. I want to remind each of you that even if you are not chosen today for an interview, your application will remain on file with our hotel for a full calendar year. I am sure it goes without saying, but not all applicants who move forward this afternoon will be suitable in the end. Thus, it is quite possible that another position may become available in the future."

Louisa and I clutch hands once more, my anxious energy mixing with her bubbling excitement. Again, I am reminded of how uniquely each of us views similar life experiences.

"Without further ado." Ms. Thompson clears her throat once more and reads from a sheet of paper. "Will the following ladies please remain present? Miss Beatrice Hampel, Miss Jane Morgan . . ."

At the mention of Jane's name, my eyes dart around the room to locate the girl I have deemed less than trustworthy since watching her climb into a chauffeured automobile. I am holding back a scoff when Ms. Thompson's voice rings out. "Miss Clara Wilson, Miss Louisa Wilson."

None of the other names Ms. Thompson calls reach my ears. Relief flows through me like the mountain runoff in springtime.

"We did it, Clara. I told you we were shoo-ins." Louisa whispers with a rapid cadence. "Have no fear, little sister. All your worrying will do you no good. It is time for you to look on the bright side of things."

Ms. Thompson pulls me from the depths of my thoughts. "Thank you again, ladies, for your interest in The Hotel Hamilton. All of you whose names were called, please remain in place. The rest of you may exit through the service hall. Mr. Olson will lead the way." Ms. Thompson inclines her head toward a tall, lean gentleman in a three-piece suit. "Mr. Olson, please show these ladies out."

The noisy gaggle of disappointed young women file from the room, their tongues wagging at an unbecoming volume and their words laced with fire from being spurned. Echoes of "What's next?" and "I can't believe I wasn't chosen" float among the crowd like butterflies in a rose garden.

Louisa waves a defeated goodbye to a girl moving toward the exit. "That's Tabatha," Louisa leans close and whispers. "I suppose she won't be joining us after all."

As the room quietens, I glance about, counting those who remain. Forty or so candidates smile nervously at one another while Ms. Thompson motions us to move closer.

"Congratulations, ladies, we have selected you to go forward with the interview process. We are seeking both full-time day staff and part-time evening staff. This afternoon, we will focus on getting to know each of you a little better. I and the hotel manager, Mr. Olson, will interview you in private. Once your interview is complete, you may leave. If we select you for the maid's training program, we will notify you at the close of your interview. Those who do not move forward will remain on our reserve list and may be called if another applicant cannot complete the training. Have I made myself clear?"

Ms. Thompson looks about the room, meeting each girl's eye. "Chairs and refreshments will be here momentarily. It is likely to be a long afternoon for some of you, so please take the opportunity for a snack and something to drink." A tight smile forms on Ms. Thompson's face. "We will do our best to be as efficient as possible, and we appreciate your patience."

As Ms. Thompson steps from the platform, Jane catches my eye and moves through a clutch of applicants, toward us.

"Clara, it is good to see you again. Isn't it marvellous that both of us are moving on?" Though her voice hints at lightness, Jane's eyes snatch glances at Louisa as she speaks.

"Yes, I am feeling quite fortunate at the moment." My hands go to my stomach to calm the butterflies jostling about. I gesture toward Louisa. "Jane, this is my sister, Louisa."

"Oh, you didn't mention you had a sister. Or that she was applying for a position." Jane's eyes shine brightly as she connects the dots. "Aren't you the girl who arrived dreadfully late yesterday?"

Louisa smiles as sweetly as ever, motioning toward Ms. Thompson and Mr. Olson. The two of them are deep in conversation, with a stack of paper application forms between them. "Not late. Quite on time, really. Gave me an opportunity to have a few words with Ms. Thompson before the meeting began," she says.

"I see." Jane feigns disinterest as she pretends to scan the room. "And what, pray tell, did Ms. Thompson have to say? Any nuggets of wisdom on how best to gain the attention of Mr. Olson?" Returning her attention to Louisa, Jane's eyes dance with mischief, and I read a hint of accusation in her question.

Louisa chuckles, brushing off Jane's untoward tone. "Nothing so conniving as that, I'm afraid." Cocking her head, Louisa examines Jane from a new angle. "Polite conversation regarding the plans for the hotel's grand opening is all. I had wondered if a spectacle the likes of the one that took place at The Hotel Georgia was planned for this opening." Louisa's casual reply allows her the opportunity to look away from Jane's stare. A clear sign the conversation, on her part, is finished.

The tension building between Jane and Louisa heightens my trepidation about the upcoming interview.

How much simpler would things be if neither Louisa nor Jane were in the running at all? In a perfect world, my application would have edged out both of them and I would have had a clear, undistracted focus on the tasks ahead of me. Now, I must balance polite conversation with my wariness of Jane's intentions and Louisa's sharp tongue.

Five young men draw my attention as they enter the room, carrying chairs and tables. "You may place the tables against the far wall." Ms. Thompson directs them with a long, pointed finger. "Ladies, please help yourself to a chair. The kitchen staff will bring the refreshments within the hour."

The clatter of tables and chairs being set up drown out further conversation. With an efficiency I have seldom witnessed, the young men position two tables near the wall and cover them in thick white table linens, freshly pressed and without a crease in sight. I turn to catch Louisa's attention but find her delivering a coy smile toward the young men. Following her gaze, I almost gasp when the tallest one, with fair hair and a handsome face, returns her smile with a crooked one all his own. He winks at her over his shoulder while exiting the room.

I am about to comment, a warning tone gathering in my throat, when Ms. Thompson calls my name.

"Clara Wilson." Ms. Thompson lifts her eyes from her papers as I raise my hand in response. "There you are, Miss Wilson." Her stern expression morphs to a welcoming one as our eyes meet. Ms. Thompson pivots and strides toward the open door. "Please, come with me."

I look toward Louisa and Jane, with unease and hesitation. As I think of all that could go wrong, a tingling sensation envelops me like a scarf tied too tightly about my throat. My mind plays tug-of-war with the attention Louisa garnered from that boy and the obvious discord between Jane and my sister.

Louisa's palm pressing lightly on my back pulls me from my indecision. "Go," she says. "You'll do great." Her brilliant smile encourages me forward.

I hand my apple and book to Louisa and follow Ms. Thompson to a small office, where she introduces Mr. Olson before offering me a chair.

"Miss Wilson, your application form is thoughtfully filled out, so we have only a few questions for you." Ms. Thompson reads the page once more before meeting my eyes.

"What would you say is your greatest asset, Miss Wilson?" Mr. Olson's voice is gentle but forthright.

Swivelling my head in his direction, I answer with an assuredness I seldom possess. "Loyalty, sir." My eyes drop to my hands folded in my lap before I remember to sit up straight and deliver a confident response. "My mother often commented favourably on my trait of loyalty." I find Mr. Olson's face to be kind and feel myself relax a touch.

"Your mother, Miss Wilson. She has passed?" Ms. Thompson clears her throat before continuing. "I don't mean to pry into your private affairs. I merely noticed that you mentioned being well versed in caring for the family home, and since you are of a tender age, I want to ensure your taking on full-time employment will not be an additional burden to your family situation?"

"No, ma'am. I am eager to work." I lean forward in my chair. "In all honesty, ma'am, my family is in need of a full-time salary." With a hint of embarrassment at my admission, I pause.

"And your sister, Miss Louisa Wilson? Has she applied for the same reason?"

"No, ma'am." Panic encases my chest, trapping a breath that is desperate to escape. "Louisa is less familiar with our family's financial need." I feel heat casting colour up my collar. "If it is all the same to you, ma'am, I would prefer to keep it that way."

"I see." Mr. Olson nods, first in my direction and then in Ms. Thompson's. "Miss Wilson, with only a few words, you have not only demonstrated a sound reason to work, but also a strong work ethic and a moral obligation that far exceeds your young age."

"Thank you, sir." The butterflies in my stomach feel as though they've transformed into frogs and are now jumping with eagerness. I draw my lower lip between my teeth to maintain a ladylike appearance.

"Ms. Thompson, Miss Clara Wilson is an acceptable applicant. If you agree, I would be pleased to offer her admittance to the training program." Mr. Olson's eyes crinkle in what I interpret to be a pleased expression, though his lips remain neutral.

"Certainly, sir. I agree with you." Ms. Thompson's words catapult my happiness, deeply woven with relief. "Miss Wilson, will you return next Monday at precisely nine o'clock to begin the training program?"

I stand abruptly, excitement boosting me from my seat. "Yes, Ms. Thompson. Yes, I will."

"Good. Then we will see you on Monday." Ms. Thompson hands me a thin bundle of papers and a pencil. "Before you go, please fill out this paperwork for our employment records and leave it on the table outside this door. Stewart will show you to a quiet room where you can complete the forms. Welcome to The Hotel Hamilton, Miss Wilson."

"Thank you, ma'am and sir. It is an honour to be

considered for the position." I leave the interview feeling as though I am gliding, floating above my troubles. I am eager for the training program to begin. The man I presume to be Stewart, though no formal introductions take place, shows me to a room across the hall. He directs me toward a desk and chair and leaves the door slightly ajar on his way out.

I turn my attention to the three sheets of paper. With my head bent over the polished desk, I am unaware of other applicants as they come and go from their own interviews. When my paperwork is complete, I exit the quiet room, deep in thought. In my relief, fanciful thoughts of things to come dance through my head. I am placing the completed papers on a small tray on the hall table when Louisa startles me by poking a finger into my ribs as she passes by. I turn to see her step into the office where Ms. Thompson and Mr. Olson are waiting. I glance at the tray that the papers rest within, then make my way back to the banquet room.

Looking around the room, I notice the gathering of applicants has dwindled and Jane is nowhere to be seen. I walk toward the refreshment table and pour myself a tall glass of water. As I wait for Louisa, I nibble on a slice of cinnamon loaf and encourage my glee to stow itself away out of politeness for those yet to be interviewed. I have no intention of boasting about my good news in front of my sister, should she not be selected. I consider her feelings and the potential damage her bruised ego may inflict on me and decide I will downplay my fortunate outcome and instead focus on consoling Louisa, should the situation require it.

CHAPTER 12

*T*uesday, May 10, 1927

My eyes trace the delicate swirling pattern of the room's carpet, coaxing my attention this way and that with its deep blues and touches of gold. As my gaze wanders, so does my mind. I remain silent as I practise words of consolation for Louisa. When she reappears from her interview, disappointment is likely to have twisted the natural beauty of her face into a pout, and I ready myself for her look of unfathomable misfortune.

I glance up from my seated position, Louisa's tall frame catching my attention through the open wood-panelled doors. Delight emanates from her being, and the gentle glow of the overhead chandeliers further highlights her rosy cheeks. She lets out a small squeal as she hurries toward me. "I made it through too."

I rise to meet her, and Louisa swoops me into an embrace. Her enthusiasm spills out of her in a rush of words and occasional shrills of excited laughter. "When I saw you in the hall, I knew you had been successful. That was all the boost I needed to ensure I would be right there beside you in this grand adventure of ours."

Louisa catches her breath, glancing around the room. Her brow furrows as she returns her attention to our conversation. "You were taking such a long time, and at first, I didn't understand why. I thought perhaps they had sent you on your way and I was going to have to search for you, forlorn and roaming the streets." Louisa brushes against my arm in a playful gesture, her imagined duties eased by our current fortunate circumstance.

I am instantly humbled by her concern for me. Louisa worried for me. I, on the other hand, spent my idle time drafting commiserating words to console my sister, half hoping she would be unsuccessful. I chastise myself silently and wonder where my kind and generous spirit has hidden itself.

"So many girls came and went, Clara." Louisa inclines her head toward the final cluster of young ladies gathered across the room. "Rather, so many girls went off to their interview and didn't return. I don't know how many others they accepted into the training program, but the stack of papers in the tray had only grown by a handful or two by the time I added my own."

My head shakes back and forth as a cloud of uncertainty forms around me. "I don't know either. To be honest, I was so focused on my own paperwork that I do not even know whether another girl was nearby." My voice grows quiet as embarrassment at my lack of awareness fills the space between us. "I—I remember having a sense of people coming and going from the hall." A flutter of unease rises within me. "But I am not sure who or how many there were."

"Here." Louisa has my novel hidden beneath her arm.

She hands it to me before extracting my apple from a pocket disguised by the layers of her fabric-rich skirt.

"Oh! I completely forgot about those. I am sorry you had to manage my belongings all afternoon."

Louisa shakes off my concern with a swift movement of her head. She reaches for my half-full glass of water and takes a sip before continuing. "You wouldn't have known. They put each of us in separate rooms to finish the paperwork."

Perplexed, my question gathers in the lines of my forehead. "How do you know this?"

Louisa takes another sip of water. "Another applicant already occupied the first room I was directed to, so Stewart showed me to an empty room further down the hall."

"I see." My thumb taps the spine of my novel. "So, there is no way of knowing who is joining us on Monday?"

"Well, I can tell you that Jane girl was called for her interview. A few girls after you were summoned." Louisa's dislike of Jane Morgan shrouds her words. She sounds as though someone has handed her a spoonful of cod liver oil to swallow. "I didn't see her again." Louisa sniffs. "Not that it will trouble me at all."

I am struck by my lack of concern regarding the outcome of Jane's interview. Louisa counts on her fingers the number of applicants who surely would have passed near me on their way to and from the office. Louisa prattles on, and I take a hard look at how threatened I've truly been by Jane's presence. It's funny how some individuals can set your teeth on edge and evict good manners and common sense from within your person.

With Jane presumably out of the equation, my thoughts turn to how Louisa might impact my success at the hotel. She secured a position in the training program all on her own. My head tilts as I weigh Louisa's impulsive tendencies against her jubilant and quite contagious joyfulness.

Louisa gestures excitedly as she talks about the fun the two of us will have working together, being able to count on one another. "Who knows." Louisa leans closer with a mischievous wink. "We might even meet a few movie stars while working at a swanky hotel such as this." A backward roll of her shoulders tells me she is attempting to fool herself into believing that being a maid will be enough for her. "That might be as close to Hollywood as I will get, after all." Pretending her comment didn't leave a bruise on her skin, Louisa sniffs the air before averting her eyes.

I chide myself for feeling put out. Clearly, I am not the only sister who is struggling to sort out where her life has landed. I catch Louisa's profile as she pivots, looking around the room. I haven't seen that sparkle in her eyes for quite some time. Even in the best moments of these past few years, grief and misfortune have marred any semblance of joy, wrapping around moments of delight like a deadly snake.

I think of all those afternoons she spent sitting on the sofa, lost and mournful. A small sigh leaves my lips as I consider how rarely Louisa speaks of Mama. I wonder how three people who love one another so dearly can keep themselves closed off and separate in such tiny quarters as our apartment. Grief demolishes a person before it reshapes you, moulding you into only that which you can tolerate, never demanding more, never pressing you toward life.

No, something deep within me argues. Grief wants nothing more than for you to stay stuck, right where you are, in a puddle of nothingness.

Louisa drains the glass of water before returning it to

the long table near the far wall. I give my head a subtle shake, willing myself toward a more pleasant mood. The least I can do is be happy for Louisa and her victory. Perhaps working together will be a blessing. Given Lou's excitement at the prospect, I suppose this could be more of an adventure than I originally thought.

I begin second-guessing myself in no time at all as I remember her earlier interaction with that boy. The far too familiar downward spiral of distressing emotions tries with a fervour to pull me under. I shake away the image, knowing I would rather see my sister filled with purpose and contentment. I nudge aside any residual animosity and jut out my chin defiantly, intent on setting aside worrying thoughts. In this moment, this happy moment, I decide to be pleased for myself and for Louisa. I link my arm through hers, pulling her toward the open meeting room doors, and congratulate her on her accomplishment.

With light banter, we walk down the staff corridor, toward the back entrance of the hotel. I allow the sensation of ease and freedom to linger around me. Childhood memories glitter with a brilliant sheen in my periphery, and I feel the magical sensation of connecting with a loved one. These are the moments I've missed so much. This is what it means to be a family.

"How pleased Papa will be," Louisa exclaims, tugging me closer to her as we near the hotel's exit.

I stop at once, a prickle of anxiety crawling up my back. "No, we can't." I search for the right words to explain myself. "We can't tell Papa anything about this."

"But why?" Louisa's nose scrunches up, like a toddler who's been given spinach instead of sweets. "He will be pleased we have succeeded so far." Louisa turns, arms folding across her chest in preparation for an argument. "Is there something you aren't telling me, Clara?"

"No." My voice does little to convey assuredness or honesty, and Louisa's tapping toe tells me so. "I—I simply think Papa will have fewer objections to us taking jobs if we are to present the news to him once our employment is secure. Either way, there is little sense worrying him or getting his hopes up until we know for certain."

Louisa's skepticism lines her face as she considers my reasoning.

"Think of it this way," I offer. "By the time we have become maids, we will have a little spending money from our training wage. Then we can surprise him with a roast beef dinner, like Mama used to make for special occasions. Won't that be worth the wait?"

"I suppose," Louisa concedes, as I consider how I will afford both the overdue rent and a roast dinner. "All the trimmings too? It's been ages since we enjoyed Yorkshire pudding with gravy."

A laugh erupts from my chest. "Of course, Yorkshire pudding and all the trimmings. It will be like Christmas in June." Our mutual fit of giggles has us bumping into one another as we exit the hotel and step into the warm alleyway.

A rustle and then a clang capture my attention. In the corner nook of the hotel's outer wall, shadows shroud a young boy sifting through a garbage bin. Both arms moving like a windmill, he pulls out newspapers and old rags, dropping them to the ground while he continues his hunt.

I step toward him slowly, curious but careful not to startle him. "Excuse me." I take another step closer, and his head pops up like a mole emerging from a freshly dug hole.

A wide smile erupts on the young Asian face before me,

and recognition leaps from my memory. He is the same boy I saw dashing through a gauntlet of hotel applicants' legs near the kitchen yesterday. His impish smile gives him away. The boy holds up an apple core, lifting it high in the air for me to see. Most of the apple's flesh has been eaten away, yet his contagious smile and dancing eyes show his perceived good fortune.

Glancing at the full, ripe apple in my palm, a stab of guilt races my grumbling stomach to the surface. I stretch my arm forward, open my palm, and motion for the boy to take the apple.

He raises the previously discarded core, his smile growing wider.

"Please," I say, "take this one."

The boy shakes his head and points to his apple.

Louisa brushes against me as she moves closer. She speaks, barely louder than a breath. "I don't think he wants it, Clara."

All my fears rise to the surface. Tears gather in my eyes as I see myself, Louisa, and even Papa in this young boy's face. We are but a short fall from a life of digging through garbage bins for daily sustenance. I understand how easy it is to find oneself in such a situation. Yet, this boy seems happy, grateful even.

I take another step closer, placing the apple in the boy's empty hand. "For you." I incline my head. "Please. For you."

The boy looks at both apples. I expect him to toss the core into the bin. Instead, he meets my eyes. "Thank you, miss."

Relief leaps across my face. "Clara," I say. "My name is Clara."

"Thank you, Miss Clara." He manoeuvres a few paces

away before lunging into a run, both arms moving quickly as he sails away from us.

The hotel's back door closes with a bang, causing us both to turn.

"Ah, I hoped I would catch you." Jane walks in our direction. "It looks as though we've all secured placement in the training program. How exciting," she coos, batting her eyelashes.

Louisa, not missing a beat, cocks her head. "How did you know they invited us into the program?"

Jane peeks over her shoulder and lowers her voice an octave. "I thumbed through the forms in the tray when I was handing mine in. It looks like Beatrice, you know the dowdy-looking one with woven braids pinned at the back of her head, will also join us." Without hiding her displeasure, Jane adds, "I guess you can't win them all."

Louisa gives a terse reply. "No, I suppose you can't."

Though I suspect Jane misses Louisa's pointed tone, I notice the ridicule in my sister's delivery and stifle a giggle. Jane waves goodbye and dashes around to the front of the hotel, where I expect her chauffeur and car are waiting.

As Jane disappears around the corner, my excitement plummets. "Looks like I will have to contend with Jane after all."

"Don't let her get the better of you, Clara." Louisa places an arm around my shoulders and ushers me toward the street. "Come on, we have our own futures to celebrate." Louisa's eyes glisten with exhilaration, and all I can do is marvel at her optimism.

CHAPTER 13

*T*uesday, May 10, 1927

  The sidewalk is bustling with activity. Those who have been held captive behind office and shop windowpanes venture into the warm late afternoon air, creating a busy crowd. The courthouse across the street stands tall, anchoring Georgia, Howe, Robson, and Hornby Streets with its formidable dark grey stone. The sun, positioned overhead in a clear blue sky, spotlights the twin granite lions on either side of the courthouse's wide stone steps.

As we walk toward home, Louisa squeezes my arm, linked through hers, and clears her throat. "Clara, what do you really think of Jane? I find her haughty and more than a little annoying." Louisa rolls her eyes in exasperation. "But I wonder what your thoughts might be."

A sideways glance at Louisa tells me she has more to say on the subject. Instead of barrelling ahead, as is her usual approach, she is chewing her bottom lip to hold back her words, and I wonder why.

We make our way past The Hotel Georgia, both of us snatching glimpses inside as we manoeuvre through the crowd, past the hotel's front door. "Well, I suppose our thoughts are in line when it comes to Miss Morgan." I feign disinterest by scanning the shops we pass, willing my words and demeanour to convey nonchalance.

"Yes, but"—Louisa checks for automobiles before tugging me across the street—"I got the sense that you feel threatened by the girl."

"Well, she comes on a little strong." I pull my arm free of Louisa's under the guise of adjusting the book tucked beneath my other arm.

"That she does." Louisa laughs out loud before her voice softens to a gentle tone. "I guess, well, you should know that you have no reason to think she is better than you, no matter what airs she puts on."

Louisa's needle-like words shimmer in the light as they unveil the purpose of our conversation. In moments such as these, my sister continues to surprise me. I often think of her as someone who prefers to ignore uncomfortable situations, both her own and others'. Somehow, though, her understanding of Jane's misguided motivations far exceeds what I would expect.

"What makes you say that?" Innocence, or rather false ignorance, is my go-to fallback.

"Don't think I can't read you like an open book, Clara Wilson."

I stifle a nervous laugh. If only Louisa knew how much I haven't told her. I suppose a person can't possibly keep every thought a secret, especially from those so knitted in one's life. Determined to regain my composure, with a purposeful blink of my eyes, I thrust the responsible and unflappable Clara to the forefront of my being. "I don't think there is anything to worry about with Jane. I am sure everything will be fine." I lightly pat Louisa's arm. "Things will work out how they will."

"What did she say that has you all in a bother?" Louisa is done nibbling around the edges, and her raised eyebrow tells me so. "I can almost see you quivering in your Mary Janes. You can't fool me, Clara, not for one minute."

With no response from me, Louisa wraps an arm around my shoulders with a pumping motion, squeezing life into my limp posture. "Whatever it is, I am sure it is time to let it go. You can't control the outcome of everything in life, Clara, so there is no sense wasting time or thought on the matter."

"Mm-hmm." I nod in agreement as my thoughts shift to their own trajectory, arguing against Louisa's comments. I am sure she means well, but I need control over this particular situation. The hotel must hire me. Ignoring my fear-induced reflex, I coax a calmness into my voice. "I'm sure you are right. I would simply hate to see an opportunity such as this go to someone who hasn't been completely honest."

By Louisa's expression, I can tell she would like to inquire further about what I mean by "honest." Not willing to give her the opportunity, I press forward. "What I mean is that Jane Morgan is a wild card, plain and simple. I am sure we could be the best of friends in another situation, but competing against her for employment is not what I would call a good time. She seems so put together, so confident, knowing what she wants and going after it without apology. I guess I wish I had a little more of that in me."

"Oh, but you do, Clara. You do." Louisa turns to face me. "You should be proud of who you are. Besides, you know what you want too. And you are going after it, aren't you?" Louisa inclines her head to ensure I hear her point. "Success comes in all shapes and sizes, Clara, and not all of them look like Jane Morgan."

"Thanks." I nudge her shoulder with my own. "I suspect you are slightly biased, being my sister and all." My teasing tone doesn't push Louisa from the topic.

"Well, you can think of it this way. Jane isn't the only girl returning for training. Surely the hotel intends to hire a fair number of maids. Otherwise, wouldn't it be a waste of their time to train us all?"

"You are absolutely right, Louisa. I hadn't thought of it that way." My hopes lift a little We begin strolling toward home again. "Good thinking. We must stand a decent chance of being selected. We will simply have to work hard and show them the Wilson girls are prepared to do whatever it takes to become maids at their hotel."

A giggle rushes past Louisa's lips. "Well, I may have to draw the line at your 'whatever it takes,' but if you really want to work, there are plenty of other opportunities out there." Louisa's voice flutters up and down like a ballad. "Perhaps this was only the first step. Now you know you want to work. That must be what matters most, not specifically this position at this hotel." With nary a breath between sentences, Louisa gushes, "Oh, but it would be lovely to spend all day within the walls of such an exquisite hotel."

I know in my head she is right. There are plenty of opportunities to work. Somehow, though, I have put all my eggs in one basket. I have staked everything in my life on securing a job at The Hamilton.

Recognition dawns on me like the beginning of a pesky heat rash, prickling near the surface and promising further havoc. I see the similarities between this and how I focused on setting up a home at The Newbury a few months ago. I was engrossed by the task. I could not see how Papa's transgressions were affecting our lives. Like a snowball gaining speed and size while rolling down a mountain, challenges only become bigger if they aren't tended to early. I am well aware of what I must do. I must be dedicated to the task of training while remaining constantly vigilant. This is the only path to ensure my success at becoming a Hotel Hamilton maid.

Louisa must sense my unease as she yanks me sharply to the right, away from home and the simple dinner I am to prepare upon our arrival. "Come on, let's stop for an ice cream. It is a beautiful day, and we should celebrate today's success. Besides, Papa won't mind dinner being tardy, as long as we bring him a treat too."

My brow furrows as I consider the few coins left in my pocketbook. I slated the money to, with any luck, help with next week's groceries. The scant coins are available only due to the too-expensive peaches I was forced to decline purchasing. My forehead perspires at the mortifying memory, and my body responds with an immediate instinct to flee.

As worry over our imminent future materializes in my mind's eye, I consider how a few coins might come in handy. I may need to purchase a newspaper to search for further employment opportunities, in the event I am dismissed from the hotel's training. As much as possible, I need to keep my options open. I am determined to stretch the little we have as far as possible. Struggling to find words to explain our inability to even consider a treat such as ice cream, my mouth goes dry. My desire to avoid burdening Louisa with the news of our dwindling financial stability engulfs me. If I am being honest, part of me is terrified of telling her.

The stress and anguish over our troubles may gnaw at me every moment, day and night, but confiding in Louisa will only underline the full weight of our precarious situation. I am not capable of giving voice to my fears. Telling Louisa would make our current struggles far more real.

Louisa's eyes sparkle as she extracts a neatly folded bill from her pocket. "My treat." Her enthusiastic smile could light up a darkened sky.

"But how? Where did you get the money?" My mind whirs with questions.

"Don't look so distraught. I sold a few costumes from the play I was in last summer. Seems another production company is putting on their own rendition, and they were eager to get some costumes second-hand." Louisa's smile fades a little as she looks me up and down. "Are you feeling all right, Clara?"

"But we— How much?" I stop myself from saying more. Louisa doesn't need to know how close we are to being penniless and on the street. I push away my frantic dismay and smooth my hair. My mind races with thoughts of the market and how I've scrutinized every penny spent. For months I've worked with so little, preparing meals to nourish rather than delight. I've stretched coins further than I would have thought possible. I've darned socks, grated soap, and made do. The exhaustion of keeping a handle on things pours out of me as uncontrollable tears.

"What's the matter? I thought a treat would be just the ticket." Louisa's hand goes to my back to comfort my tears away. "I've been saving the money for a special occasion." She leans her head toward mine, touching my forehead to hers. "Today is a special occasion, Clara. It would be nice to celebrate with you."

My head bobs as I sniffle. "Yes, you are right. We should celebrate. I don't know why I am blubbering on so much." I offer a lighthearted laugh as embarrassment at my emotional outburst spills from every pore.

Louisa stands up straight, placing one hand on each of my shoulders. "You have been worrying yourself sick over this hotel thing. Really, Clara, you need to learn to let go a bit. That worry will eat you up inside." Louisa gently shakes my shoulders, grabbing my attention. "Enjoy the moments as they come. Let's get some ice cream."

I swipe the tears from my face and look Louisa in the eye. "Well, if you insist." I loop my arm through hers and pivot us in the fountain shop's direction. "But . . ." I pause to formulate my words with care. "Let's not take any home for Papa today. I don't think he would be happy with a puddle of ice cream, and that is sure to be all we'd have left with today's sun." I force a smile and add a conspiratorial wink for good measure. "Then you can save the rest of your money for another day to remember."

Louisa's delight is obvious. "I won't tell if you don't."

CHAPTER 14

*S*unday, May 15, 1927

The choir sings and I find myself mesmerized by the way their voices lift toward the wood-slatted rafters, echoing and flowing like the cascade of a waterfall, powerful yet soothing. Christ Church Cathedral, though far from my usual Sunday destination, is a welcomed stop this spring morning. The music pulled me in through the open door as I strolled by on my way to the water's edge. The stained glass draws my eyes past the hanging, gold-encased lights, the stately pipe organ, and the shadows cast by the oversized wooden beams.

After spending the past several days talking with Louisa about the opportunity that lies before us, my excitement at our potential employment at the hotel has grown in spades. Louisa's vision for our future has ignited my imagination, filling my heart and soul with notions of comfort and stability. She dreams out loud of somehow being discovered as an actress while working at the hotel, and I don't have the heart to rain on her parade. I have learned that sparing her feelings is a natural part of our sibling relationship.

My spirits lifted even higher when Papa announced on Thursday afternoon that Mr. Murray had asked for his assistance at the estate. He asked me to pack him a lunch, and off he went, bright and early Friday morning. Papa stayed busy on Friday and Saturday, during long days of spring planting and pruning. The work and travel took him well into the night, meaning Papa is home sleeping off tired muscles instead of a drunken stupor, and for that, I am immensely grateful.

Upon waking late this morning, Papa headed back to the Murray estate. He kissed the top of my head as I handed him a lunch pail packed with sandwiches and an apple. His voice was raspy from sleep, but its singsong tone held joy. My heart flipped inside my chest, desperate for him to find his way once again.

A few extra dollars are sure to reach the grocery tin this week, given Papa's lack of wayward spending, in addition to the influx of paid work. If I am able, I plan to squirrel away some money to pay down the overdue rent. Or perhaps, I muse, I will save the extra coins for our special roast beef dinner. I plan to keep my promise to Louisa once we have secured full-time employment.

Until Papa releases the funds, though, I can only guess at what will be available to me. I watch with quiet resonance as the choir and congregation settle into their seats. The shuffle of hymn books and the creak of wooden pews accompany the transition.

The subtle glow of candles flicker around the room. At the front of the church, the reverend takes his position at the pulpit before scanning the crowd. "May God be with you." The reverend's voice booms all the way to the back row, where I have snuck in from the side entrance so as not to disturb the service.

"And also with you." The congregation replies in unison, and I am reminded of how Mama always knew what to say and when. She grew up Anglican, and it was important to her that her daughters be baptized and regularly attend Sunday services.

"Let us pray," the reverend continues as the congregation bows their heads as one.

The prayer washes over me, blanketing me in contentment, and I am filled with a deep desire to see Mama sitting beside me, her shoulder gently brushing mine as she speaks the Lord's Prayer. Her voice would be light and filled with the love she embodied in all things said and done.

I squeeze back the moisture brimming in my eyes and wish I had invited Louisa to join me on my walk this morning. I hadn't noticed the absence of this weekly ritual until now. I am reminded of the small cog I truly am in this great big world. The church can humble and shelter those within its tranquil environment. My heart expands with this knowledge, and I find myself lost in a silent prayer of gratitude until the reverend closes the sermon, his youthful face lit up like a lantern.

KNOWING I WILL SPEND MY WEEK TRAINING AT THE HOTEL, I dedicate my Sunday afternoon to household chores. The hours pass as I scrub the floors and wash the laundry, all the while fretting about what tomorrow will bring. Louisa joins me in conversation, though not in effort. She follows me from the bathroom to the kitchen, passing me the soap when I ask as she prattles on about tomorrow's training and repeats for the hundredth time how exciting it is to be women of the working class.

Wiping sweat from my brow after scrubbing a particularly dirt-soiled shirt of Papa's, I offer Louisa a pointed look. "You know we will both have to pitch in with the household chores from now on."

"What are you talking about?" Louisa's face wrinkles, her dream-filled tangent cut off.

"If we are both going to work at the hotel, then we both need to help with the chores at home." I stand up straight, wiping my hands on the apron tied around my waist. "You can't expect me to work all day and then also cook and clean here by myself."

Her fantasy abruptly shoved aside, Louisa's mouth puckers as though she's eaten sour grapes. "Nobody expects you to do all the cooking and cleaning."

"Really?" I smother a sharp remark and rest my hands on my hips. "When was the last time you cooked a meal, Louisa?"

She examines the contours of the ceiling. "I—I made lunch just last week." She gives a determined nod like an exclamation point, intent on proving me incorrect.

"You made a peanut butter and jelly sandwich, Louisa, and you made it for yourself."

"Well, I still took the initiative, and I managed quite well, I'll have you know." The huff in Louisa's voice holds more hurt than anger. Pushing this conversation would be futile, no matter how carefully I craft my words.

"All I am saying is that we need to work together. At home and at the hotel." A pout has fastened itself to her otherwise porcelain-perfect face. "I need your help. I won't be able to stay on top of everything here while also keeping our training secret from Papa."

"All right." Louisa grabs the bucket of water from the floor, taking it to the sink and dumping it down the drain. "I will do what I can to help."

I resist the urge to tell her I was not yet finished with the water and instead force a smile of appreciation into place. "Thank you. That is all I ask of you."

"What's next, then?" Louisa spins around, surveying the kitchen and living space. "What chore do we have to tend to?"

"You could polish the furniture. It shouldn't take too long since there are only a few pieces in each room." Directing Louisa with a rag and jar of polish, I send her to the living room with instructions to polish the kitchen table and the dresser in each bedroom. "Don't forget to move all the items off of the furniture before you dip your cloth in polish." I hope the reminder will help her avoid a messy accident.

With only one of my dresses left in the basket, I decide to skip the rest of the washing and instead set up the ringer. While Louisa polishes the wood, a show tune dancing on her lips, I crank the ringer to remove as much moisture as possible from the wet heap of clothes. Then I hang them to dry, one by one. With the help of a warm breeze, the clothes should be dry and ready for folding by morning.

Several hours and tasks later, Louisa and I collapse on the sofa. A sea-laced breeze from the open window washes over us. I check my wristwatch and smother a groan. It's already four twenty, and I still have dinner to scrounge up before Papa returns from his afternoon of work.

"I can't believe how fast the afternoon has gone." Louisa's right arm drapes over her forehead dramatically.

"Time flies when the tasks are many," I agree, wondering how either of us will manage the household duties with much busier schedules. Perhaps I haven't considered the details of my plan thoroughly enough. A dull thud pulsates at my temples, signalling a headache is about to usurp logical thought. I rub my forehead with my fingers.

Besides the added weight of the household chores, my concern over keeping Papa's awareness of our new schedule at bay niggles at me. "I hope they will need Papa on more days than not at the Murray estate. Otherwise, I am not sure how we will explain our daylong absences and new scheduling of household chores."

Louisa looks at me as though I'm talking nonsense. "I'm not sure he'll notice. At least, not for a little while."

I sit upright and pivot to meet her gaze. "Why on earth would you say such a thing? Of course he will notice."

Louisa shakes her head. "Sadly, I don't think so." A defeated shrug tells me she is more than a little aware of Papa's daily rituals. "The past few weeks, he has been sleeping late most days. He barely utters a coherent word until the afternoon, when he perks up and announces he is heading out for a walk."

I am stunned into silence. Louisa is right. I am hardly aware Papa is home until he appears in the late afternoon, dressed and ready for his daily walk. I busy myself most days with household chores, ensuring our home is clean, with fresh bread at the ready.

"I don't think he even notices me curled up, reading on the sofa." A touch of sadness laces Louisa's words.

"He comes home for dinner though." I attempt to weave together a semblance of family life, so my sister can see our work isn't all for naught.

"Yes, and then it is off to the gin joints. Both the legal and illegal ones, I'm afraid." Louisa gauges my reaction from behind an arched eyebrow.

"Illegal too?" I have wondered about this but haven't yet confirmed my speculations. "How can you be certain?"

Louisa's face transforms, and her vacant expression sends a shiver up my spine. Chill bumps emerge on my arms, and the sinking sensation that another blow is about to be delivered hangs in the air like a foul smell.

"I followed him." Plainly spoken but carrying immense weight, Louisa's words reverberate inside my head before travelling to my heart, where they land like a hammer.

"Followed him?" My mouth turns dry as the words edge forward, one at a time. "Where?" I pause, the sensation of the room rotating sending me off balance. "When?"

"Three weeks ago, I guess." Louisa shrugs again, and I wonder if she doesn't remember or if she is trying to forget.

"Wh-where did you follow him to?" All this time, I have thought that I was the one holding this family together, by the skin of my teeth, no less. The room spins faster as my belief that I had our situation handled slips through my fingers like sand.

"A warehouse," Louisa says flatly, "in Chinatown."

"Chinatown? What on earth was he doing all the way over in Chinatown? Was there work at that warehouse?" My eyebrows knit together, gathering with them the tension headache that is growing more persistent by the second.

"It was a blind pig, I presume." Louisa lets out an irritable sigh, her distaste for the topic colouring her words.

I cock my head to one side, stretching and massaging my neck. I poke and prod at the tightening muscles distractedly. "What exactly is a blind pig?"

"A nickname for establishments that serve illegal alcohol, while offering activities such as gambling and—"

Louisa chews on her lower lip, and I assume she is contemplating how much to share with me. "And what?" I ask, both wanting to know and wishing to never need to have such a conversation.

"Women."

"What do you mean 'women'?" I fold my arms across my chest in defiance. "Seriously, Louisa, can you be any more cryptic?"

"For hire." Louisa's eyes examine her hands folded and twined in her lap. "Men pay to be intimate with them." Louisa's eyes flick up to mine. "They are called prostitutes, Clara."

"No, you don't think . . ." The gasp leaps from my lips. "Papa would never. He still grieves for Mama, and we can barely afford all that we require. No, Louisa, you are wrong. Papa would never spend the money we need to survive on women or gambling."

"I didn't say he would. Settle down, Clara." Louisa's expression screams exasperation. "I was merely answering your question about what a blind pig is. I didn't see Papa do anything other than go into the place."

"He wouldn't. I know he wouldn't do such a thing." My straight-backed posture sinks a little under the weight of this new disappointment. I cannot deny Louisa's evidence. "He has a problem with the drink. Of that I am aware." I thrum my fingers against my folded arm. "I imagined being able to fix this, getting a job at the hotel and fixing it all."

"Oh Clara, this isn't your problem to fix." Louisa shifts closer to me on the sofa and wraps a protective arm around my shoulders. "Papa is responsible for his own actions. All we can do is be responsible for ourselves."

"I thought, or hoped, that if I got a good job, Papa would see the error of his ways and return to us." I lean into Louisa as the tears gather in my eyes and I become the little sister I would rather not be. "I want so much for him to be the man he was before. To be the father I need him to be."

"I know you do. I do too," Louisa coos into my hair. "You might be right, after all." Louisa's voice brightens as she pulls back, forcing me to meet her eyes. "Perhaps we can. If we work hard." Louisa wipes tears from my damp cheeks. "If we work together, both here and at the hotel, just as you suggested, then I don't see why your plan couldn't work."

"You really think so?" I sniffle and wipe my nose with the back of my hand.

"I really do." Louisa rests her forehead against mine. "What have we got to lose?"

I nod, inadvertently bumping my head against Louisa's. We both laugh, releasing the tension from the serious conversation.

I gather my emotions and hug Louisa fiercely. I wash my face before heading to the kitchen, with the daunting task of creating dinner from what little is left from the week's grocery shop. Despite Louisa's mention of working together, her lack of assistance in the kitchen does not go unnoticed by me. Choosing to ignore the slight, I let my larger worries dissolve as I scour the cupboards and icebox for inspiration and necessities.

I chop an onion as I think about what tomorrow might bring. Setting the onion aside, I move on to peeling and dicing a few potatoes. The mashed potatoes will hold together my economical meal of bubble and squeak.

Mama had bubble and squeak as a little girl, growing

up in the outskirts of London. She used to make the traditional English dish for Monday lunches, to exhaust leftovers from Sunday's lunch or dinner. As the potatoes boil, I chop our remaining vegetables into fine morsels, knowing full well that Louisa would turn up her nose at the dish if she were aware of the turnip I've snuck into it.

As I add the chopped vegetables and a small helping of leftover ground beef to the skillet, I recall a few lines from one of Aunt Vivian's letters. *Being a maid is the most useful I have felt in all my life. My confidence in my thoughts, words, and actions has grown immeasurably. I must think on my feet while maintaining a polite demeanour and occasionally a placating smile.* I relish the strength of those words. Aunt Vivian has provided me with constructive advice. Even when I do not feel confident, I must present myself as such. Confidence, real or imagined, must be key to my success in becoming a Hotel Hamilton maid.

The door to our apartment opens and Papa walks in, hat in one hand and jacket in the other. "Hello, darlin'. I see I have arrived on time." Papa steps into the kitchen and peers over my shoulder at the skillet full of tonight's dinner. "I'll wash up and be ready in a jiffy."

My head pivots as my eyes meet his. "I still have to fry up a couple of eggs to add on top." I smile at his kindly face, thankful he is home, safe and sound. "You have a few minutes yet."

Papa leans closer, planting a kiss atop my head before retreating toward the bathroom to wash up for dinner. That is when I smell it. The liquor on his breath lingers in the air, and I know that home was not his first stop after a day of work. Even more discouraging is the knowledge from my conversation with Louisa. No government-licensed establishments are open on Sunday, which can only mean one thing. Papa has been in the company of other deviants at a blind pig somewhere in this city. My disappointment drips like molasses from a spoon—thick, formidable in scent, and sure to stick to everything it touches.

I crack an egg, a little more vigorously than I intend to, into a hot fry pan coated with oil. Despair's drowning sensation engulfs me as I pick eggshell fragments from the sputtering pan. I shake my head and force myself to focus on the remaining eggs, reaffirming that which I am committed to controlling. Like steering a ship toward port, I direct all of my thought and attention to the hotel and the training that will be upon me in a matter of hours.

CHAPTER 15

*S*unday, May 15, 1927

The sky, black beyond the bedroom curtain, hasn't lulled me into a much-needed sleep. I step from the bedroom into the hall so as not to disturb Louisa's slumber with the tossing and turning that accompanies my overthinking mind. Moving toward the bathroom, I am halted by the dim glow sneaking from under Papa's closed bedroom door.

I inch closer, not wanting to intrude but with worry, or perhaps pure curiosity, drawing me forward. Leaning closer to the door, I hear Papa's voice murmuring soft and low. Who can he be talking to?

Weighing my options, I am turning to leave when a strangled sob emerges from his room, catching my attention and my heart. I place a steadying hand on the door frame and bend my head toward the closed door.

"I am unmoored, Lizzie, and I am disappointing everyone around me. I am a disgrace as a husband, a father, and a man." Papa's anguished words reach my ears, and I feel my heart crack within my chest as Papa calls out his pet name for Mama in desperation.

"I am so very sorry, my love. I have ruined things yet again. First the cottage and now the apartment. Another home lost to my grief. How am I to do this without you? Our children need a mother, and I need you to steer me straight again. Tell me, Lizzie, what would you have me do? Tell me and I will do it. Whatever it is, I will do it for you."

My own tears steam down my face, dropping in rhythm to Papa's words as they hit the hard floor. I stifle a hiccup behind a clenched fist as Papa's voice cracks in a sombre laugh.

"We had it good. My life was never so easy before you entered my world. Oh, my darling, we lived like kings, didn't we? We may not have been rich in worldly possessions, but our house was filled with love and we never went without. Our girls never felt a day's struggle. Not until you vanished from our lives."

Papa's heartbreak and distress force me backwards from the door, my bare feet stumbling slightly. I pause and wait for his anguished wails to subside before pressing my ear closer again.

"How I've found comfort in the bottle is nothing to be proud of. I imagine you are disappointed with me, and you have every reason to be. But Lizzie, it is only with the drink that I see you the clearest. My troubles fall away, and all that is left is you and me, my darling. I wish it could be so again. I miss you with every fibre of my being."

Papa's torment strikes my core. We've all missed Mama's presence in our lives deeply, but Papa's description of his broken and distraught state shows me just how impossible his life has felt these past five years. I can't help but have more empathy and far less judgement for my father, who has been existing in a living hell.

"I know what I must do, Lizzie. Truth be told, I am terrified to let you go. Letting go of the drink is the only way I can do what I must for our girls, but letting go of the drink means letting go of our time together too."

Though I cannot see him, I feel Papa's body convulsing in agony as grief whips him like an unforgiving master. I swipe at my wet face and retreat to the kitchen, unable to listen further and knowing I've already heard too much.

Pacing the short distance across the kitchen, I let my emotions flow. I am more convinced than ever that acquiring a job at the hotel is the right course of action, if only to save Papa from his own demons.

SEVERAL HOURS LATER, AS THE MORNING LIGHT FILTERS through the kitchen window, I am kneading my third loaf of bread. I spent the wee hours of the morning calming my thoughts while I mixed, kneaded, and baked. I am still in my pyjamas, hands covered in flour, when Papa surprises me with his presence.

"Well, good morning to you, Clara." Papa's tender smile is contrary to his tormented cries from last night, catching me off guard. "You are getting an early start."

"Nothing like fresh-baked bread to start a morning right." My words are infused with lightness, but I turn my face toward the dough to hide the true nature of my thoughts. I busy myself with placing the dough in an oiled bread pan before covering it with a kitchen towel. "The first loaf should be cooled and ready to eat within the hour."

"I am looking forward to it." Papa leans against the

counter, eyeing me with curiosity. "Say, if you've got a moment, do you think you could help me with something?"

"Of course. What do you need help with?" I wipe my hands dry with a fresh towel, folding it in two before hanging it over the oven's door handle.

Papa lifts one finger, motioning for me to wait a moment. He returns to the kitchen with a necktie in each hand. "Which one looks best with my white shirt and brown jacket?"

"A tie?" I feel my brow furrow. "What do you need a tie for?"

"I've an appointment at the city today, and I'd like to look as presentable as is possible for an old bloke like me."

I can't hide my amusement. "First off, you aren't old." I step toward him, taking the dark blue tie from his right hand. "And second, this one will go best with your brown jacket."

"Thank you, darlin'. I will go with the blue." Papa saunters toward his bedroom as Louisa emerges from ours, and I pray that all really will be well.

CHAPTER 16

*M*onday, May 16, 1927
We arrive at the hotel a few minutes
before nine o'clock. Louisa and I disputed during our
journey how early we should arrive for our first official day
of employment. Temporary or not, today is as close to a
working life that either of us has ever experienced, and I
am invigorated by the thought. Our quarrel over arrival
time felt like lighthearted bantering since the weekend
enthused a fresh air of camaraderie between us. I am at
peace knowing I am once again invited into the fold of my
sister's life. Though I wouldn't consider admitting it to her, I
am reassured by the bond that exists between us.

Aunt Vivian's note about confidence is my secret shield
today, and I plan to wield it as often as necessary. After
Papa's detour in both destination and moral aptitude, with
his visit to a local watering hole, followed by his late-night
emotions and what felt like a fresh start this morning, I feel
as though I've been strapped into the rollercoaster at the
fair.

At the hotel, I force a straight back and what I hope is an assured smile as I open the employees' entrance door and step inside.

We gather again in the banquet room—more than twenty girls and Ms. Thompson. Wearing another striking two-piece suit, this one with dark grey pinstripes atop an even darker grey backdrop, Ms. Thompson works her way through the gaggle of young ladies to the front of the group.

"Ladies, may I have your attention, please?" Ms. Thompson waits a moment as all whispering ceases. "Today, we are going to break into small groups. Some of our more experienced maids will walk each group through a few basic tasks." Ms. Thompson glances at her notes. "The Hotel Hamilton has three hundred and twenty rooms on its eight floors. This includes the twenty-six signature suites on the eighth floor. Those suites offer our more affluent guests an exceptional experience, with a living area and a separate bedroom. The views of the city and the North Shore Mountains are quite spectacular, I assure you. Our most experienced maids tend those suites."

A few gasps and murmurs arise from the group of trainees. Ms. Thompson shushes the room with the slight wave of her hand.

"As previously mentioned, you will train for a position as a fifth-floor maid." Ms. Thompson's chin edges upward as she peers purposefully at us. "We are seeking to hire eight full-time maids for the fifth floor. I believe it goes without saying that we aim to hire only the most suitable candidates. Though the signature suites are exquisite, and we expect many special guests on the eighth floor, all hotel guests and rooms are to be treated with the utmost respect and care." Ms. Thompson checks her notes once more before donning an even sterner expression. "No guest or room deserves anything less than sensational service, ladies. Is that clear?"

Murmurs of agreement filter through the cluster of trainees, and the bubbling excitement gains momentum with every detail Ms. Thompson unveils.

"I should also mention," Ms. Thompson says, "that each floor, one through seven, has four dedicated part-time afternoon maids who will take care of turndown service and evening duties. All maids hired will train extensively in both the daytime and evening duties so that, at a moment's notice, one can be called to fill in for another position, should a maid fall ill or be otherwise unable to tend to their tasks."

"Ms. Thompson." A girl from the back row raises her hand. "If we are unsuccessful in gaining one of the full-time positions, will we be considered for the evening post?"

"We have already begun training the last of the evening maids, but I see no reason we would not consider those not selected as a daytime maid for an evening position." Ms. Thompson writes something hurriedly on her papers. "I will need to inquire further as we move through the training, as I will not be aware of all the part-time positions that require filling until we are closer to the hotel's opening."

"Thank you, ma'am," the girl replies with a dip of her head.

"As I was saying," Ms. Thompson continues, "daytime maids will also master the evening turndown service. A full-time maid can expect to work either Monday to Friday, Tuesday to Saturday, Wednesday to Sunday, or Thursday to Monday from eight to five, with a thirty-minute break for the midday meal. Once we have been in operation for some time, we plan to rotate schedules so that all employees will have varying days off each month."

Ms. Thompson clears her throat and flips several pages back and forth before addressing the group again. "The Hotel Hamilton offers housekeeping twice a day and, as mentioned, evening turndown service. The evening maids will work from four o'clock to nine o'clock, with an overlap between daytime and evening maids so they can transfer pertinent information to one another at the handoff of services."

Louisa and I exchange a look, both of us presumably buoyed by the prospect of available positions. I am doing the math in my head, calculating how many girls will not receive an invitation to join The Hamilton staff. A slight breeze tickles the hairs on my neck, and I angle my posture for a glimpse toward the cause of the disturbance.

A young man, dressed in what I presume to be a bellboy uniform, stands at attention in the open doorway.

"Ah, Mr. Simpson." Ms. Thompson's gaze, along with every other head in the room, pivots toward the young man. "Are we ready, then?"

His cheeks flush with a hint of boyish colour, all eyes scrutinizing his presence. "Yes, ma'am."

"Thank you, Mr. Simpson. Please tell Mr. Olson we will be on our way shortly."

"Yes, ma'am." Mr. Simpson bows at the waist and turns to leave, but I catch him sending a quick wink in Louisa's direction. My sister's smile widens, her hands folded in front of her as she sways slightly—a coy gesture I've seen her use in the company of other handsome young men whose attention she would like to garner.

My insides turn to mush, and a wave of unease courses through my veins. Criticizing thoughts flash through my mind. I should have known better than to trust Louisa to stay on task for something as important as our family's well-being. I scold myself for not having sought employment on my own. It will be a miracle if she doesn't get us both dismissed by the end of the week. Flirting with the male staff has not been specifically disallowed, but I can't imagine an establishment such as The Hamilton would tolerate such shenanigans.

I am angry with both Louisa and Papa for putting us in such a precarious position. I had hoped Papa would work for more than two days at the Murray estate. If he were busy with work, the happy result would be extra money in the grocery jar and a lack of time for him to venture anywhere but home and the estate.

Today, though, he has thrown me another curveball by mentioning a meeting in the city. I wonder if the happy thoughts I allowed should actually be worry. Emotions simmer beneath the surface of my skin, spitting like hot oil in a fry pan. Worry, anger, betrayal—I've no idea which wounded sensation leads the charge, only that my manufactured confidence is crumbling with speed.

"Before we begin our training, I will take you on a tour of the hotel." Ms. Thompson's words break through my whirling thoughts, wrenching me back to the task at hand. "I suggest you pay close attention, as going forward you will be required to navigate the hotel with discretion while staying on top of your duties. The employee service halls are your roadways through the hotel. Though they are not always the quickest route to a destination, they are the only pathways available to you." Ms. Thompson's warning expression indicates the seriousness with which we should take this direction.

"Well then." Ms. Thompson steps forward. "Form a line, ladies. Two by two, if you will."

We shuffle into place, organizing ourselves into position behind Ms. Thompson like a brood of ducklings, prepared to follow our fearless leader. Louisa beams at me, her excitement overriding her awareness of the incensed judgements burning behind my eyes.

As we exit the banquet room, I do my best to shake off my souring mood and decide to keep my lacklustre perspective to myself. I will manage all the things I can control and focus on the tour of the hotel. After all, this may be my only chance to explore the stately hotel before it is filled to the brim with guests.

Ms. Thompson leads us down the corridor we have entered through each time we've arrived at the hotel. A murmur of surprise moves through the line of maid trainees as Ms. Thompson pushes the back door open.

"This way, ladies." Ms. Thompson's voice flutters over the group, and we follow suit until we find ourselves at the hotel's grand front entrance. The polished brass handrails gleam brilliantly, and the bright sun illuminates the red-carpeted steps and the glass doors.

Ms. Thompson waits for a few stragglers to catch up before proceeding. "It is of the utmost importance to Mr. Hamilton that all staff members are familiar with the guest's perspective, and the best way for us to do that"— Ms. Thompson's mischievous smile gives away her amusement—"is to show you what a guest will experience. We are going to walk you through the guest experience from beginning to end."

A ripple of excitement consumes us, and Ms. Thompson's motioning hands do little to quiet the chatter erupting from the group. Her words rise an octave higher to penetrate the babbling voices. "Of course, no tour of the hotel would be complete without showing the working side. Ladies, the hotel is glamorous and exquisite." Ms. Thompson's eyes narrow slightly as she tilts her chin up. "But so must our service be."

I make a mental note, catching Ms. Thompson's meaning. We should appreciate the hotel and its glory so every time we step within its walls, we exemplify The Hamilton's distinction. Ms. Thompson moves past the front steps and motions for us to follow.

The two oversized glass doors accented by shimmering brass handles, each in the shape of an H, open as if on cue. Young men in freshly pressed hotel uniforms, complete with shoulder tassels and pillbox hats, stand at attention. They hold open the doors as a man in full formal wear steps onto the centre of the landing.

With a look from left to right, the man spreads his arms wide and bows at the waist. "Welcome to The Hamilton, ladies. We hope you enjoy your tour." Without another word, he guides us through the doors and into an expansive, marble-floored lobby that looks slick enough to skate on.

To the right is a dark wooden bellboy stand, complete with a bellboy, a bell, and a gold-plated sign. To the left stands a large potted tree, beside which is a narrow table with a desk lamp and a telephone. I step closer, peeking at an ornate box containing sheets of paper with the hotel's name and address embossed in gold. A collection of pens and envelopes fills the box's other slots.

We are directed forward as a group, the line splitting as we move around an immense round table. Its only purpose, as far as I can tell, is to hold a massive vase filled with fresh flowers. Ms. Thompson's voice cuts through my delight at the spring bouquet. "I'd like you to pay special attention to the flower arrangements throughout the hotel, ladies. Fresh flowers are an important aspect of the hotel's decor, and maintaining them is a daily task for all maids. Regardless of their location, should you see a flower arrangement appearing down in the mouth, I expect you to take the initiative and remedy the situation at once."

Heads bob at Ms. Thompson's advice. "Next, we have the registration desk." Spanning the right-hand side of the lobby, the stunning structure has intricately crafted front panels and a marble countertop. Ms. Thompson places a hand on the dark marble surface. "This is where guests check in. Once registered, the guests receive a room key. A bellboy then escorts them to their rooms while managing their luggage and any initial requests."

Ms. Thompson signals to the tall, slender gentleman behind the desk, and he moves to the wall of dark cabinets behind him, extracting a key from a discreetly hidden cubby. He hands the key to Ms. Thompson. "Thank you, ma'am. We hope you enjoy your stay at The Hotel Hamilton."

Ms. Thompson slips the key into her suit jacket pocket before drawing our attention to the lounge across from the registration desk. An unbecoming gasp almost emerges from my lips as I step onto the deep plush carpet, its swirling blue-and-grey pattern a mere piece of the well-appointed space. Luxuriously ornate sofas and chairs adorn the room in complementing patterns and colours. If asked to choose a favourite, I am quite aware I could not.

Delicate, thin-legged tables stand at the ready beside each cushioned seat. In stark yet stunning contrast, a

fireplace anchors the room with its expansive hearth,
promising warmth on cool rainy days. Ms. Thompson takes
us toward the lift, and one by one, we step inside. A man
dressed in a lift-operator uniform holds the door ajar for us.
A quick look at the mirrored and gold-detailed box has my
head spinning as I consider how such a contraption works.
Though lifts have been popular for some time now, I have
yet to travel in one. Even if given the opportunity, I suspect
I would continue to choose the stairs and the assuredness of
my own legs.

Louisa nudges me with her elbow. "Still not your thing,
Clara?" she whispers while smothering a giggle.

I shake my head but offer her no further comment for
fodder.

Ms. Thompson leads us through several banquet rooms,
some larger than others but each complete with a platform
for musicians, a wooden dance floor, and chandeliers. We
tour the restaurant at the rear of the hotel, on the lower
level. White linen wraps each table, and candles wait
patiently for a match and intimate dinner conversation.
The restaurant's menu is of keen interest to all of us, as we
salivate over the delicacies many of us have never thought
to dream of tasting.

"This concludes the guest experience tour. You will, of
course, see plenty of the hotel's guest rooms later, so we will
view the fifth-floor rooms after lunch." Ms. Thompson
motions us toward the hotel's kitchen, separate from the
restaurant's more compact set-up. Ms. Thompson tells us
this is where banquet food will be prepared for specially
catered events.

We explore the basement laundry, the supply
cupboards, the pathway of service corridors and back-of-
house stairs before arriving at a stockroom, its walls lined

with cubbies and hotel staff uniforms. "After lunch," Ms. Thompson says, her voice gravelly and likely beginning to tire from speaking over excited squeals and conversation, "we will meet back here. I will sign out two sets of uniforms for each of you. Let me be clear, ladies. Should you not become an employee at this time, you will return your uniforms intact in exchange for your training wage. No uniform, no salary." Ms. Thompson's chin rises, and I recognize this as her way of asserting her authority. "No exceptions."

Ms. Thompson pulls a pocket watch from her jacket and opens its worn cover. "The time is now eleven fifty-five. I will expect you back at this location by twelve thirty." She slides the watch back into her pocket and eyes us sternly. "I suggest you note the time it takes for you to use the service corridors to exit the building to ensure you are not tardy on your return."

I glance at my wristwatch and plan to do as instructed. Louisa pulls on my arm as the group disbands, each of us heading through the same corridor. At least if we lose our way, I think to myself, we will be lost together.

"You know, I've already seen it all before." Jane's voice, overly sweet in my ear, startles me. She bumps against me to gain my attention.

"What have you seen before?" Louisa doesn't miss a beat, interjecting herself into the conversation before I can come up with a suitable response.

"The hotel, silly." Jane rolls her eyes. "My uncle toured me around last week when he learned I was keen to work here."

"How nice." Politeness wins out as I press down the ill feeling rising in my stomach.

"Well, I've got to grab some food from the White

Lunch, so I'll catch up with you soon." Jane weaves through the crowd, clearly not concerning herself with the fact that everyone in the group needs to obtain lunch or find a suitable location to eat.

We exit the hotel via the alleyway door. Louisa's displeasure is certain. "Can you believe that girl?"

CHAPTER 17

*M*onday, May 16, 1927

Settling into a corner of the expansive stone steps at the front of the courthouse, I squint my eyes against the bright noonday sun, relishing the warmth while attempting to shield my vision from the glare. Men in suits scurry past us carrying brown briefcases.

Unpacking our lunch, I hand Louisa an egg salad sandwich. She unwraps it, peeks between the thin slices of bread, and pokes a finger at the filling, her nose crinkling.

"I thought you liked egg salad?" My sandwich lingers halfway to my mouth.

"Not really. I prefer ham and cheese, but I'd settle for a peanut butter and jelly over this." Louisa purses her lips before taking a reluctant bite.

I don't even attempt to hide the roll of my eyes. "Well, ham and cheese wasn't an option today." With my stomach grumbling, I bite into my sandwich before shooting a comment, laced with sarcasm, at the ungrateful recipient beside me. "I can forever send you with peanut butter, then. Or better yet"—my voice dips into a mocking tone—"you could make your own lunch. You claim you can put together a peanut butter sandwich, after all."

Louisa shoots me a sharp look as she drinks from our shared flask of water. "What's gotten your knickers in a knot?"

I take a deep breath and am about to lay it out for Louisa, despite my better judgement, intent on calling her out for flirting with the bellboy. Jane's high-pitched voice announcing her arrival halts my words.

"The lineup at White's was mad," Jane says, inserting herself into our conversation and our lunch spot without considering that she might be interrupting.

She squeezes between Louisa and me on the step, pushing on as if her words are the only ones that matter. "But I can't resist White's specialty sandwiches. Look at this." Jane holds a grilled sandwich up to eye level. "Grilled ham and cheese. I mean, who would have thought a warm sandwich could be so delicious?"

Louisa's glum expression catches my attention as her eyes travel between her own lukewarm egg salad and Jane's almost steamy, melted cheese delicacy, lifting the corners of my lips upward. I hide my amusement behind another bite and purposefully look away, scanning the wide grassy area between the courthouse steps and Georgia Street.

"You know that White Lunch does not take a kindly view of others?" Louisa raises a single eyebrow accusingly toward Jane, her dismay over the sandwich she desires but cannot have thrust aside.

"Whatever do you mean?" Jane asks.

A small huff of indignation escapes Louisa's lips. "They

refuse to serve anyone who doesn't look like them." Louisa's bobbing head adds emphasis. "They won't hire anyone who isn't white either."

"Where in the world did you hear this?" Jane asks before turning her attention back to her lunch.

I can't tell whether Jane is unaware of the business's well-established status or isn't concerned by it. But I sense the rumblings of a potential showdown and interject so as not to witness a scene on the courthouse steps. "Our father." I motion for Louisa to drop it, with a flick of my wrist. "He works in a field of many ethnicities and has several friends from varying backgrounds. All Louisa is saying is that White Lunch is not a business we are comfortable supporting."

Jane shrugs as she nibbles at her sandwich, dabbing the corners of her mouth with a napkin after each bite. She's mannered enough for proper table etiquette, but oh, how she appears clueless when reading situations. Or perhaps she simply has little concern for others, hence her bullish behaviour.

I let several moments pass, to sidestep what could have been a heated disagreement, while I eye her with curiosity. As I watch her delicate but efficient consumption of her restaurant-purchased lunch, I contemplate Jane's motivation for applying to work at the hotel.

"So." Jane sips from her half-pint bottle of milk. "What did you ladies think of the tour?"

"The hotel is a beautiful establishment," Louisa begins, recovered from her outrage. "I am in love with the dark wood, and oh, those furnishings in the lounge area . . . Their beauty took my breath away." Louisa fans her hand in front of her face, and I imagine her mind leaping to a daydream of her in the hotel's lavish lounge area, front and centre and famous.

I hardly needed reminding of Jane's whispered announcement as we exited the hotel for lunch, but Louisa's comment all but begs me to press for further information. Gathering my courage, I take a sip of water and press my inquiry forward. "How is your uncle connected with the hotel, then?"

Lou's head snaps up, clearly surprised at my forthright and less than polite question.

Jane dips her head with a timid gesture, though I am inclined to think it is an act. "I'm not really supposed to say, but I suppose if we can keep it between us girls . . ."

Louisa and I nod our heads in unison. "Of course." My interest piqued, I encourage Jane to continue.

"My uncle is a dear friend to Mr. Hamilton, the owner of the hotel. He asked for a private tour for himself and me, and that was all it took." Jane takes the last bite of her sandwich before wiping her hands on the napkin resting in her lap.

I can almost hear the gears turning in Louisa's head, as she considers how to ask the burning question. "So, does that mean you are a shoo-in? For the job."

"Well, I couldn't say for sure." Another modest inclination of Jane's head does little to convince me her words are true. "Someone has certainly mentioned me to the hotel management. But I suppose I'll have to complete the training to the same exacting expectations as every other girl in order to be hired."

Louisa catches my eye, her expression transforming into one of scrutiny, though I doubt Jane would ever be aware enough to suspect so. My sister, the actress, can fool almost anyone with a lighthearted comment or a nonchalant wave. Well, anyone save me, that is.

Jane continues, slapping her hand on her lap in mock hilarity. "Of course, Ms. Thompson did see me sitting on one of those brand-new sofas in the lounge. The furniture had just arrived, and my uncle teased that the sofa needed a trial run, so I obliged him by settling onto one." Jane snickers behind her palm. "Got to give her credit though. Ms. Thompson didn't say a word, and she managed quite the job of hiding her surprise at seeing me reclining with my feet up on the sofa."

Tilting her head back, Jane drains the last of her milk. "I have to say, the room may appear exquisite and welcoming, but that sofa was nothing short of uncomfortable." Jane shakes her head in disapproval. "Perhaps they are meant to be sturdy rather than comfortable." Without another word, Jane stands and descends the steps to locate a garbage bin for her sandwich wrapper and napkin.

I exchange glances with Louisa and find her left eyebrow raised, in either question or disbelief. I stifle a giggle at my sister's wriggling eyebrow and busy myself by taking large bites from my apple and checking my wristwatch for the time.

Jane and Louisa chatter back and forth, Lou wrangling their conversation and steering it toward the safer topic of Vancouver's mild May weather. As their small talk deviates to spring fashions, I factor the threatening nature of Jane's earlier words into the equation for calculating my chance of employment at the hotel.

Jane is unpredictable. I am certain of this. I mull over her telltale comments, quickly stacking up on my mental tally, and stiffen my posture. I believe I am a suitable candidate for a maid's position, and I refuse to let Jane's entitlement unfurl my plans. I need to gain employment and am more than prepared to work hard. My work ethic, I am sure, is far more substantial than anything Jane offers. I still wonder, though, why she of all people is desperate for a job. By all appearances, employment is not the natural step in a life such as hers.

I eye Jane and Louisa as they exchange conversation about waistlines and hem lengths. Of course, I think, placing my hands behind my body and leaning back, we have yet to showcase any work ethic at all within the walls of The Hamilton. With a quick shake of my head, I attempt to shrug off my desire to locate stability in my life. I try to reason with my agitation. One morning spent at the hotel is not sufficient for anyone to secure a position.

I lift my chin in defiance of my mental chatter and coerce a thread of confidence into my being, rising from the worn soles of my shoes to the top of my head. No matter what, I remind the frightened girl who lives within me, I must think clearly and do whatever is necessary to ensure I am awarded employment. If I must, I will edge Jane out of the equation. I glimpse my sister's profile with a sideways look, considering her unpredictable nature and, more recently, her flirtatiousness. If need be, I will put myself and my capabilities ahead of Louisa too. As the disingenuous attitude settles over me, I feel my body recoil at the ill-mannered view of my sister and the world.

Clara, I scold myself. You are better than this. You are loyal and kind and generous. Shame on you. Before the unkind thought toward my sister can burrow further beneath my skin, I check my wristwatch and decide the time to return to the hotel is upon us, if only to save me from my own destructive thoughts. I place the cloth food wrappers and empty bottle in my bag and stand with an authority that is borrowed rather than owned. "We should get back." I fix my sights on the hotel's facade before Jane or Louisa can look my way.

"Time already?" Jane checks her own watch. "A half hour isn't quite what it used to be, now is it?"

Without waiting for a response, Jane rises and offers Louisa a hand. Noticing the gesture and interaction between them, my body stiffens with a stab of jealousy. I hadn't considered the possibility that the two of them could become friendly. My mind, like a train running the wrong direction on a one-way track, reels with the distasteful prospect. With the awareness of yet another potentially perilous situation, exhaustion washes over me like an ocean's wave. Weary from dodging a continually growing number of obstacles, I wonder how I will ever make it through a day, let alone an entire week of training.

Louisa and Jane discuss their mutual lack of experience with household duties as we wait to cross the street. "How difficult can it be, really?" Jane asks as we step forward. "I've seen our maid make my bed a thousand times."

The roll of my eyes and the smirk on my lips go unnoticed by Jane and Louisa as I fall in behind them.

"I've made my own bed," Louisa says, a touch of pride coating her words. "Not every day." She hesitates, catching my gaze over her shoulder. "But I have done it."

Jane smiles with confidence as we near the hotel's front entrance. "They have to train us, after all. I really don't think we have anything to worry about."

Several other maids-in-training join us at the turn toward the hotel's back alley, and the conversation erupts in volume, reminiscent of a colony of gulls circling the sky above the ocean's edge, all eager to be heard.

We are about to step through the back door when I hear Jane's voice above the rest. "We could help one another if we need." She nudges Louisa's shoulder. "You know, in training. Then we will both be at the top of the class when selection time comes."

Louisa steps to the side, including me in the conversation with a wink. "I suppose we should all work as a team, since I imagine that is what we will be as employed maids."

My head bobs in agreement with Louisa's words. "Yes, I believe teamwork will be an essential part of our every day."

Jane squeezes Louisa's hand in a brief show of solidarity, as though forming a pact of sorts. Pivoting and striding ahead with the others, Jane adds, "If that doesn't work out, I can always ask my uncle to make certain I am hired in the end. He knows how desperately I need this job, and he is always eager to help his favourite niece."

I stop in my tracks, and those a step behind bump into me. I offer a muffled apology and resume a slightly slower pace, less than eager to catch up with the conniving Jane.

Lost in my troubling thoughts, I am aghast as I follow the group, numbness deadening my limbs. How bold. What a brazen statement. It is utterly distasteful.

We filter into the hall by the supply room, spreading out like an oriental fan around the room's entrance. I stow myself into the folds of the group, wishing I could disappear altogether.

Like a fish swimming against the school, Louisa picks her way through the group until she reaches me. "I told you that girl was something else." Louisa seethes with a downturned expression. "In all my life, I have never seen someone so uncharitable. Can you imagine? Who thinks of asking someone to work together and then slaps them in the face with her own self-serving solution?" Louisa fumes as her arms cross over her chest. Her toe taps with building frustration.

I see Ms. Thompson threading her way to the room's entrance and realize I have little time to calm Louisa's mood and avoid a public outburst, which would surely have us both shown to the door with haste. "You were right. Jane is apparently out for Jane alone." I bite my lower lip. "All we can do is trust one another." I offer Louisa a reassuring smile.

"I am more determined than ever." Louisa's eyes narrow as she leans closer to me, lowering her voice to a whisper. "Clara, I will do what I can to help you be successful. If anyone deserves a position here, it is you."

Louisa squeezes me into a brisk hug, and moisture seeps into my eyes. Shame rises within me like mercury on a sweltering summer day. My earlier preoccupation with beating my sister out of a maid's position cloaks me in self-loathing. Right or wrong, I believed I was the more worthy, solely because my goal was more serious, more altruistic than hers.

I sigh, seeing Louisa's heart on full display and ready to fight for my desires. In this moment, I realize, nothing will stand between her love and protection of me. In a few hastily spoken words, Louisa has shown her true nature. She may want success in her own way, but if push comes to shove, she will be the encouraging hand on my back. Yes, it is true. Louisa's opportunity at the hotel may be sacrificed for the greater good of our family, and she doesn't even know why.

I hug her back, tightening my arms around her shoulders with a determined squeeze. I don't want to release her from our hug or from her own ambitions, whatever they might be. The relationship between sisters is full of complications, I think, and yet it is exceptionally simple.

CHAPTER 18

Monday, May 16, 1927

"Hazel Greenwood?" Ms. Thompson's voice rises with her head from her clipboard and papers. The girl called Hazel steps forward. The slight hesitation in her approach tells me I am not alone in feeling the jitters this afternoon.

"Ah, yes. Miss Greenwood, there you are." Ms. Thompson gestures for her to follow. "Come with me, please." The two of them disappear into the stockroom, and a few minutes later, Hazel emerges with a small pile of neatly folded fabric in her arms.

Ms. Thompson, referencing her list, calls out each name and issues each trainee two sets of maid's uniforms, complete with a fringed cap and two starched white aprons. Louisa and I stand shoulder to shoulder as we wait for our names to be called, bound by blood and by purpose.

Ms. Thompson calls Jane's name. Apparently delighted, she nearly skips into the supply room. She returns a few moments later with freshly pressed uniforms draped over one arm. She strikes a pose with her crisp white-and-navy cap already secured atop her head, garnering her a few chuckles before she returns to her place among the group.

Louisa's arm, butted up next to mine, tenses in a fleeting display of what I imagine is annoyance with Jane's theatrics. Ms. Thompson calls my name. I lift a foot and am ready to step forward when Lou catches me, my dress held tight in her fingers.

She hisses in my ear, "I think we will serve ourselves best by working together with Jane. As she suggested." Louisa forces a smile in Jane's direction.

The slight narrowing of Louisa's eyes quells my instinct to argue. "Jane isn't the sort of person we want as a friend. Nor do we wish to have her as a foe." Louisa infuses false sincerity into an even broader smile to ensure her message has reached me.

"Miss Clara Wilson." Ms. Thompson pops her head out of the supply room and scans the group. "Ah, there you are, Miss Wilson. Please step inside to collect your uniform."

"Yes, ma'am." The prickle of impending conflict shivers through me as I step forward. I find myself distracted as Ms. Thompson asks me about my usual dress size. She runs a finger along the labelled shelf, extracting all pieces of my new uniform before following me back into the narrow hall to call on Louisa, the final trainee to be summoned.

Their voices filter into the hall. Ms. Thompson comments, "You are a tall one, dear, but I think we have just the thing."

The echo of rummaging boxes spills through the supply room door. "Ah, yes, here it is." Ms. Thompson's voice, breathless with the effort of her search, softens. "The last one."

"It is meant to be, then," Louisa says, and I can hear a true and pleasing smile in her tone.

"I am so pleased you view it as a good omen, Miss Wilson. I am afraid to say there is only the one. I will see how you get on and order another uniform to accommodate your taller frame by the week's end, if need be. In the meantime, be sure to deliver the dress and apron to the basement laundry each afternoon. I will let them know they are to launder it at once so it is ready for you each morning."

"Thank you, ma'am. No worries at all. I am pleased to manage with what is available, though I have little doubt that a second uniform will be required in the end." Louisa beams at the hotel matron as they exit the stockroom together.

I stifle a giggle as Lou dips into a brief curtsy before taking her place beside me.

Jane slices us with a scathing look, her contempt barely hidden beneath a forced smile. Louisa may be right. On all counts, Jane appears out of control and untrustworthy, at best.

We gather in the now familiar banquet room for further instruction. I reposition Louisa out of earshot of the group, eager to hear her plan regarding Jane.

"But what are you going to do? Lou, please. Do not attempt anything rash. Truly, I need this job. I need to feel sturdy ground beneath my feet. I know I can find a sense of peace again as soon as I—"

"As soon as you what, Clara?" Louisa asks, her eyebrow arched like the curve of a question mark.

I search the patterned carpet for a reason good enough to quieten her inquiring thoughts. Louisa's toe taps and the walls seem to close in around me. My unwillingness to enlighten my sister as to our family's dire situation forces me to contrive a white lie—one I hope will satisfy her curiosity while not damning me directly to hell.

"The busyness will do me good," I say, pulling my shoulders back to gain the advantage of a confident posture. "If I can focus on something other than Papa and worrying about where he is and what he is up to . . ." My words falter. In the end, they hold truth, fear, and an honest amount of the powerlessness weighing on my heart.

Louisa squeezes my shoulder in comfort. "When will you learn, Clara? You can alter another person's choices about as much as you can change the weather. Papa is a smart man. He won't live like this forever, you know."

I offer a solemn tilt of my head. I've heard Louisa's words, but I find myself unable to believe they ring true. Salvation, I am more than certain, will come from me gaining authority over our family's financial status. Once that has been achieved, I am hopeful Papa will return to us. And life, a real happy life, will resume.

Lou taps a finger to her lips in thought. "I may not be able to curb Jane and her privileged attitude, but we can certainly bring our best to each task and outshine her. We are capable girls, and the world is our oyster."

A clatter of noise draws our attention. "You may leave those right there," Ms. Thompson says to a young man dressed in a bellhop uniform, before returning her attention to the group. "Ladies, please fetch a chair from the rack Mr. Jones has delivered and sort yourselves into a circle. Our next task this afternoon is to examine the proper etiquette with which you will interact with hotel guests."

∽

AN HOUR AND A HALF LATER, I FEEL AS THOUGH I'VE BEEN through a crash course designed for a young debutante about to be presented to society. As "yes, ma'am" and "no, ma'am" roll off my tongue—with an added "three bags full, ma'am" recited within the confines of my head—I note Jane's aptitude for all things high society. I presume her own previous etiquette lessons are now paying off. She converses and curtsies with ease. Her responses are on point and delivered with a confident smile to Ms. Thompson, whose pleased expression confirms Jane's ability.

Reading my silent thoughts, Louisa leans close and whispers in my ear. "Everyone has a talent for something, Clara. Don't let it concern you." She squeezes my hand in what I suspect is an effort to bolster me. Louisa reminds me of my good nature, hidden somewhere among my discouraging thoughts.

Mama's voice rings in my memory, fortifying Louisa's assurances. *Never begrudge someone their talent, even if it displeases you.*

I press a smile into place and acknowledge my sister's reminder.

Ms. Thompson claps her hands to gain the group's attention as she stands and pushes her chair back from the circle. "Ladies, ladies, please." The room quiets as all heads swivel in the matron's direction. "We will take a quick break before journeying to the fifth floor, where we will spend the afternoon learning the intricacies of making a proper bed, from beginning to end."

A murmur buzzes through the circle. Ms. Thompson clears her throat and continues. "I will ask each of you to replace your chair on the rack and then follow me to the basement, where you will change into your uniform. They will launder your uniforms here, at the hotel, with you wearing a clean uniform for each shift. This is an expectation, ladies, which The Hamilton takes seriously." Ms. Thompson peers around the circle, making eye contact with each maid-in-training. "We do not permit you on guest room floors in anything other than a tidy uniform. Am I clear?"

A round of "yes, ma'am" erupts before the sound of clattering chairs fills the room.

Jane appears at my side, a delighted grin charming her natural beauty to the surface. "I am surprised she did not ask us to walk round the room with a book balanced atop our heads." A light laugh accompanies her words, clearly enthused by her success in today's activities.

"Oh my. I am afraid I wouldn't have been much good at that." I stifle a nervous giggle.

We move through the banquet room door, following the others toward the basement. Louisa falls in line beside us as I gather my nerve and push forward. "Jane." I hesitate as we squeeze through the much narrower door leading to the staff corridor. "You mentioned the other day that you are desperate for a job at the hotel."

"Oh yes." Jane touches my forearm. "I absolutely must emerge from the training with employment in hand."

I formulate my words with the politeness Mama instilled in me, aware my boldness in questioning Jane's motives is discourteous at best, likely crossing the line toward rude. "It's just, I suppose I don't quite understand." I sneak a sideways glance to gauge Jane's reaction to my prying.

Jane, either unaware or unconcerned with the impertinent nature of my question, does not hesitate to respond. "What don't you understand?"

"Well, clearly you are familiar with the dialogue and

etiquette of someone who wouldn't normally need to seek employment." The heat of embarrassment rises in my cheeks. "Your social calendar is a tad fuller than any of ours, I imagine." I swing my arm wide, gesturing to the flock of girls making their way to the hotel's basement.

Jane's giggles echo about the low-ceilinged corridor, garnering a few over-the-shoulder looks from those ahead of us. "Of course I have a full social calendar, silly." Jane pauses to let others' attention pass by. She lowers her voice and continues. "According to Mummy, my social calendar is precisely the problem." A sigh and an exaggerated eye roll emphasize Jane's distress.

"My parents informed me a few weeks ago that since I have refused to marry the dreadfully dreary, and far too old for me, suitor selected by them, I am required to find something productive to do with my life." Jane sighs, wiping her eye, though I cannot tell if the tears are real or feigned. "Apparently, I have embarrassed the family to the ends of the earth and—" A strangled sound emerges from Jane's throat, causing all three of us to stop walking.

"And what?" Louisa asks, placing a steadying hand over Jane's arm.

"If I don't find something Mummy deems suitable, I am to be sent to England and hidden away with an ancient relative so I can do no further damage to the family name." Jane's shoulders hunch forward. "My uncle is the only one rooting for me at the moment."

"Oh Jane, I am so sorry." My innate empathy oozes out of me, and I feel the shame of my wretched thoughts toward Jane. She too has struggles, and my single-minded focus has been steering me in a less than charitable direction.

Louisa and I exchange a look as Jane dabs at the actual tears gathering in her eyes.

Stepping to the side, Louisa hooks her arm through Jane's, encouraging me with a gesture to do the same. "Come now. Cheer up, Jane. You've got the Wilson sisters to help you along." Louisa winks mischievously and Jane giggles.

Together, the three of us walk down the corridor, arms linked, chins lifted, and determination reinstated in our bones.

We catch up with the others at the service lift, just in time to hear Ms. Thompson giving us permission to descend via the stairs, if we wish, and meet the others in the basement. Without hesitation, I follow the few girls heading to the stairwell. "Meet you there," I say over my shoulder to Louisa and Jane, the fresh breeze of a favourable mood lightening my steps.

In the basement, Ms. Thompson shows us to the changing area. With plain, navy-blue day dresses pulled over our heads, the hotel matron directs us in assembling the rest of our uniform. We are to tie the apron in a neat but sturdy bow. The cap is to be pinned straight in place. Our shoes, though far from pristine today, are to be buffed to a shine before every shift.

"My my, you look an impressive bunch." Ms. Thompson's neutral expression takes on a hint of a smile as she strolls the length of our assembled line. "Now, let's see how we get on with making a bed."

By the time I climb the stairs to the fifth floor, my effort has created warmth under the starched uniform. I surprise myself by considering the benefit of the service lift for future ascents. I enter the hotel room located across from the guest's lift. Louisa snickers at my pink checks as I stand beside her in the semicircle that has formed around the bed.

Ms. Thompson demonstrates the process as she flicks a crisp white sheet above the mattress, allowing it to billow and float toward the bed. "The key to a well-made bed is the hospital corner." Ms. Thompson gathers and folds the sheet into a tight and uniform position beneath the mattress.

"Once one corner is in place, you will repeat the process on the other three corners. You will note the importance of ensuring your sheet has an equal amount of fabric on each of the long sides of the bed, along with an ample amount of fabric to tightly secure the head and foot sections. They have not yet positioned this mattress with a headboard and footboard. I will caution you that the task becomes slightly more challenging when tugging and smoothing against a hard wooden bed frame."

Ms. Thompson ensures the group is following along. "The sheet should remain in place for a sleeping guest, if situated properly. The guests will sleep under a plush duvet of Italian quality and design." Ms. Thompson's eyes dance as she lingers on the word "Italian," and I wonder if she dreams of travelling abroad, as is becoming more common.

Ms. Thompson moves around the mattress, tugging and straightening. While she does, I let my gaze roam about the room. The pale grey-blue walls accent the dark wood of the dressing table and bedside tables, ensuring the room is spacious yet cozy. The drapes gather like a pool beneath a waterfall atop the plush cream carpet, highlighting the tall windows and the view beyond.

Enamoured as I am by the luxurious guest room, my hand shoots up when Ms. Thompson asks for a volunteer to try fitting the sheet to the mattress. My rapid response interrupts her question, and Ms. Thompson smothers her amusement behind a tight-lipped expression. "Clara Wilson, you seem eager. Please, Miss Wilson, will you show us how to make a hospital corner?"

"Yes, ma'am." I add height to my posture and step right past my timid nature. Determined to prove my ability and reach the sought-after outcome for my family's future, I pray my show of willingness and gumption will garner me the hotel matron's favourable notice. A deep, steadying breath relaxes me as I stand at the foot of the bed and lift the sheet with one long, swooping motion. I move with purpose, tucking, tugging, and smoothing until the sheet lies neatly above the mattress at all four corners. I step back and admire my work. The sheet stretches across the mattress, taut and possibly firm enough to bounce a quarter on.

"Well done, Miss Wilson. Well done indeed." Ms. Thompson's appreciation of my effort floats around the room, with subdued applause from a few maids-in-training.

Pleased as punch, I beam in Louisa's direction, well aware of the courage I've displayed. Stepping back into the fold of the group, I find Jane chatting conspiratorially with another girl, behind a raised palm. I swallow hard, the sinking awareness of her lack of loyalty to Louisa and me torpedoing my joy. Jane's head inclines in my direction before she shares a laugh with the other girl. She hung onto the camaraderie we three created for less than an hour, her self-important nature returning with fervour. Jane is out for Jane, I remind myself with a disheartened shake of my head. My short-lived elation recedes into the background prattle coming from the group as a splinter of unease settles beneath my chest.

We assemble into groups of four, Ms. Thompson dividing us between several fifth-floor guest rooms, and spend the afternoon taking turns with a mattress and a sheet. Thankfully, Jane partners with a different group, but my enthusiasm for the task has lost its lustre. I watch the others, only commenting when required.

Louisa and two other girls laugh and carry on as they work tirelessly on their hospital corners, each of them peering over the other's shoulder. One accidentally placing the sheet in the wrong direction leaves them all in stitches. I smile politely at their mischief but find myself with worry on my mind.

As the day ends, determination to succeed consumes my thoughts. I won't let Jane ruin things. I need this job. Despite knowing the reasons for Jane's want of employment at the hotel, I cringe only a little when I affirm that I need this more than she does.

CHAPTER 19

*M*onday, May 16, 1927

Papa is waiting for us on the landing, arms crossed over his chest, a dour look upon his face. We labour up the stairs, our tired feet and aching backs slowing our progress. "Where the devil have you two been?" His words are laced with anger, but I sense a small measure of concern coating his question.

"Papa." Louisa jumps in before I can respond, planting a kiss on his clean-shaven cheek. "You wouldn't believe the adventure we have had today. Let us get settled inside and I'll tell you all about it." Louisa directs his elbow toward our apartment's entrance before lifting the wide-brimmed hat from her head.

"Clara will make us tea. Won't you, Clara?" Louisa's evasive smile is followed by a purposeful wink in my direction. The message to go along and let her do the talking reaches me as clearly as if she had spoken the words out loud.

"Yes, of course." I move to the kitchen, filling the kettle

with water and preparing the teapot. While I wait for the water to boil, I rummage through the cupboards in search of something appealing to nibble. I wish I hadn't put off making the scones. I got so carried away with the methodical and comforting nature of baking bread this morning the scones didn't even enter my mind. I move jars of beans, rice, and oats as I search, intent on finding something that might please Papa, or rather distract him, while Louisa weaves a tale. I find myself both intrigued and apprehensive to hear her story.

On tiptoe, with my body leaning against the counter to gain a bit of leverage, I touch a familiar rectangular box. On a shelf taller than my petite stature allows me to see, the graham crackers are exactly what I am looking for. I arrange the sweet treat on a small plate, dabbing a few with honey while leaving the rest plain for dipping in tea.

As I settle everything on the tray, I notice the chipped and dowdy nature of the sugar bowl. A small groan whispers across my lips and I scold myself for such ungrateful thoughts. We are blessed with a sugar bowl and all the rest, after all. I push back the words "for now" from my ruminating mind, refusing to allow them entry while I lift the tray and move toward the living room.

Louisa is in animated conversation, pausing only for a moment to thank me for the tea. "So you see, Papa, we walked all the way to the waterfront tent expecting to find the theatre group rehearsing there." Louisa's burst of laughter startles me as I pour the tea, resulting in a few drops landing on Papa's saucer rather than in his cup.

With hardly a notice, she pushes on, wrapping a hand around Papa's forearm. "So, there we were, fanning our faces in the warm noonday sun, at the absolute wrong location." Louisa exhales theatrically as her beaming smile grows wider. "I just knew they had to be gathering out by the university. You know the place?" An arched eyebrow begs the question. "The building I used to rehearse in when we lived at the Murray estate?"

My head snaps up, knowing all too well how these words must cost Louisa emotionally. A sip of tea expertly covers the slight hitch in her insistent chatter. Papa offers her an understanding nod as he bites into a honeyed graham cracker.

"Anyway." Louisa's hand gestures in mid-air, waving off any hint that her thoughts were derailed. "I was kicking myself for not following my instincts. I am sure Clara was none too pleased with me when I insisted we make the trek toward the university."

Papa looks to me, and I offer my best rendition of the annoyed sister with an eye roll and a jerk of my head, garnering me a soft chuckle and a warm smile from him.

"But you see, Papa"—Louisa draws his attention back —"I was taking your advice. It was your idea that I volunteer with the theatre group, after all."

I can almost taste the honey dripping from Louisa's words, and I lick my lips. Marvelling at her genuine acting ability, I feel myself being captivated by the story she has woven, before a tremor of trepidation rattles my body, causing the teacup and saucer to quiver in my hands.

Papa's features no longer hold an ounce of displeasure. "I see. I suppose I can understand how the day became a long one. Still, I wish you had told me before you left."

"Oh, but Papa," Louisa is quick to answer, "you had already left for the day when we ventured out."

"Well then, we'll let it rest." Papa dunks a graham cracker into his tea before eating it whole with one bite.

Louisa draws her lower lip between her teeth, and I

wonder whether she is holding back delight or concern over the lie she has delivered.

"I expect we will be busy with volunteering at the theatre full days for the rest of the summer." Louisa takes another sip of tea, then dives further into her untruths. "They have taken on quite a task with this year's production, and all hands are needed."

"Both of you?" Papa's question lingers in the air.

"Well, yes." Louisa falters, hitting the first snag in her web of lies. "Clara has a knack for all sorts of things." Another pause from Louisa increases the speed with which my heart is beating.

"I have taken a shine to working with the props." I cringe as the words fall from my lips. "You know me." With a quick shrug, I attempt to hide my trembling limbs. "I enjoy seeing everything in its place."

Louisa rescues me by taking my cue. "Oh heavens, Clara is a godsend for knowing precisely where every prop must be situated while on set, not to mention how organized things are backstage now that she is in charge of it all."

"Well, I never." Papa's head bobs in approval. "It is nice to see my two girls working together so well."

"I promise to keep on top of the chores and the cooking." My responsibilities to our family being positioned at the top of my list is the furthest thing from a lie, and my confidence returns as I say the words. "Louisa has offered to help some."

"I have indeed." In demonstration, Louisa stands and clears the tray from the low table.

"I am pleased to hear it." Papa checks his watch. "I imagine we can do with a late dinner, given the tea. I don't suppose either of you would care to join me for a walk."

"Oh, Papa." Louisa's voice shrills above the clatter of the tray as she struggles to return it to the kitchen. "We have walked all over the city today. Please say you won't be upset if we decline."

"Of course not." Papa stands to retrieve his hat from the rack. "I'll be off, then." Papa tips his hat and walks through the door.

Louisa, having settled the tray in the kitchen, collapses onto the sofa in a heap. "Whew, that was a close call."

"I don't know how you manage it." I slump back in the chair, exhaustion from the day multiplied by the deceit lingering about me like an unpleasant odour.

Louisa brushes the hair from her face before craning her neck to meet my eyes. "I did it for you, Clara."

"Me?" I sit up in surprise. My nose crinkles at the distasteful nature of our lie. "Why? What do you mean?" My words are a jumble as overwrought emotions from the past twenty-four hours rise to the surface.

Louisa pulls herself upright. "You told me you didn't want Papa to know about the hotel. At first, I thought he wouldn't notice at all. But since he missed us today, I figured it would only be a matter of time before he had more questions regarding our whereabouts." The smirk on her face tells me she has had this fictional story in her back pocket, just in case. "Papa is lost in his own thoughts much of the time, but he is a bit more observant than I expected."

"I didn't think we would have to lie." The softness of my words gives away my unease at the situation.

"What did you think would happen?" Louisa scoffs, clearly put off by my lack of appreciation for her sacrifice.

"I—I suppose I thought, or maybe I hoped, he wouldn't notice. Or perhaps"—The words stutter out like water spurting from a kinked garden hose—"perhaps we might have avoided his questions by nibbling around the edges. You know, I could have said I was at the market or something truer to my nature."

Louisa rolls her eyes and shakes her head at my childish notion. "Really, Clara, I don't think even you could spend all day, every day at the market."

My head hangs low in defeat, wishing there was another way.

"To be honest," Louisa says, giggling at the contradiction between her words and our untruth, "I expected we would make it through at least one week of training before Papa noticed our absence. I certainly didn't expect him to miss us on the very first day."

"No, I suppose not." I slump against the back of the chair, beaten by disappointment and buried by the shame of our lie.

"Well, seeing how Papa questioned us so soon, I figured we had better have a solid alibi going forward." Louisa reclines, laying her arms across the sofa's back, regaining command of the situation. "He won't question our absence any further, and you won't get lost in a tailspin of white lies."

I blush in response to the truth of my sister's statement. A terrible liar I have always been. Perhaps there wasn't a lying bone left, I muse, after Louisa was born. Her own surely makes up for my lack of lying ability.

"Besides," Louisa says, her mind a one-way track, "I've heard it said one should stick as close to the truth as possible when delivering a falsity."

My head drops into my hands as my mumbled question emerges. "How in the world is us volunteering at the theatre remotely close to the truth?"

An indignant expression consumes Louisa's features,

while an air of haughtiness fills the space around her. "I would have been at the theatre all summer if we weren't spending our days at the hotel."

"It's not too late." The cheeky comment leaves my lips before I can admonish it.

Louisa stands, arms crossing over her chest. "You know, Clara, you could just say thank you."

"Lou, I'm sorry." I stand to face her. "I'm not comfortable lying to Papa is all." Rubbing Louisa's arm, I attempt to reconcile with her. "You are right. Thank you for protecting our secret."

"At any rate, it's squared away, for now." Louisa sniffs dismissively. "I think I'll lie down for a bit. Call when dinner is ready."

"Of course." I watch Louisa retreat to the bedroom and wonder if she has given any thought to how we will emerge from this lie once our fate at the hotel is secure. Feeling the need for Mama's words of wisdom, I remember my plan to write to Aunt Vivian. I check my watch and decide there is enough time to reread Mama's last letter to me before I begin dinner. Bolstered by her love, I am certain I will find the words to draft my letter to Aunt Vivian. I have no clue what I will say, but what I desire is crystal clear. Aunt Vivian is a link to Mama, and I can't deny that pull for a moment longer.

I extract the cookbook from its spot on the counter and slide the letter from its pages while smoothing the folds. I bring the paper to my nose out of habit, wishing her scent still lingered among the words. Coming away disappointed, as always, I let my gaze fall to the page and read the words that both heal and cut to the bone, twined together in a braid of immense love and overwhelming grief.

CHAPTER 20

*F*riday, May 20, 1927

      Four days later, Ms. Thompson announces a staged test will take place after the midday break.

"I will time the test." Ms. Thompson dips her chin, lowering her head to meet our eyes. "I do not say this to frighten you. I only wish you to be in possession of all the facts."

The murmur of nervous chatter erupts around me, and I feel my heart climb into my throat. I cast a wary sideways glance toward Lou.

Without so much as blinking, Louisa squeezes my hand before whispering her typical point of view in my ear. "Good news for us, then. Less time for you to fret over it."

I force a meagre acquiescing smile, wondering how my sister manages such an upbeat perspective on life's challenges. Searching Louisa's face, I wonder whether her outlook comes from her natural go-with-the-flow disposition or a delusion regarding the importance of such a task. In a flash of understanding, another thought occurs to me. What if Lou's positivity is for my benefit only? I swallow, shoving my heart back in place within my chest, deciding to do better by my sister.

"You are right," I say, my whispered words backed by dogged determination. "We will be better off quizzing one another during lunch, going over all we've learned to prepare for the test."

Louisa eyes me, a curious expression lining her features. "I meant there is no point in working ourselves up about it." She places a hand on my forearm. "We arrive at such a test with the skills we have gained. Nothing more. Nothing less. At most, we are responsible for our grasp on the training. Little else can be done about the rest. I thought we would be well served by remaining calm."

I feel every fibre of my body scream in protest to Louisa's words. I cannot fathom how one could remain calm without preparing for a test as important as this one. Even if the outcome were not intricately linked to employment at the hotel, wouldn't everyone wish to do their best on a test? And doesn't that require worrying over details? My puzzlement at Louisa's comments flushes my skin with emotion and heat. Like an uncontrolled flame, the warning of danger simmers, and I find myself powerless against its unruliness. A pool of dampness gathers beneath my apron's tie.

An abrupt clap of hands interrupts my fretting. "Ladies, ladies, please." Ms. Thompson quietens the room with a firm voice. "I will not deny the importance of the test." Ms. Thompson's eyebrows shoot toward the glittering chandelier a few feet above her head. "However, if you had waited a moment more, I would have explained further."

Volcano-like rumblings filter through the group.

Ms. Thompson lets out a huff of air. "Ladies, this is the

last time I will ask for silence." Ms. Thompson's pursed lips emphasize that she is less than impressed. "As I was saying, you will be happy to know you will work in pairs for the test. You will not be required to do everything yourself, so please, everyone, take a breath and relax a moment."

The matron's warning scuttles through the group. The maids-in-training hold their tongues while grasping hold of the additional details surrounding the test.

"Very well, then," Ms. Thompson says. "Consider yourself dismissed for lunch. Please return to floor five at one o'clock. We will meet by the guest lift." With a last nod of her head, Ms. Thompson pivots on her heel and walks away.

Though we are more relaxed, by all appearances, our dialogue remains subdued as we exit the hotel via the back-of-house corridor, fearing Ms. Thompson's wrath. Stepping into the sunshine, Louisa links her arm with mine. "I told you we had nothing to worry over." She nudges me with her hip, replacing my frown with a giggle. "Now, let's go find a bit of grass to settle onto for lunch."

Thankful we have ducked Jane during the break, I relish the quiet while I go over the tasks required to set a guest room right. Louisa and I eat in companionable silence on the courthouse lawn. Louisa, lost in her own thoughts—or perhaps minimizing conversation out of respect for my obsessive nature—nibbles her sandwich as she scans the horizon, occasionally pointing out something of interest.

With tummies full and bodies warmed into relaxation from stretching out in the sun, we cross over the street and return to the hotel and the test that awaits us there.

Ms. Thompson rattles off the list of tasks to be tested. "I am looking for a well-appointed guest room, ladies. You will approach this test by completing the following."

Clearing her throat, she begins, "Make the bed, which is currently a bare mattress, into a neat and inviting place of comfort." Ms. Thompson lifts her head from her clipboard. "This includes the implementation of hospital corners on all four corners of the mattress." With a tilt of her chin, she adds, "Don't think I won't lift the duvet to check.

"The carpets are to be vacuumed and finished in the criss-cross pattern we learned on Tuesday. The desk, bench, and night tables are to be dusted and positioned with their dedicated items." Ms. Thompson pauses as she points a finger toward the ceiling. "Remember, ladies, you may refer to your notecard to check that you have everything in hand. All maids are required to carry the notecard detailing the expectations for a well-appointed guest room to reference as needed."

A neutral expression smooths the lines of her face. "There is no shame in referencing the tools you have at the ready. We all experience moments of forgetfulness from time to time."

Louisa elbows me in the side. "See, I told you. Nothing to worry about at all."

I finger the notecard in my apron pocket, thankful for its reminders and support.

"Once the bedroom is nicely situated, I suggest you move on to the lavatory. Since our hotel is only the second in all of Vancouver to offer guests their own personal washrooms, it is our job to keep them sparkling and functional." The few lines about Ms. Thompson's eyes crinkle, though I cannot ascertain whether the gesture indicates humor or distaste. "We wouldn't want water and whatnot making its way to a freshly pressed bedsheet, now would we?"

The image of such an occurrence resonates, and all

heads in the semicircle of girls shake their heads in appreciation of Ms. Thompson's vivid insight.

"The duties required in the lavatory should be fresh in your mind from yesterday, but if need be, refer to your notecard." Ms. Thompson consults her list. "Oh, and one last thing, ladies. Be sure to open the drapes so that they frame the view beyond. It will be the first thing guests are likely to notice when they enter their room. We certainly wouldn't want to leave that experience as a missed opportunity."

Ms. Thompson flips a page atop her clipboard and assigns a guest room to each pair of maids-in-training. "Miss Louisa Wilson and Miss Carol Potter will work in room 503."

My hopes are a little dashed as I realize Louisa and I will not work together. I know how well we could do, with my experience and Louisa's willingness to follow my lead in this environment. Our communication as sisters would have been a definite advantage.

Louisa squeezes my shoulder, offering a demure smile as she joins Carol in front of room 503. I consider how I might work with someone less familiar, who might have a different skill set. I contemplate how I could navigate a successful outcome regardless of my partner's ability.

"Miss Clara Wilson and Miss Jane Morgan, you will work in room 512." Ms. Thompson's voice rises above my thoughts, piercing my confidence like a pin puncturing a balloon.

Before I can remove the dejected surprise from my face, Jane is beside me, linking her arm with mine and dragging me toward room 512.

Ms. Thompson rattles off the remaining pairings before her voice soars across the fifth floor. "Ladies, you will have one hour to complete your room." Ms. Thompson extracts her pocket watch and stares at its face as the seconds tick by. Without further warning, she sends us on our way. "Ready, set. Go!"

Jane and I bump shoulders as we both reach for the door handle of room 512, swinging it open before turning our heads to the trolly filled with supplies and cleaning equipment.

Stepping into the middle of the plush carpet, I survey my surroundings. I pull the notecard from my pocket and decide to begin by opening the drapes, figuring the extra light will make the room a tad brighter. I am fiddling with the drapes' positioning when I notice Jane slip into the washroom. Relief trickles through me at seeing Jane take the initiative to begin work on the washroom. I push aside my concern at not following Ms. Thompson's suggested order of tasks and instead focus on the bed.

I smooth the bedsheet atop the mattress and begin making my nearly perfected hospital corners. The fifth-floor linen closet holds a fresh duvet, and I dash to retrieve it before smoothing it into place. I return the cushioned sitting bench to its home against the footboard and give the bed a final once-over.

After wiping all the dark, gleaming wooden surfaces with a damp cloth, I centre the lamps on each night table. Standing at the foot of the bed, I use a keen eye to ensure the symmetry of the bedroom is intact. I open the drawer of the left-hand night table and place a copy of the King James Bible within.

I turn my attention to the vacuum, pushing and pulling the cumbersome piece of equipment across every inch of carpet space, despite the room having had few visitors. My eyes twitch toward the door, and I glimpse

Ms. Thompson as she retreats from peeking into the guest room.

I work the vacuum, creating the criss-cross pattern over the carpet. The vacuuming takes more time and effort than I expect, and the heat from my exertion snakes down my spine. I wrangle the heavy machine back onto the trolly in the hall as Ms. Thompson's voice booms out. "Fifteen minutes, ladies."

I check my watch, not believing how fast the time has gone. "Right," I say to myself, inspecting the room again. "Pillows and a throw blanket are the remaining items on the list."

I return to the fifth-floor linen closet, where I find myself surrounded by others attempting to secure the remaining items. With four pillows stuffed under my arms and the throw blanket draped over one shoulder, I totter back to room 512.

I enter the room to hear the toilet flushing. Thankful Jane is making progress of her own, I place the pillows and the throw blanket on the bench seat and tap on the washroom door. "Almost finished in there? I don't know if you heard, but we've only about twelve minutes left."

The door opens with a swift whoosh of air. The motion catches me off guard and forces me to step back as Jane emerges, a cream-coloured drying towel in her hands. Tossing the towel onto the counter behind her, Jane straightens her skirt and apron, a smirk turning up the corner of her lips. "Whew, I couldn't wait any longer to visit the privy. And with the staff facilities being all the way down in the basement . . . You won't tell, will you?"

Terror engulfs me, stealing my words. I swallow hard, determined to maintain composure in the face of Jane's inappropriate behaviour. "Please tell me you tidied up in there." I can barely keep the panic from my voice, and I clutch my midsection. The reality of my performance being tied to Jane's is more than I can stomach.

"No." Jane shrugs, her lack of concern feeling like a slap across my face.

"Do—do you not understand?" The words stutter past my lips. "We are training to be maids. Surely, you must know, as maids, we will be required to clean?"

"Honestly, Clara, I thought you would do better with the washroom." Jane's sweet smile lights up her porcelain face. "You go do that and I'll finish the bed."

"Eight minutes, ladies." Ms. Thompson's warning sounds like a fire alarm, thrusting me into action.

I push past Jane, unconcerned by the rough connection our shoulders make. Thankful the hotel has not yet reached operational level and the washroom does not need a deep clean, I wipe the counter, sink, and toilet. I peek inside the bathtub and decide it will have to do. Taking a fresh cloth from my pocket, I polish the mirror until no streaks are visible.

I glance at the soap dish and find it empty. I scurry to the trolly and fetch a fresh bar of soap and clean-pressed towels. The towels are almost straight on the rack when Ms. Thompson announces, "One minute."

A quick glance in the mirror tells me I am out of sorts. My apron has twisted around me like a disobedient toddler, while my hair and cap, once pinned in place, are coming undone in an unruly mess. After righting the bedroom, vacuuming, and making the bed, save for fluffing the pillows and placing them against the dark wooden headboard, it is no wonder I look unkempt.

"Time." Ms. Thompson is in the guest room doorway as I step from behind the washroom door, hastily securing my hair beneath my cap. I step into the middle of the room, cheeks flushed and beads of sweat trickling from my temples.

Anger pulsating beneath my skin, I look straight ahead, avoiding Jane's eyes as she moves to stand beside me while Ms. Thompson examines the room. I hear the nightstand drawer open and close. I smile inwardly, knowing I am responsible for placing the Bible in its proper place. The whoosh of the duvet lifting ticks another box on my list of accomplishments. With or without Jane's help, I am capable. I have the situation well in hand.

Ms. Thompson peers into the washroom, nodding as she steps back into the living area. "Well done, ladies."

"Thank you, ma'am," we say in unison, though I cringe inside, knowing the truth of whose hard work initiated the compliment.

"Only one thing is out of place." Ms. Thompson draws our attention with an outstretched arm to the corner of the bed. The previously hospital-cornered bedsheet, folded and tucked by my own hand, is now undone, its crisp white edge brushing the carpet.

A gasp escapes my lips as anger crawls up my back, showing itself in the gathering of moisture in my eyes.

"No need to fret, Miss Wilson," Ms. Thompson says. "Seldom do I expect perfection the first time around. However, seeing how well you've both done, I daresay I will look for everything in its place next time."

"My apologies, ma'am." Jane's voice is steady, with a mournful edge. "I was only checking Miss Wilson's work when time was called. I didn't yet have the opportunity to fix the bedding."

"No apologies necessary, Miss Morgan. It is how one learns, after all." Ms. Thompson's eyes meet mine for a

fleeting moment, making my heart plummet to the
basement faster than the hotel lift could have delivered it,
before she steps through the door and dismisses us for
the day.

Furious with Jane, first for her lack of help and now for
her bald-faced lie, I storm out of the guest room, pushing
the trolly to its designated parking space within the linen
closet. I am determined not to cause a scene, holding in the
anger that threatens to emerge as loud, hiccupping bursts
of tears.

Halfway down the hall, I remember my sweater, stowed
on the low shelf of the cleaning trolly. I glance about the
hallway before proceeding back to the closet, unable to
think what may come if I encounter Jane.

Emerging from the linen closet, sweater in hand, I see
Ms. Thompson pull aside four girls from our training
group. A few stragglers filter past, toward the employee
stairs and corridor.

"I am sorry, ladies." The sympathy in Ms. Thompson's
voice elicits a response within me that is surely opposite of
her intent. "We do not wish to waste any more of your
time. I am sad to say we have removed you from the
training program."

I scurry down the hall, out of sight and earshot. I have
no desire to be party to the delivery of such dreadful news,
nor to the resulting disappointment. My emotions tucked
out of sight, I reach the bottom of the stairs and hear the
others as they leave the stairwell and enter the employee
corridor, their movement signalled by the thud of the heavy
door.

I find myself alone and out of breath. I sink to the
bottom step, clinging to the wooden railing as the eerie
hush of the abandoned stairwell wraps around me.

Disappointment and devastation mix with a tinge of relief at not having been dismissed.

Unable to comprehend the day's events, I pat my face with my palms. I am at the cusp of a spiralling state and am desperate to shake free before it consumes me. My eyes wander over my uniform apron, damp with water spots from cleaning the washroom. With a resigned sigh, I rise and allow reason and common sense to set in, if only for a moment. I move toward the basement, prepared to change out of my uniform and find Louisa. I am aware of the irony that I feel comforted by the thought of my sister. She may very well know what to do.

CHAPTER 21

*F*riday, May 20, 1927
        By the time I reach the basement, the women's changing room is all but vacant. I say a less than enthusiastic goodbye to the quiet girl, Hazel. She is out the door before I even have the chance to remove my cap. A pout settles on my lips as I consider the others' eagerness to move on with their afternoon, having been released a few minutes early from training.

My uniform drops into the bin. The radiator hisses beside me, startling me from my cheerless mood. I hear voices beyond the door and realize the four girls who were dismissed today have yet to change. I swing my bag over my shoulder, stuff my cloche hat atop my frazzled hair, and pull on the door handle, determined not to find myself swept into their disappointment.

Louisa's voice rings out over the others as they step toward the change room. "There you are. I've been looking for you everywhere." Her piercing tone, a tad too jubilant, draws all eyes. Louisa seems unaware of the awkwardness as her enthusiasm sparks the air.

I step to the side, allowing the girls passage into the change room. Embarrassment colours my cheeks at my inability to find soothing words. Instead, a curt nod is my solitary acknowledgement of their dismissal from the training program.

Stepping toward me, Louisa pulls on my sleeve. "What was that all about?"

We walk with slow steps toward the stairs that will lead us to the hotel's back entrance. "Ms. Thompson dismissed them today. All four of them."

"What?" Louisa pauses in her stride, a hand rushing to her lips. "I didn't know." A brief glance over her shoulder shows her concern. "Oh dear, I feel bad now. I didn't realize."

My shoulders rise and fall. Words capable of explaining how I feel fail to appear. I chew on the inside corner of my lip, searching for an appropriate place to begin. My emotions get the better of me, rising to meet my swirling thoughts, so I hold my tongue. With forced patience, I wait for us to leave the confines of The Hamilton before unburdening myself of my worries to Louisa.

As we climb the stairs, Louisa says in her singsong voice, "I wanted to tell you. I saw your little friend."

"My friend?" I am in no mood for guessing games, and I fail to etch the annoyance from my words.

"Yes, the little Asian boy. The one with the apple." Louisa presses on. "He is an adorable little fella. He was outside, chasing his shadow about the alleyway, when I peeked out the door to see if you were waiting for me there."

"Oh. I see." I recoil at the reminder of how much worse life could be for the Wilson family.

"Something's gotten under your skin. I can tell." Placing an arm through mine, Louisa draws me closer. "Other than the girls who've been dismissed, I mean." Leaping from one conclusion to another, she continues with a whoosh of explanation. "I didn't mean to worry you over my whereabouts. I had to deliver my uniform to the laundry. Since I only have the one." Louisa hesitates a moment. "I thought you would remember that."

An exchange of loud voices at the far end of the corridor wrenches our attention from our conversation. I lift my free arm, pointing toward noise, while offering Louisa a woeful smile. "We'll talk outside," I say, catching the inside corner of my lower lip once more in an effort to hold myself together.

The white walls of the employees' back-of-house maze ends at the junction where the kitchen entrance opens wide. "Like I've stated before, Chef, you have your way and I have mine. I will run my pastry kitchen how I see fit. Now, off I go. I have things to do, and I'll not have a disagreement with you keep me from the demands of my day." A woman's stout frame appears in the threshold, her pinked cheeks glistening with dampness or fury.

A startled expression crosses the woman's face at the sight of us. "Oh dear. I apologize, ladies. That wasn't meant for outside ears." The woman wipes her hands on the long white apron draped over her round frame before offering a sheepish smile. She steps toward the much smaller square kitchen we peeked in during our tour of the hotel. A giggle emerges from behind Louisa's palm, and we shuffle out the back door in a hurry.

As the hotel's heavy back door closes behind us, tears

prick my eyes as the emotion from the day's events rushes up to greet me. Unable to manage a stoic demeanour for one moment longer, the tears gather and stream down my face, not even waiting until we round the corner of the alley.

"What is it?" Louisa's arm wraps me in a firm grip about my shoulders. She moves me closer to the building's exterior, searching my face for understanding. "Things can't possibly be that bad, now can they?" Leaning her forehead toward mine, she draws me closer, our heads bumping with my every hiccup. "Come now, Clara," Louisa coos.

"Those girls. The ones who were dismissed . . ." My words stammer out between gulps of air. "That could have been me." Fresh sobs rattle my body, unmooring me like a ship caught in a storm.

Louisa straightens her arms to full length, holding me by the shoulders and imploring my eyes to meet hers. "Sad as it may be for those four, I can't see how this is anything but good news for you. We've made it through the first round of testing. Shouldn't that be a reason for celebration, not consternation? To be honest"—Louisa's voice shifts from concerned to snooty—"I thought you'd be delighted that I passed. And without you at my side, guiding my every move, I might add."

"But—but so did Jane. She passed the test too." My voice is but a whisper, making me cower at my crumpling assuredness.

Louisa's eyes narrow. "What did Jane do?"

The story spills out of me like an overturned glass of milk. Between bursts of tears, hiccups, and the occasional childlike stamping of my feet, I tell Louisa about every detail of the afternoon's test.

"I can't believe she would stoop so low, and for what?"

My words peter out as my anger and dismay are finally uprooted. I simply can't understand why anyone would behave as Jane has.

"Oh Clara, I am sorry this happened to you." Louisa urges me forward with slow steps. "I can't imagine she will be a suitable fit for employment anywhere, much less at the hotel."

Resolve forces its way up my spine. "I would think not. I have never encountered anyone quite like Jane." Exasperation rushes out of me, and I snatch a sideways glance at Louisa as we cross the street. Desperate to hear her thoughts, I hope she will have a solution at the ready.

"I have seen it before." Louisa's shoulders rise and fall in a defeated shrug. "Not as ardent as in Jane's case. Nor with such an ill intent, I might add. But I have seen others, desperate to direct an outcome in their favour, go to great lengths to achieve what they seek." Louisa's eyebrow lifts as she directs her words toward me.

We fall into silence, each lost in our thoughts, as we wander toward our apartment. Occasional glances from Louisa poke at me, and I feel as though I am under Lou's microscope, though I do not know why.

A block from home, with a fair bit of thinking behind me, I decide on my course of action. I clear my throat and announce my plan to Louisa. "I can't let Jane sabotage my efforts. I will have to make certain Jane and I are not paired together again."

"Um, I'm not sure how you plan to accomplish that," Louisa says, "but then again, maybe we will have new partners for each training exercise."

"I won't let her take this opportunity away from me, Lou. If I can't keep from being paired with Jane again, I will know to handle everything. I will take charge and ensure I complete all tasks by my standards. I will just have to be perfect at everything I do while keeping a watchful eye on Jane and her sneaky side." I pull my shoulders back with determination as the beginning of a headache throbs at my temples.

Louisa releases a quiet sigh. "I'm not so sure about your plan, Clara. It's awfully difficult for anyone to be perfect all the time, let alone while watching their own back. You must admit that you weren't successful in keeping an eye on Jane today."

"That is because I didn't know she would be so underhanded." I rub two fingers at my hairline in an attempt to dislodge the throbbing from my head. "I know better now. There are no other options, Lou. I have to succeed." I give up on my head and squeeze my hands instead. A rumble of discomfort settles in my stomach as Louisa's words of caution unpick my resolve like a frayed stitch. "I must do everything I can to gain employment at The Hamilton, Louisa. Everything I can."

"I understand, Clara, but—" Louisa pauses as she considers her words. "Perhaps it would be better to speak with Ms. Thompson. I can't imagine the matron would be happy with Jane. She should know what is going on, and once she does, the situation will be in her hands."

"I disagree." My head shakes decidedly from left to right. "I cannot take the chance that Jane's connections will fall in her favour. Ms. Thompson may have already been instructed to let her pass the training, and then where would that leave me? No, I am sorry, Louisa, but Ms. Thompson won't be privy to my troubles with Jane."

"Well, I hope things go the way you expect, Clara. Really, I do." Louisa places a gentle hand on my forearm. "I am just not convinced it will be as easy as you think."

We climb the front steps to The Newbury side by side. "I never said it would be easy." I bump Louisa with a hip check, my attempt at lightening the mood between us. A roll of her eyes tells me that, despite our disagreement, we are okay.

By Saturday afternoon, my throbbing head has consumed me, pounding in rhythm with every stroke of the brush as I scrub the kitchen floor. Each movement ensures another jab of pain while unravelling my frazzled brain. I consider a visit to the pharmacy, located three floors down and conveniently attached to the corner of our apartment building. But the expense of headache powder holds me in place, with the scrub brush and soapy water at my side.

I woke with a purpose this morning. While Louisa ventured out into the sunshine for a visit with theatre friends, I set to scrubbing the apartment from top to bottom, determined to use the time to identify every way in which Jane could cause trouble for me. By the time the bathroom is clean, though still dated and well used, I am exhausted from the exertion and my mind's reckless wanderings.

Without a doubt, Jane has gotten under my skin. I sit back on my heels and swipe at the heat gathering across my brow before tossing the brush into the bucket with a splash. My pulsating head and rapidly dwindling mood have already ruined my day.

"Time for a break?" Papa's voice startles me as he steps into view in the hallway. "Didn't mean to surprise you, Clara."

"Oh, Papa, I'm sorry. Did all my commotion wake

you?" I admonish myself for having been lost in my brooding all morning. I hadn't even thought to check on him. Standing, I lift the bucket onto the counter for emptying.

"Wake me?" Papa's smile grows mischievous. His cheeks lift, etching lines at the corners of his eyes, like a half-folded fan. "I've just returned. Left before either of you were up and about."

"Oh." I twist my head over my shoulder to meet his gaze, splashing a trickle of dirty water as I move. "I—I assumed you were still sleeping." Mopping up the water with a rag, I place the bucket in the sink. "Where were you off to so early this morning?" I add a note of fabricated cheerfulness to my words, a veiled attempt to compel a pleasing answer from him.

"Here and there, really." Papa moves toward the kitchen table. "I went to see Mr. Murray. I thought perhaps he might have work coming up this week."

"A job. Well, that is good news." I fill the kettle and set it to boil, encouraging the conversation as I bustle about the kitchen. "How is Mr. Murray? And the children, of course. Oh, I miss them all."

"Fine, fine. Everyone is getting on well, it seems." Papa clears his throat and lowers his gaze. "I don't want you to be getting any ideas, Clara. Mr. Murray has made it clear that the new groundskeeper is working out well, and he has no intention of replacing him."

The sugar bowl settles on the table without a sound. Careful with both my words and my actions, I respond quietly. "I see."

"Clara, I am sorry. I know how much you and your sister wish to return to the estate, but I am afraid that will not be the case." Papa laces his fingers together, rubbing his thumb like a worry stone. "Now, Mr. Murray is a fine man, and he has offered me work for the next few weeks. With all the planting yet to be done, I can lend them an able hand, and I am happy to do so."

"Of course, Papa." I place two cups of steaming tea on the table. "I am sure it will feel good to get your hands in the dirt, among the fresh flowers."

"You must know by now that I am a proud man, Clara." Papa hesitates, his head drooping low. I sit across the table from him, holding my breath as he continues. "I know I've let you down."

"Oh, Papa." I reach across the table and place my hand over his, searching for the words to comfort his heavy heart.

"As I said, I am a proud man, but I promise I'll do better by you and your sister." His chin drops another inch as he examines his tea, adding a spoonful of sugar and stirring with care before lifting the cup to his lips.

Papa is a good man, I tell myself as my eyes roam between his downcast face and my teacup. Troubled, but decent all the same. Guilt over Louisa's and my make-believe story about our daily whereabouts raises a white flag within me. My desire to unburden myself of our lie plays tug-of-war against the duty I feel to help rescue my family from financial ruin. Is a lie ever justified? The question hangs around my neck, heavy and ominous.

We sip our tea in silence, too many words left unsaid and my lack of courage keeping them so. The little girl inside me wishes for a fortunate outcome. Perhaps Papa's employment over the next few weeks will be enough to lend us a brighter reality—one with stability, and routine, and adequate grocery money.

"Thank you for the tea, Clara." Papa rises from the table, coming around to offer my shoulder a warm, gentle squeeze. He places a handful of coins on the table. "For the groceries." His hand trembles atop my shoulder, and my sense of calm wavers. "I'll have more to offer next week, so you can plan on stocking up on necessities then."

Papa leaves me sitting at the table, my eyes glued to the smallest allotment of grocery funds he has given me to date. My mind whirs with the unlikelihood of making the money stretch for an entire week. My hands rest damp and clammy atop the table, while my legs feel as though they are fixed with cement, restraining me in place.

Papa's voice wrenches me back to the room. "I'll be out tonight. A few of the yard boys from the estate are meeting up for a pint. No need to wait on me for dinner."

A chill slices through me. Out of habit or loyalty, I promptly blame it on my sweaty dampness from the vigorous cleaning. My hopes for constancy plunge like a rock into the depths of the ocean. The battle inside of me smolders to the surface in a rolling boil.

Half of me is desperate for him to notice the little girl inside of me, crying out for reassurance. All I crave is for the world outside to disappear while Papa pulls me into a hug and tells me everything will be okay. My fear of our reality fuels the other half of me. The desire to scream at him is overwhelming. He must know the strain we are under. I can't imagine him to be unaware of the cost of groceries or the cost of life—and all that hangs in the balance. Surely even a grief-stricken man would feel his own stomach rumble with hunger, his own head dampened by rain should he find himself without shelter.

I tamp down the urge to let fly the growing number of caged, angry words. I must make him understand. We need him, in every sense of the word. I gulp my tea, frantic for the warmth to give me courage. Placing the empty teacup on the table, I force myself to stand and face him for the conversation we've tiptoed around for far too long. The words are on the tip of my tongue. I turn to call out to him but am left speechless as I watch the apartment door close behind him as he leaves.

CHAPTER 22

$\mathcal{M}$onday, May 23, 1927
"Ladies. Ladies, your attention, please."
Ms. Thompson stands before us, having corralled us in the
basement hallway outside of the change room doors. "I
have an announcement to make."

The whispers and shuffling feet put me on high alert.
With ragged nerves from a weekend of restless sleep, I turn
my distracted attention to Ms. Thompson's commanding
voice.

"I am pleased to say"—Ms. Thompson's posture relaxes
a touch as she clasps her hands in front of her, the soft
rounding of her shoulders giving her a gentler appearance
—"you have all made great strides over the past week."

Excitement echoes through the cluster of uniformed
girls. Louisa bumps my elbow with her own, a confident
smile accompanying her wink. I offer her a feeble smile,
wondering for the hundredth time whether I should have
confided in her about the eviction notice. In the end, I
convinced myself there was no need to burden Louisa,

especially since Papa will soon bring home a full week's wage from the Murray estate. I squeeze my eyes shut and will myself to focus on those funds.

"We have decided that this will be our last week of formal training." Ms. Thompson holds out her hands to maintain calm within the circle, the girls ready to pop open like a champagne bottle on New Year's Eve. "Mind your outbursts, ladies. We have much work still ahead of us." The matron's steel-rod posture reasserted, she quiets the ripple of excitement.

A hand shoots up and all eyes turn in the girl's direction. "Yes, Miss Potter. Did you have a question?"

"Yes, ma'am. I was just wondering when we will know your decision?"

"Thank you, Miss Potter." Ms. Thompson's head dips in quick but assertive nod. "We will remain in training for the duration of the week. Over the weekend, a decision will be finalized by myself and Mr. Olson regarding the fifth-floor maids." Ms. Thompson's pride in the hotel shines like a lighthouse on a dark evening.

"We ask that, unless you are told otherwise prior to the weekend, you return next Monday morning at nine o'clock, at which time we will announce the successful candidates. I should also like to mention that for all of you who remain through Friday, your training wage will be waiting for you come Monday morning. Be sure to collect your alternate uniforms from the laundry and have them with you."

A chorus of "yes, ma'am" reverberates through the group. The reminder of the expected training wage provides an essential and welcomed breath of relief. There is no doubt we desperately need funds. This weekend, worry over the past due rent and the lack of this week's grocery money consumed me. Knowing too much can be tormenting.

"Do your best, ladies. This is the time to shine." Ms. Thompson leads the way to the service lift. The lift will require multiple trips to deliver all of us to the fifth floor, so I, along with a handful of other girls, head for the stairwell.

On the fifth floor, we gather in front of the lift doors, crowding together like sardines in a tin can. The delicate nature of my surroundings comforts me, and I breathe a small sigh at the beautiful environment. The hallway is painted sky blue above the decorative chair rail. Every table, wall sconce, and detail weaves together to impress, delight, and calm any individual fortunate enough to find themselves here.

My attention lingers on a recently added painting beside the lift's brass-caged opening, and I consider the expense of such a thing. The Wilsons have never afforded a luxury such as fine artwork. I find myself unable to determine the painting's purchase price, but I know full well that it is worth more than all of my worldly possessions combined. In my fragile state of mind, I leap to the realization that one painting among the many now adorning the hotel's walls could fund our rent for several months.

I admonish myself for such unbecoming thoughts. *Different social classes have unique life experiences*, Mama used to say, always adding that *having more is not a guarantee for a life of happiness*. Ms. Thompson checks her clipboard before addressing us. "Today, we will turn our attention to the care of the spaces outside of the guest rooms." Pacing the width of the hall, she continues. "This may seem like a small task when compared to the care and attention that goes into the guest rooms, but rest assured ladies, guardianship of the hall, lift, and even the stairwell will be part of your daily duties as fifth-floor maids."

I pinch the skin at my waist while pretending to adjust my apron's tie as I strong-arm my scatterbrained attention back toward Ms. Thompson, certain her instructions will be necessary to today's work.

"Walk with me, ladies. We will start at one end of the hall and follow the lines of the hotel to ensure nothing is overlooked." Ms. Thompson guides us through the hallways in the hotel.

We fall into place around the matron as she stops. "We always begin at the left-hand top of the H, just as you would when writing the letter." Ms. Thompson points to the brass room number positioned on a guest room's door. "Or, for those of you unable to picture the letter *H* while standing within the hotel, I'll simplify things for you. We begin the cleaning of the hall at room number 501."

The girls share a giggling murmur, and Ms. Thompson inclines her head. "Just to be clear, ladies, you will count your way through the hall until you've reached the last room on the floor. Now, let's go over the list of tasks that you will complete along the way."

Releasing a bundle of notecards from her clipboard, Ms. Thompson hands them to the girl closest to her and asks her to pass them along. "Take one card each, ladies. These cards, like your guest room notecards, act as your reminder. Your guide, if you will, on each surface that needs cleaning and every task that is to be completed in the hall and corridors during your shift. These tasks are in addition to those in the guest rooms under your assignment, so be sure to allow enough time for the completion of both sets of duties each day.

"Miss Morgan, please fetch me a cleaning rag from the

cleaning cart we passed around the corner." Ms. Thompson
returns her attention to the group as Jane walks toward the
cart. "I realize the list may seem to have more items than
there is time to accomplish, but all of you will work
together in the communal areas of the hotel.
Communicating with one another will be essential to
getting on with shared tasks."

Jane hands Ms. Thompson the rag before returning to
the group. "You will note we have added several paintings
to the hotel's walls over the weekend. You are to use a dry
rag to wipe clean any dust from the edges of the paintings."
Ms. Thompson demonstrates her technique on a muted
pastel painting of children at the seaside, detailing how to
support the artwork as we clean. "Be sure to take a step
back once finished to ensure the painting hangs straight on
the wall. Who would like to try it?"

Ms. Thompson hands the cloth to the first girl in line
and comments favourably, offering only a nudge of
correction as each girl moves the rag carefully around the
painting's edge.

"The only way to stay on top of the cleaning, ladies, is
to attend to it every day." Ms. Thompson thanks the last girl
for trying her hand at wiping down the already spotless
frame. "Now, as you can see, the woodworkers have carved
an intricate pattern into the chair rail." Ms. Thompson
runs her hand along the sculpted strip of wood that
separates the top and bottom halves of the walls.
Interrupted only by guest room doors and the lift at the
epicentre of each floor, the chair rail is an extravagant
design element matching the grandeur of the hotel.

With the dry rag in hand, Ms. Thompson wipes down
each section of wood. "We begin at the top so any debris
can fall below. Follow the flat edge first on one section of

wall, like this." Walking the length of a section of chair rail, Ms. Thompson uses a smooth motion as she moves.

Ms. Thompson returns to her starting point. "Next, from top to bottom of the rail, you will trace the curves and flourishes, removing dust as you go. Again, a dry rag is best for everyday cleaning. Those ladies who remain with us as maids will learn about the deeper cleaning that will take place monthly." She hands over the rag, and we go through the paces of cleaning and recleaning the same section of chair rail.

As each girl follows the swooping pattern of the wood molding, Ms. Thompson continues with her instructions, checking off her list as she goes. "The baseboards are to be wiped clean daily as well." She looks up from her list to make another point. "And of course, ladies, should you see a mar on the wall, do your best to wipe it clean. If a mark proves stubborn, you are to bring it to my attention so a suitable solution can be found."

Once everyone has had a turn at the chair rail, Ms. Thompson moves on to the plush carpet. "Just as you do in each guest room, you will vacuum the common area carpets in a tidy and tight criss-cross pattern. Take care not to bang into guest doors or the walls with the vacuum." Ms. Thompson raises her eyebrows. "Or we will have to add repainting the trim to your list of duties as well."

Referencing her list again, she says, "Ah yes, and ladies, there are long, slender tables in a few locations throughout the hall. You will dust and polish them daily. You will also check the vases and flower arrangements that sit atop those tables." Ms. Thompson steps past us into the wider space where the short hall leads into the main one. "After lunch, we will tackle the entire fifth floor together. For now, follow me. Let's go over the care and attention of the lift and stairwell."

Like ducklings following their mother to the water's edge, we arrange ourselves into pairs and walk behind Ms. Thompson toward the stairwell. We come across a long, slender table of brilliantly polished dark wood. A wide-based crystal vase holding a bouquet of spring flowers sits atop the table. "That reminds me." Ms. Thompson stops abruptly, causing those of us further down the line to bump into those in front of us. We stifle laughter as we reposition ourselves to allow for a little breathing room.

"As I mentioned earlier, the flowers are to be checked each morning and evening." Bending at the waist, Ms. Thompson examines the clear glass. "These could use fresh water, don't you think?"

From my position near the back of the line, I watch as a few heads closer to the table bob up and down. "A maid with an eye for detail will pluck any decaying flowers and rearrange the bouquet to ensure it appears full and lush." Ms. Thompson motions with her hands. "Ladies, please step back and form a circle so those in back can see what we are talking about."

As my turn arrives to inspect the flowers, I notice a few blooms with more stick than flower to them. I hesitate, unsure whether tending to the flowers in this moment is appropriate. A girl behind me taps me on the shoulder for her turn at a peek. I step aside, reasoning that the others must have noticed the same as I did. Stepping in line beside Louisa, I decide to pluck the offending flowers from the vase as soon as the matron dismisses us for lunch.

Jane steps forward from the group. Without hesitation, she picks the twig-looking flower from the bouquet. "Like this, ma'am?" An angelic smile spreads across her face.

"Yes, Miss Morgan. That is precisely what I meant." Ms. Thompson nods her approval.

The blow hits me in the stomach, sucking the breath from me for a moment. With swirling thoughts, I admonish myself for my hesitation to act. Ms. Thompson was still talking, I reason, irritated at being one-upped by Jane again. I am quite certain that interrupting her might have seemed rude.

Lou pokes me in the side, drawing a scowl from me. She inclines her head toward the matron, silently mouthing, "Ms. Thompson."

My head swivels and my eyes meet Ms. Thompson's. "Miss Wilson?" she says.

"Yes, ma'am." Heat rises to my face, warming me most uncomfortably.

"Are you well? I asked if you and Miss Morgan would take the vase to the kitchen and give it a wash before replacing the flowers? I left a fresh bouquet on the counter this morning."

"Of course, ma'am." I step forward, diverting my eyes to the floor, but not before catching the smug look on Jane's face.

"Off you go, then." Ms. Thompson hands the vase of flowers to Jane and returns her attention to the group.

We descend the back-of-house stairs toward the kitchen. I can't bring myself to look at Jane, let alone speak to her, so I allow her to go first as I hang back, following her lead while racking my brain for a way to work with her.

Jane pushes open the kitchen's swing door with the back of her shoulder and turns to examine me as the corner of her lip lifts in a mocking smile. "Daydreaming, were you?"

I feel the warmth of a fresh blush rising and turn away

from Jane's watchful stare, with the pretence of searching the counters for the flowers.

"I don't blame you." Jane laughs and jostles my shoulder, inviting me into a jovial moment at my expense. "I can't imagine needing much more instruction on how to wipe down a picture frame, either."

"We better get to the flowers." I head toward the oversized kitchen sink and begin unwrapping the string from the bouquet.

Jane dumps the old bouquet in the garbage, water and all. "Wait!" I call out a little too late. "We could have used the greenery. Not to mention the water should be poured down the drain. Now someone else will have to deal with a heap of wet garbage."

"Oops." Jane shrugs, her concern over her misstep either well hidden or non-existent. She hands me the crystal vase without another word.

Jane leans against the prep counter in the middle of the expansive kitchen and folds her arms across her chest, a clear sign she has no intention of helping any further. A breath of relief passes my lips. I am better off handling things myself.

I wash and dry the vase and fill it with fresh water before searching for a sharp kitchen knife. Unbundling the flowers, I lay them out across the counter and trim the ends of the stems.

"Why do you do that?" Jane asks. "Wouldn't it be easier to just leave them all tied together and put them in the vase?"

I shoot Jane a curious look over my shoulder. "Haven't you ever put flowers in water before?"

"No, someone else does that at home." Jane's forehead crinkles. "Though I am not sure who." I force back an eye roll at her perplexed expression. Flowers and their management are clearly new considerations for Jane, and I wonder yet again what aspects of being a hotel maid appeal to her.

"You cut the stems so the flowers are better able to soak up the water. They live longer that way." I carefully place each individual flower in the vase, arranging them as I go. I rotate the vase, repositioning a few stems to ensure a full and even display from all angles.

"There. Doesn't that look better?" I turn with the vase, pleased by my arrangement.

Jane smiles. "Sure does." Without hesitation, she takes the vase from my hands and moves to leave the kitchen, opening the swing door with her backside. "Coming?"

"We have to clean up this mess first," I call after her, but my words and irritation are shut out by the swinging door.

Jane pokes her head back through the door as it swings in. "I'll run these up, then." Before I can say another word, Jane is through the door and on her way, ready to take credit for my carefully arranged bouquet.

CHAPTER 23

*M*onday, May 23, 1927
  Left alone in the vast kitchen, I drop my chin to my chest in stunned disbelief. Frustration courses through my veins. Both my physical appearance and my internal compass are mere moments from coming unhinged. My world seems to tilt as I mutter admonishing words to myself.

I survey the mess of flower stems and greenery I have yet to clean from the counter while searching my mind for another option. I can't even stop myself from being helpful. How in the world will I be assertive enough to stand against Jane? I am beside myself with worry. I alone am to blame for allowing Jane to take what she wants and continue on her way. I shake my head, disappointed with myself for handing her the win, right along with the vase of flowers.

Feeling duped yet again by Jane's opportunistic abilities, I grab the garbage bin by the handle and drag it across the hard floor. The metal bin squeals as it scrapes against the floor, determined to defy my efforts. "I can't win this way."

My voice emerges in a whine, increasing my irritation and sending this morning's hopeful thoughts sailing out of reach.

Angry tears burn to the surface, pooling and threatening to spill over. I swipe the leaves and the short ends of the cut stems into the bin with such force that they overshoot the bin's edge. Cut flower pieces scatter across the polished kitchen tiles like spiders scurrying from a downpour.

With little resolve left, I sink to the hard floor. Tears stream down my face as my world, my hopes, and my emotions all run amok, making a mess of my composure and my confidence.

"Come now, it can't be all that bad."

I jump at the voice.

"I didn't mean to startle you, dear." A plump woman with a round, kind-looking face stares down at me.

"Sorry, ma'am. I didn't hear you come in." I shift to my knees and begin gathering the stems and flower bits, tossing them into the garbage bin with uncoordinated haste.

"Ma'am? Don't think anybody's called me ma'am in years." A soft chuckle accompanies her words. "Ruby is my name, but you can call me Cookie."

"Cookie?" I look up and wipe my cheeks, aware how dishevelled I must appear.

With a groan of exertion, Cookie squats to meet my eyes. "Yes, it's because cookies are what I am good at. I am the assistant to the pastry chef here."

Recognition dawns on me, and I offer her a weak smile. "I remember now. I saw you the other day, while my sister and I were leaving. You seemed a mite bit flustered by something or"—I hesitate, wondering if I have said too much—"someone."

"Ah, you witnessed the unfortunate exchange between me and Chef." Cookie's red-flushed cheeks deepen in colour. "I wish I could say it was a rare occurrence." A sigh escapes her lips.

Though I am curious about the cause of such a disagreement, I sense the need to change the subject. "I imagine it is wonderful to be good at something like making pastries and such."

Cookie heaves herself up into a standing position before offering a hand to me. She places the garbage bin at its home beside the prep table without a sound. "Everyone is good at something. You just have to find what that thing is for yourself. Now, why all the tears?"

"Oh—well . . ." My gaze shifts around the white walls of the kitchen before finding comfort in the view of my shoes. "I suppose I've realized that my abilities won't be nearly enough if I am set on working here at the hotel."

"I don't believe that for a moment. If you are good at something, that talent will shine through. Are you with the training maids, then?"

"Yes, ma'am. I mean yes, Cookie. I am a maid-in-training for the fifth floor."

"Well, Ms. Thompson was telling me this morning that she has an excellent group of girls and her decision will be a difficult one. Wishes she could hire you all, she said."

The compliment lifts my eyes, along with my spirits. "I best be getting back. Thank you for your help with the flower trimmings. Ms. Thompson will wonder where I've gotten to if I don't hurry."

"Don't let me keep you. But dear, I hope you know when a situation isn't going the way you wish, it doesn't mean all is lost. More times than not, you can locate an opportunity to start anew. Whatever the situation, the place where you find yourself is simply a new location from which to begin again." Cookie's ruddy cheeks lift as a smile twitches at her lips. "Chin up now, you hear?"

"Thank you, Cookie." I grasp the sides of my apron and dip in a quick curtsy, as Ms. Thompson taught us to do when addressing distinguished hotel guests. Though neither a guest nor, in most social circles, distinguished, this kind lady has offered me comforting words and a new perspective from which to view my current predicament. I pivot toward the door and move quickly through the back-of-house corridor and up the stairs to the fifth floor.

Ms. Thompson is dismissing us for lunch as I take my place beside Louisa in the semicircle of maids. The arrangement of flowers on the slender table near the lift looks well positioned but offers me little joy. I quell a rogue harrumph, about to slip out, behind closed lips.

We depart for lunch, retrieving our bags from the employees' room before heading into the warmth of the day. Stepping into the alley, a voice calls out to us. "Louisa, Clara, wait up." Jane is waving from the shadow of the heavy back door.

"What nerve." The words leave my lips in a whisper, but the disdain lacing them does not go unnoticed by Louisa.

"I've just got to grab my purse. Back in a jiffy." Jane calls out, a delighted expression stretched across her face.

The back door closes behind Jane, and Louisa directs her attention toward me. "Is there a problem, Clara?" Her signature raised eyebrow questions me as the other girls filter past us, leaving for their thirty-minute break.

A huff slides past my pursed lips. "I did the flowers."

Louisa looks at me, a question behind her expression. "Yes."

"No, I mean I cleaned the vase, cut the stems, and arranged the flowers." My annoyance is barely in check, and I feel as though it may explode from the top of my head.

"Yes, I know you took care of the flowers." Louisa rubs a comforting hand over my upper arm. "Jane told all of us how you showed her how to cut the stems."

"What?" My head spins as though Louisa has shoved me backwards.

"When she returned with the flowers, Ms. Thompson commented on how well put together they were. Jane babbled on about trimming the stems, removing the low-lying greenery, and adding fresh water. Then she said you had told her why it was important to do so."

"She did?" I am left to flounder in the confusion of my misunderstanding, unsure whether to be ashamed for calling Jane out in error or to double down and guard myself more diligently. The threat and uncertainty surrounding Jane is not shrinking to the shadows, as I would prefer.

Louisa laughs, the cheerful sound tinkling like wind chimes in a breeze. "She did. Ms. Thompson even made a point of telling all of us how we could learn from one another and what a good example the two of you had provided." Louisa drops her chin, searching my face. "See, Clara, things aren't always as awful as you imagine them to be."

The back door closes, drawing our attention. "There she is now. This would be a good time to pack away your sour mood so we can enjoy the sunshine and a pleasant chat." Louisa calls Jane over with a welcoming wave.

"Thanks for waiting." Jane beams at us. "I packed a lunch today. Well, actually, our cook packed me a lunch today." A sheepish look comes over her at the truth of the matter.

"Why don't we head over to the lawn?" Louisa points to the courthouse lawn across the street. "We have a blanket, and there is plenty of it to share."

"That sounds terrific," Jane says, her perky mood smoothing out my disdain for her and replacing it with wary optimism.

Before crossing the street, Jane purchases a newspaper from the boy on the corner, waving it above her head in excitement. "I've been waiting for more news of this. Isn't it exciting?"

I catch the headline as we step onto the grass.

LINDBERGH LANDS AT PARIS.

Louisa squeals beside me. "Oh, how exciting indeed. Can you imagine it, flying in an airplane all the way to Paris? How dreamy that would be?"

I spread out the blanket as Louisa and Jane babble on about the transatlantic flight.

"Over thirty-three hours. How incredible," Jane says, her head bent toward the black newspaper ink.

"How exhausting," I say. The thought of being trapped in a tin can, frozen to the core and alone, is less than appealing.

Louisa laughs and looks up from peering over Jane's shoulder. "You won't even ride in the lift, for goodness' sake. An airplane is definitely beyond your comfort."

I settle myself on the blanket, pulling out sandwiches and a bottle of water. With a short supply of essentials at home, my sandwich comprises more homemade bread than filling. I stifle a disappointed groan and position my face toward the sun.

"They say here that tens of thousands greeted him at

the airport when he arrived in France." Jane, distracted by the news article, sits on the edge of the blanket, almost crushing her packed lunch beneath her.

Louisa, caught up in the thrill, lets out a yearning sigh. "I would love to have tens of thousands of people come to see me. It is what I have always dreamed of."

Jane cocks her head to one side. "Really?" Noticing her packed lunch beside her, she pulls out a sandwich and nibbles at its edges.

Louisa replies with an ardent nod, swallowing her bite in a hurry before gulping a splash of water. "I do. I dream of the stage every day." Louisa lifts her face to the perfect angle, showcasing her most favoured pose. "And probably most nights too," she admits from behind a raised palm, quelling a giggle.

I smile at my sister's dramatic flair. In every room she enters, she is a breath of fresh air. She is the sunlight on a cloudy day. Louisa deserves so much more than being relegated to working as a hotel maid. Like the banter of gulls at the water's edge, Jane and Louisa's back-and-forth chatter fades to the background as I contemplate how to make both of our dreams come true.

Cookie's words echo in my mind. I look from Louisa to Jane and wonder where my new starting point is. With Jane's recent about-face, I am compelled to give her a second chance, an opportunity to right her wrongs. But can I trust her? Is this morning's honesty another part of her game, with her as the cat and me the mouse?

If only I were as steadfast as Mama, then the answers would be easy. These past years, I've tried to mimic her thoughts and actions. I've held her ideals tightly, determined to do as she would have done—or at least what I imagine she would have done. Sometimes, when I feel small and alone, uncertainty consumes me. Was it all a dream? Was Mama really the angel I've made her out to be? Or are my remembrances the wishful memories of a child? I can't be certain that my memory does not play games with me. Perhaps it is easier to remember her as perfect so I always have an example to lead me forward in life.

"What do you think, Clara?" Lou is looking at me, the incline of her tone catching me off guard.

My head swivels toward her out of reflex, her voice yanking me from my blurry-eyed view of the city beyond. "Sorry, what did you say?" I busy myself by repacking our bag.

"You were miles away." Louisa lowers her voice, tilting her body to muffle our exchange.

"Lost in the sun's warmth is all." I poke my head around Louisa's shoulder and address Jane. "It is wonderful, isn't it? The sun I mean."

"Huh?" Jane looks up from the newspaper, now spread wide in front of her. "Oh, yes. The sun, it's nice."

Thankful I am not the only one in a state of distraction, I offer Louisa the last of the water before sliding the bottle into the bag. I check my watch, surprised at how fast the time has gone. "Well, I suppose we should head back. I wouldn't want to miss anything." I stand and wait for the others to rise from the blanket so I can fold it and squeeze it into the bag.

Jane folds her paper in half before securing it beneath one arm, her face erupting with a playful grin. "Oh, heavens no. I would hate to miss one second of how to wipe down a door frame." She giggles at her own mockery of this morning's training.

"Well, it may not be especially difficult, but it's

important to know nonetheless." Louisa says, grabbing one side of the blanket. She steps toward me as we work together to fold and straighten it.

We take one last look at the lawn, ensuring we've collected all of our belongings, and make our way back to the hotel and an afternoon of further training.

CHAPTER 24

*M*onday, May 23, 1927

I walk with purpose, my mind stretched to the limits, mirroring my white knuckles as they flex and ball within my jacket pockets. Louisa catches up with me, grabbing hold of my sleeve. "Why didn't you wait for me? Didn't you hear me calling you?"

I shake my head. "Sorry, no." I pause for a streetcar before heading across. Louisa remains at my side, waiting, I presume, for further explanation. "I want to get home."

"Why the rush? Aren't your feet tired from the day? I know mine are." Louisa's questions pummel me, and the assault unseats me with the strength of a gale-force wind.

"I need to do some thinking is all." Embarrassment at my thoughts slinks in, making me feel grimy from the inside out. My internal temperature rises, and in less than a blink of an eye, I regret this morning's decision to wear my raincoat. The offensive mackintosh now wraps around me like a straitjacket.

"Thinking?" Louisa matches her stride to mine. "About what?"

"I need to make a plan, and I want to get home so I can sort it out." A huff threads through my words, but I am powerless to curtail its presence.

"What kind of plan?" Lou scrutinizes me with a sideways glance. "What are you up to, Clara?"

"I would really rather not talk about it right now, if you don't mind." My pace quickens as I deliver my best none-of-your-business stare before hurrying forward.

"I do mind." Louisa's smile falters, and she walks faster to keep up.

Unable to shake the unease surrounding Jane, I am eager to arrive home. Our lunch together did little to convince me of her newly turned leaf. Something isn't adding up. Yet with evidence to the contrary, I will appear unhinged if I voice my concerns.

"I'm waiting," Louisa says. Her ability to put on a mothering manner when a situation calls for it unnerves me, and I question, not for the first time, if her acting skills really are that convincing.

"If you must know, I am thinking of ways to eliminate Jane from the training program."

"Clara Wilson, I am shocked by you." Louisa, clearly not finished lording her assumed parental role over me, seems to grow in height as she admonishes me. "Why on earth would you think such a thing, let alone act on it?"

Louisa shakes her head disapprovingly as we pass the barber shop with a cheerful red-and-white-striped awning. "This isn't like you. This isn't like you at all, Clara."

"You can't possibly understand, Lou." The desperation to save my family from poverty shakes my words free. "I have no choice. I have had time to think this through and I have determined that I won't be able to edge Jane out by being polite and kind. That became more than clear today."

"You are right. I don't understand. Jane was nothing but honest and delightful today. I thought we shared a pleasant lunch." An exasperated sigh whispers through Louisa's lips. "Geez, Clara, whatever happened to giving a person a second chance?"

"That's just it, Lou. If today showed me anything, it is that Jane is not to be trusted. Her whims are simply too unpredictable to be relied upon." I swallow hard, trying to push down the discontentment expanding within my chest. "It is time for me to think like Jane does. That is the only way I know to fight back in her game."

"But Clara, why do you need to fight back?" Louisa stops walking and pulls me closer to the exterior of a brick building. "We've worked so hard to get where we are. Jane's actions are all on Jane. She isn't our responsibility."

When Louisa recognizes her statement is not making its intended impact, she presses on with a haughty demeanour. "Besides, I have worked hard too. I have scrubbed toilets, made beds. I have shirked no duties or complained about them, regardless of how bone weary I've felt. For heaven's sake, Clara, I put a ridiculous-looking hat atop my head every morning as part of the uniform, and for what?" Louisa's voice rises an octave. "I'll tell you what. For you, dear sister. I have done it all for you. Because you were the one so desperate to secure a job at The Hamilton."

A snowstorm of emotions courses through me. Anger at Louisa for inserting herself into my original plan of gaining employment at the hotel. Fear over our current inability to fill our cupboards with enough food to last the week. Hopelessness at the unlikeliness of paying our overdue rent

without a job. Shame for not having the courage to tell
Louisa the details of our dire situation. This woman before
me is more than able to deal with a difficult situation. She
has stepped up when I did not expect her to. She made her
own way into the training program, and for all
appearances, Louisa seems to be learning, growing, and
truly rising into the role of hotel maid.

My chin drops to my chest. The shame I carry
outweighs all other feelings. Here I am, responsible for
telling myself the untruth that Louisa wasn't up to the task.
I convinced myself I was protecting her by hiding our
situation. I have been fooling myself all along.

In a matter of weeks, I've seen my sister reclaim her
inner joy. I think back to her melancholy days and wonder
if I've been misreading her all along. Everyone is entitled to
a little pity party once in a while. Lord knows I've had my
share of them in the past two weeks alone. Louisa was
simply grieving the loss of her beloved lifestyle. I look at my
sister, and it is as if a light has turned on within her once
more. She is far stronger than Mama or I gave her
credit for.

"We were wrong about you." The words resist being
spoken, but I force them out, anyway.

"What are you talking about?" Louisa's anger toward
me is replaced by confusion. "Who was wrong about me?"

"Mama and me." I look past my sister, ashamed to meet
her eyes. "In a letter, Mama asked me to look out for you.
She told me I was the strong one." My shoulders sink with
the understanding of how wrong I've been. "She didn't
have the chance to see you grow into your strength, Louisa,
but I did. I should have stopped listening to her advice. Not
because it wasn't good advice at one time, but because it is
outdated. You've—we've moved beyond everything Mama

could have known about us, because she did not know who we would become without her here."

I wade through swirling emotions, searching for the words to share with her. I must tell Louisa why I am determined to be hired at the hotel, though I know she may very well throw a fit. If I can muster the strength to see the conversation through, it is almost impossible to imagine an outcome where having Louisa on my side would be anything but a benefit.

"I'm sorry. I've let you down, Louisa."

"Honestly, Clara, I thought you would have more to say for yourself." Louisa tosses her hair over her shoulder and moves toward our apartment.

"You are right." The words squeak out from where they've been hiding, with my anxiety attempting to hold them hostage. "I have more to say. I have much more, in fact."

I glance about the street, left and then right. "But not here. We should walk on. I promise to tell you everything when we get home."

Not willing to lay down her disappointment with me yet, Louisa replies, "I am holding you to that."

A nervous smile lowers my eyes while lifting the corners of my mouth. "I have no doubt."

We walk in silence, Louisa still in a huff and me thinking through the best way to tell my sister that we are broke and on the verge of total collapse. How does one begin? I ask myself before returning to the image of the red-stamped eviction notice. After a few more blocks and several minutes, I decide to start at the beginning. I will tell her about the notice and then walk her along the path that led us to this day.

We approach The Newbury. Though my ringing nerves

have encapsulated me in a cocoon of dread, I have a plan, and that is the best I can hope for.

"Ah, Miss Wilson." The voice startles me from my thoughts, jerking my head up.

"Mr. Watkins," I say, recovering myself, intent on masking my internal dialogue with a polite appearance. "How nice to see you. You are taking advantage of the fine weather." I glance toward his broom. "After this morning's clouds, I wasn't sure we would see the sun today." I catch Louisa's expression, which seems to question my sanity as I babble. "It appears I've overdressed for the day, after all." I tug at my raincoat, fiddling with the tie at my waist.

Mr. Watkins looks to his shoes before offering a sad smile. My stomach clenches as my jaw comes unhinged, gaping at what I am certain is about to be bad news.

"Nice day indeed. Miss Wilson, I was actually hoping to catch you this afternoon." Mr. Watkins leans the broom handle against the building's front step railing before moving close and lowering his voice. "You see. Well—I've heard word from the management." His eyes shift up and to the right, glancing briefly at The Newbury beside us. "I am sorry to say there is no inclination to offer much of an extension on the rent."

I hear Louisa's small gasp. A ripple of hopelessness runs through me, and my knees feel as though they will buckle where I stand.

I turn my full attention to Mr. Watkins and press on. "What exactly are they willing to offer?"

"The past due amount," Mr. Watkins says, his eyes pleading with mine for understanding, "in full, is due by the end of next month." Mr. Watkins works his hands together, a worried gesture if ever I saw one.

"I understand." The weight of the world seems to land

heavy on my shoulders, along with Mr. Watkins' news. I planned to be caught up with the rent by August, but now I must somehow find a way to pay back our debt a full two months earlier than I hoped.

"My sincere apologies, Miss Wilson." Mr. Watkins pats my shoulder with a gentle hand. "I wish I had better news for you."

"Thank you, sir. Please know I appreciate all you have done for me and my family." The urge to dash to the seclusion, if not security, of our apartment is overwhelming. A quick glance at Louisa informs me she will remain on my heels, no matter which way I run. "We had better go." I force a smile that I hope appears grateful. "Thank you again, Mr. Watkins. I will do everything I can to remedy the situation."

Mr. Watkins tips his hat as we head for the stairs. The sound of his resumed sweeping follows us past the first floor, where the silence between Louisa and me becomes deafening.

Louisa closes the apartment door behind us, words ready to fly from her lips. I hold up my hand, urging her to bite her tongue a moment longer. I remove my jacket and hang it on the hook, feeling the relief of air touching my skin. My bag finds the floor at the entrance to the kitchen as I search the two bedrooms, the bathroom, and the living room of our small home, ensuring Papa is not present.

My search complete, I turn to Louisa and gesture to the kitchen table. "Shall we?"

She settles herself at the table while I pour us each a tall glass of cold water.

My bottom has not yet graced the chair when Louisa starts in, her voice shrieking higher with every question. "What on God's green earth is going on, Clara? Past due rent? How can that be? How far in arrears are we? Does Papa know? Oh heavens, whatever will happen to us?"

An exasperated sigh leaves my lips, taking with it every ounce of the determination I have been clinging to for weeks. "This is what I was going to talk with you about when we arrived home."

"I certainly hope so." Louisa fires words like a fastball. "What I can't fathom is why I am hearing of this for the first time today."

When there are no airs to put on, no part for her to act, Louisa seldom guards her emotions. Instead, she makes her thoughts and feelings known in concise, direct, and often clipped sentences.

Knowing I was wrong to keep this from my sister, I stutter an apology. "I should have confided in you. I am sorry. I suppose I didn't want to worry you." Reaching for my glass, I run a finger up and down its outside surface, wiping the thin layer of moisture developing there. "I found the eviction notice in Papa's jacket the day you followed me to the hotel. The day we submitted our applications." My lip quirks as I attempt to hold back the emotions rumbling through me. "I figured I could find a job and take care of things."

"By your unwillingness to fill him in on our recent adventures, I am guessing Papa isn't aware that you know about the eviction letter?" Louisa's head bobs methodically as she pieces together the events of the past few weeks.

"He doesn't know that I have seen it." The dam breaks within me, and the disquiet and worry I've kept hidden forces its way out in a feeble explanation. "All I knew was that the grocery allotment was shrinking by the week. Had been for months. I tried my best to manage with what I had at my disposal, but—" I find myself at a loss for how to make Louisa understand.

"It wasn't enough." Louisa finishes my sentence, her understanding far greater than I expect. "Oh Clara, you shouldn't have been burdened with such things. You should be in school, not pinching pennies and working to pay a rent that's not your responsibility." Louisa's mood shifts from angry to devastated. "Oh Lord, what would Mama say?"

Louisa's sentiment pushes me over the edge of the cliff I've been staring down. All I can do now is fall. Tears roll down my face as my entire body convulses with grief. "I—I was only trying to do what Mama would have." I gulp in air, trying to calm myself. "She would have found a way around, all the while keeping a smile on her face and a spring in her step."

Kneeling beside me, Louisa wraps me in a fierce embrace. "We will get through this. We will, Clara. Together." Minutes pass with us entangled in each other's arms, holding one another up in a desperate attempt to stay afloat.

"Can't we confront Papa? Tell him we know about the eviction notice and demand that he find a job, temporary or otherwise?" Louisa is searching for an answer to the questions I've been asking myself for weeks.

"You saw how he reacted when you called him out on being unemployed. He walked out." A weary sigh wraps around my words. "He knows what he needs to do. He is just struggling with how to get there. I think he is moving in the right direction, not fast enough is all. Besides, wasn't it you who told me I am not responsible for other people's choices?"

Louisa rolls her eyes as I thrust her own words back at

her. "Maybe that rule should be applied on a case-by-case basis." Shooting me a bashful smile, Louisa launches into a laundry list of questions.

I fill her in with everything I know. We put our numbers to paper over cups of tea, calculating the training pay amounts due to us on Monday. We lay out our options, calculating how much we will earn by the end of June if they hire both of us as maids. I breathe a little easier seeing the numbers add up. With two salaries between us, we can pay back most of the overdue rent by the deadline, but we will still be short for May and June, keeping us two months in arrears. That leaves us even less than the meagre grocery funds we've become accustomed to. I promise Louisa I can manage the groceries with a smaller allotment for as long as we need.

If they hire only one of us, we cannot find a solution within the math. Viewing the reality from several angles, my nerves become even more frayed. "If only I had thought sooner about planting a small garden on the rooftop, we might have had enough vegetables to at least make a go of this."

"That's it." Louisa jumps up from the table and runs toward our bedroom. "I forgot all about it."

"What?" My brow wrinkles over my tear-stained cheeks.

"I have this." Louisa holds out her hand, several coins resting in her palm. "I put away the change after we had ice cream and haven't thought about it since." She shrugs, with a sheepish expression. "I know it isn't much, but I am sure it will allow us to purchase seeds for a small rooftop garden."

"Thank you, Louisa. I will make it stretch as far as

possible." I take the coins from her and place them securely into my pocketbook.

"Hmmm, I wonder if . . ." Louisa taps her bottom lip with a fingernail. "Not to worry, Clara, I will see what else I can come up with. Besides, I think you and I both have what it takes to make it as hotel maids. Only four more days to go."

"I hope you are right." I squeeze Louisa's hand, the burden of my secrets lifted. Though our problems remain far from solved, it is true that troubles carry less weight when shared with another.

The apartment door clicks as the knob turns, and I scoop our papers from the table in a hurry, holding them behind my back as I stand to greet Papa.

"Well, hello there." Papa's face and arms are deep with colour from an afternoon spent in the sun. "I hope I'm not too late. We wanted to get as much planting in as possible while we had the daylight."

"Not late at all. We were waiting for you before making dinner." Louisa tears the papers from my hands before scurrying to our room to hide our afternoon calculations. I let out a slow breath and move toward Papa, pecking his cheek. "I imagine those sandwiches have worn off by now. Why don't you clean up and I'll get started?"

"Yes, ma'am, you don't need to ask me twice." Papa nods his agreement before turning to leave the room.

"That was close." Louisa hisses in my ear upon her return. "What exactly is for supper?" I sense the trepidation in her voice, knowing what she knows now.

I open the refrigerator and peer inside. "Vegetable hash," I say, pulling out a small carton of eggs. "With a fried egg on top."

"Okay then. Tell me what I can do?" Louisa reaches for

an apron, tying it behind her back as she joins me at the stove.

"Lou, you really are one in a million." The love I have for her bubbles up within me. "I am so glad you are my sister."

"You might want to hold that sentiment until you've seen what I am capable of in the kitchen," she says with a nervous laugh. "If it were up to me, we'd be having peanut butter and jelly sandwiches."

She bumps my hip with her own in jest, and we work side by side, preparing a dinner our family can be proud of.

CHAPTER 25

*T*uesday, May 24, 1927

I tiptoe from the bedroom, notepad and pencil in hand. Louisa's soft snores remain steady as I close the door. The early morning light filtering through the thin curtains offers me a shadowy path to the kitchen. I flick on the least offensive bulb, located over the sink, and pause for a moment, waiting for my eyes to adjust to the yellow hue.

I sit at the table and revisit the numbers Louisa and I came up with yesterday afternoon. The numbers don't lie, and no matter how many times I tally them up, the only solution is for both of us to secure maid's position and start work immediately. We require every penny of two full-time salaries to pay the overdue rent by the deadline. Louisa's tenacity about applying for jobs together could be about to pay off. I wince at the memory of my less than hospitable words the day she inserted herself into my plan.

I hold my head in my hands as I dig the heel of my palms into my eye sockets. "Be strong, Clara," I whisper to myself as I flip the page and begin anew. If I am to dominate the field of maids-in-training, it is time to set aside nice, polite little Clara and assert myself at every opportunity.

My hand moves with fervour across the page as I detail my strengths, my knowledge, and my skills. I turn my attention to how to put Jane in her place. Never knowing which version of Jane I am to face, I feel compelled to cover all bases in order to ensure I am the maid who moves forward.

I am so immersed in my list-making that I don't hear Louisa come into the room.

"What are you doing?" Louisa's question startles me, causing me to jump out of my chair, swiping the notebook along with me.

"Why are you up?" I know better than to answer a question with a question, heightening Louisa's keen ability to notice cues of deception. "I didn't mean to wake you," I say, hoping to curtail her curiosity.

"How about you answer my question first?" Louisa tilts her head toward the notepad in my hands.

I sit back down at the table, a defensive mood building in my chest. "Fine. I was doing what I said I would, during our walk home yesterday. I am working out how to prepare myself should Jane decide to pull a bait and switch with her morals."

"Oh, Clara." Louisa sits down in the chair beside me. "I wish you could understand. You can't direct the world according to how you think it should work."

A scoff leaves my lips. "I am doing no such thing." Hiding the annoyance in my voice is not a priority. "I have no desire to manage the entire world. I do, however, wish to give myself the best possible chance." My chin juts forward.

"It seems to me that dealing with Jane and her untrustworthy nature is simply a part of the process."

"It isn't in you to be cunning. Or unkind, for that matter." Louisa leans forward, placing her elbows atop the table, steepling her fingers as she considers her next words. "You're asking for trouble if you keep on this path."

"What are you saying? That I am not capable of putting Jane in her place?" I fold my arms across my chest, knowing all too well that Louisa's stage training has taught her how to portray and read nonverbal communication. I imagine her reading me like a magazine.

Softening her tone in response to my guarded stance, Louisa prods me. "You know what? You may be right. Jane may get a job at the hotel. But even if she does, that doesn't mean we won't. This isn't an either-or situation. The hotel needs maids." Louisa snickers. "If you think about it, given Jane's lack of gumption, the hotel will certainly need more maids than her."

Louisa's humour at the situation coerces me to drop my guard. I roll my eyes and stifle my laugh.

"Earn a position the right way." Louisa's stare pushes its way into my periphery. "Work hard, but stay true to the wonderful, kind, giving person you are." Louisa's hand reaches for mine, squeezing my fingers reassuringly.

I offer her a weak smile, determined not to commit to either direction. Perhaps Louisa is right. Jane may have turned a corner and found a higher moral ground. If she hasn't, though, and I find myself caught in her web, I know precisely what I will need to do.

THE MORNING AT THE HOTEL PASSES WITHOUT INCIDENT AS we work together as a group, filling the linen cupboard with fresh towels, sheets, and pillows. Several trips to the large hotel laundry room brings perspiration to our necks. We climb the stairs again and again, carrying heaping piles of pristine white fabrics varying in size, shape, and plumpness.

We share a collective chuckle when someone mentions we could use the maid carts and the service lift to lessen the workload and the time spent on our task. I catch Ms. Thompson's eye as I pass her on my way to the lift, pushing a cart filled to the brim with hand towels. "Ma'am." I offer her a polite dip of my head. Her pleased expression tells me she was waiting for the efficient solution to occur to us.

Lunchtime finds us sprawled on our blanket on the courthouse lawn again, both of us hot and tired from the morning's activities. Our water bottle emptied within a few minutes, I make my way to the line at the drinking fountain for a refill. As I watch others fill their cups and bottles with the crisp water from the concrete lion's mouth, I am delighted by a memory. On another warm summer day, long ago, we visited the site as a family. I was thirsty from our walk, and Papa lifted me up for a drink straight from the lion's mouth. I smile at the remembrance, repositioning the happy thought into my heart and letting it lighten my spirits.

I take my seat beside Louisa. I am reassured by the knowledge that Papa is once again at the Murray estate, planting the gardens for the bulk of the day. The thought of his potential salary lights a sliver of hope within me. I allow the sensation to rest in my belly, along with my peanut butter sandwich.

"I was thinking." Louisa breaks into my silent thoughts.

"With Papa working this week, we may have more funds available than we originally accounted for."

"I am hoping so too, but . . ." I cannot finish the sentence. Incessant worry of the unknown pushes aside the shred of hope I was keeping.

"But we may not see the likes of it if he chooses instead to visit"—Louisa checks over her shoulder and lowers her voice—"a blind pig."

My sandwich churns in my stomach, the word leaving a sour taste in my mouth. I sip from the water bottle, eager to wash the sick feeling away. All I can offer my sister is an empathetic look.

Louisa places a hand on my forearm. "I understand now why you kept the news from me. When the words are said out loud, it somehow makes our situation more real."

"I know, and I am sorry."

Louisa gives my arm a quick squeeze. She turns her face away before swiping a tear.

We return to the hotel, freshening up in the ladies' washroom before ascending the stairs once more.

Ms. Thompson gathers us together, clipboard in hand. "I want to go over what you can expect for the coming days. We are nearing the end of our training, and your efficiency and ability to work together have been assets to both the schedule and the hotel."

We share joyful glances with one another as Ms. Thompson flips pages on her clipboard.

"Ah, here it is." Ms. Thompson taps a finger against her board. "Since we are more than half a day ahead of schedule, I have decided we will assist another group of trainees for the rest of the afternoon."

Another group? I question how we have not been aware of other maids-in-training. I have seen the bellboys, the kitchen staff, and even the doorman a time or two, always giving them a wide berth so as not to interfere with their duties or mine. I wonder who has been training these maids, since Ms. Thompson rarely seems to leave our sides.

"You won't have seen these ladies before, as they completed their training the week before you began. However, we've had to make a few recent staffing changes." Ms. Thompson sniffs, showing her distaste for the predicament. "Thus, a few of the less experienced girls require some extra training before the hotel opens. I trust I can count on each of you to help in all manners necessary."

A chorus of "yes, ma'am" accompanies several bobbing heads.

"Very well, then. If you will follow me, ladies, we will travel via the guest lift to the eighth floor."

As if on cue, the lift arrives with a ding. The attendant steps forward to hold the cage and door ajar as the first cluster of girls enters the box, quelling the excited chatter.

"Ma'am?" I take a step forward. "I can take the stairs if you like. Meet you there."

"Miss Wilson, don't think I haven't noticed your reluctance to use the lift. I appreciate your willingness and ability to climb stairs like a mountain goat. However, the entrance to the eighth floor is best experienced by the lift. Who knows when you will have this opportunity again?" Ms. Thompson spreads her arm wide, gesturing to the open door. "After you, Miss Wilson. After you."

I swallow hard and clutch my hands together to still their shaking. "Yes, ma'am." I step inside the box suspended mid-air, saying a silent prayer as the doors clang closed.

"Eighth floor," the short man with the round hat calls out at a volume unnecessary for the confined space.

Ms. Thompson's estimation of the best way to experience the floor of suites is correct. My shoes sink into the plush, deep-red carpet as I step from the lift, my relief at having arrived safely shoved aside as my eyes take in the opulent eighth-floor hall.

The quaint, calm elegance of the fifth floor's muted blues and greys is in stark contrast to the bold and rich-looking fabrics, art, and finishes before me now. The walls' flock papering beckons for a hand to run across the velvety gold and burgundy pattern. My eye follows the height of the wall to a wide ornate border molded into the upper wall and ceiling.

Though the dark, luxurious colours could have made the space seem heavy, shimmering crystal chandeliers combat the lavish design, while the cream-coloured crown molding and ceiling give the hall an airy feel. The lift dings again, distracting me from my evaluation of the eighth floor. Louisa and several others step out, with oohs and aahs of their own.

Ms. Thompson thanks the attendant and motions for us to gather around her. "I am pleased to see the delight on your faces, ladies." Her eyes scan the hall and ceiling. "The eighth floor of suites is certainly the cherry on top, so to speak."

Ms. Thompson peers over our heads toward the back of our group. "Ah, there you are. Ladies, let me introduce you to Miss Smythe, Miss Patterson, Miss McKinley, and Miss Roberts." All heads swivel. "These are the maids of the eighth-floor suites whom you will assist this afternoon."

The eighth-floor maids offer us kind smiles. My mouth forms an O shape as I take in their appearance. Each of them wears a dark blue, three-quarter-length smock, tight at the waist with an elegant half apron. Each pocket

embroidered with a small blue *H* in the corner, and a touch
of red piping lines the neckline and cuffs. I imagine the
smock would pass as a very presentable day dress without
the apron.

Louisa nudges me with her elbow. "We need to see
about becoming eighth-floor maids."

I question her with a furrowed brow.

"No funny hats," she whispers.

I stifle a giggle as Ms. Thompson details our duties for
the afternoon.

"Miss Wilson," Ms. Thompson says. Louisa and I both
turn to the matron. "My apologies. Miss *Clara* Wilson. You
will assist Miss Smythe with her hospital corners."

"Yes, ma'am." I curtsy, feeling as though the luxury of
the space demands the formal gesture.

Ms. Thompson rattles off several other duties, assigning
fifth-floor maids and eighth-floor maids as she goes. Most
of our group will work in teams. It seems Miss Smythe and
I will be the only ones to work as a pair.

"Your eighth-floor counterparts know where to go, so
please, ladies, gather in your groups and press on. I will be
in to see each of you on a rotating basis." Ms. Thompson
takes a step back, allowing us to scuttle toward our assigned
groups and working destinations.

Miss Smythe waits for the chaos and chatter to calm
before stepping forward and extending a hand. "Lovely to
meet you, Miss Wilson."

"You as well, Miss Smythe." I offer a light squeeze of
her hand, finding it a bit cooler than my own.

"We are this way." She gestures. "Suite 803." I
acknowledge my understanding and follow her down the
hall. "I've managed every one of my duties with high
marks." Miss Smythe twists one hand within the other, and

I sense a shiver of nervousness about her. "The hospital corners seem to be the only thing to elude me, and Ms. Thompson has assured me you are a gifted teacher."

"That is very kind of Ms. Thompson. I am sure we will have you in the swing of things in no time at all." I offer an encouraging smile, hoping to put the girl at ease.

As we near suite 803, I am surprised to hear sounds coming from inside the room. The suite has occupants already. Catching my concerned expression, Miss Smythe says, "It's no trouble, Miss Wilson. Another group is working on a separate task in the suite. Not to worry, the suite can accommodate us all."

As we step into suite 803, the noise grows louder, and it takes me a scant moment to identify the cause of the commotion. Jane is in the centre of the suite, spinning in circles, her arms held out wide. "Finally, something that feels like home," Jane laughs as she stumbles slightly, coming out of her spin. "I could certainly get used to working on this floor."

Miss Roberts, whom I identify as another eighth-floor maid, is beaming at Jane. "Oh Miss Morgan, I think you would fit in nicely here on the eighth floor."

Miss Smythe and I exchange looks before she steps forward and motions Miss Roberts to one side. Their words are indiscernible behind a rush of whispers. I stand, awe setting in at the room and its furnishings. "Wow," I breathe.

The beautiful suite is far greater than I expected, even after seeing the hall. In expanse alone, the suite is nearly the size of our entire apartment at The Newbury, though far grander in design. My eyes linger on each sofa, chair, table, and lamp. I almost gasp at the sight of a well-positioned chaise lounge. The perfect reading spot.

Jane's words float my concerns about her to the surface

again. I scoff at her brazen comment, given it is likely that no other maid in the hotel's employ lives in a home remotely like the environment in which they clean. How foolish and boastful that girl can be. My blood feels close to boiling as I watch Jane reel in the others with her joyful chatter.

"Not a friend of yours, I take it." Miss Smythe reads my mind as she touches my elbow to gain my attention.

"Is it that obvious?" I ask, hoping it isn't true.

"Not to worry, Miss Wilson. I am aware of such things only because I find myself in a similar position." Miss Smythe inclines her head toward Miss Roberts, and I understand I am not the only maid here with little use for those not up to The Hotel Hamilton's standards.

CHAPTER 26

*T*uesday, May 24, 1927

Miss Smythe and I move toward the oversized bedroom, anchored by furniture standing tall and grand. We begin with Miss Smythe showing me her current bed-making skills as the ruckus on the other side of the wall settles to a low din.

I spot Miss Smythe's error in judgement at once but hold my tongue until she has completed the task in full. I watch with a discerning eye as she tugs and folds, busying herself about the expansive mattress. Jane's voice pierces the air with a burst of laughter, garnering an eye roll from me. Another inflated statement draws my attention. "Well, truth be told, I am a shoo-in for the position."

My head swivels to the open door to take in the scene. Jane has positioned herself on the arm of a sitting room chair, balancing her petite frame as though she were here to host a tea party instead of clean the suite. "Had I known about the eighth floor, though . . ." She gestures around the suite with a sweep of her hand. "I would have insisted I work here instead of on that dowdy fifth floor."

Fuelled by irritation, I turn back to the bed. As she smooths the pillows in place, Miss Smythe meets my eye with a sympathetic glance.

Miss Roberts chimes in, her nasal tone grating on my every nerve. "Oh, Miss Morgan, what fun it would be to work side by side with you."

Miss Roberts sniffs and I imagine her snubbing her nose toward the vaulted ceiling. "Some of the other eighth-floor maids don't even know what the word 'fun' means." Though Miss Roberts is out of my sight, I hear the disdain dripping from her words. Miss Smythe's expression contorts as the comment lands at her feet. "They aren't worth the extra quarter a day, I'm certain, but they sure think highly of themselves."

I fight the urge to step into the living area and put both Jane and Miss Roberts in their place, choosing instead to bite my lip, drawing a sliver of blood as my anger rises. A subtle shake of her head tells me Miss Smythe feels my sentiment. She encourages me to stay calm by meeting me beside the bed and gesturing for me to hold my tongue with a finger to her lips.

A dawning of realization interrupts Jane's laugh. "What do you mean, extra quarter a day?" She lowers her voice to a whisper. Miss Roberts and Jane exchange a flurry of murmured words before Jane's voice rings out. "Really?"

"Ladies, is this a social gathering or a place of work?" Ms. Thompson's voice cuts through the room like a hot knife through butter.

Miss Smythe and I step into the living room to greet the matron. All heads turn toward her barking inquiry.

I watch Jane with a sideways glance as she rushes to

stand, clasping her hands behind her back and fixing a demure smile on her face.

"Miss Roberts, as the eighth-floor maid, I put you in charge of this group, allowing you to prove yourself as capable as you claim to be, and what do I find when I check in?" Ms. Thompson's pencil taps the hard surface of her clipboard. "A gaggle of gossiping girls instead of the ladies I know to be in training for a coveted position at this hotel."

"Yes, ma'am." Miss Roberts fidgets with her hands as her eyes drop to the floor. "We were getting to know one another is all. As colleagues, ma'am."

Ms. Thompson takes one step forward. "Let me remind you, Miss Roberts, I am well aware of how you enjoy getting to know the other staff members. You are already skating on thin ice."

Ms. Thompson's eyebrows stretch further into her hairline than I have ever seen, and I wonder which of Miss Roberts' bees has gotten under Ms. Thompson's bonnet. "There are no more second or third chances left for you, my dear. This is your one remaining opportunity to redeem yourself."

"Yes, ma'am." Miss Roberts' eyes flick up once. "Thank you, ma'am."

Ms. Thompson turns her attention to Miss Smythe and me, stepping past us to enter the bedroom. "Looks like we have made some progress." Bending at the waist, Ms. Thompson examines the lower half of the bed. "Though not quite there yet, I see."

"Yes, ma'am." Miss Smythe's reply is threaded with disappointment.

I clear my throat, garnering the matron's attention. "I have watched Miss Smythe, ma'am, and she is quite accomplished at the task. There is a minor adjustment required, but with a tweak, she will be well on her way to delivering perfect hospital corners."

Miss Smythe offers me a grateful smile, relief smoothing the creases embedded in her forehead.

"Thank you, Miss Wilson. I trust you have everything well in hand." Ms. Thompson checks the state of the sheets once more. "Perhaps try fetching a fresh set of sheets from the linen closet. These appear as wrinkled as if they'd been slept in. Fresh linen might help the situation."

"Yes, ma'am." Miss Smythe nods with confidence, her back straightening a fraction with the additional advice.

Ms. Thompson turns her attention back to Miss Roberts. "I trust you, too, are ready to resume? Fifth-floor ladies, you are here to assist Miss Roberts with an entire cleaning of this suite. I suggest you band together and show her the most efficient manner in which to move through a room, as she has in the past struggled to complete her tasks in the time allotted."

Several of the fifth-floor girls I know to be good workers signal their understanding toward the matron. I reach for the notecard in my apron pocket and catch Hazel Greenwood's attention with a wave of the notecard. Hazel's understanding is clear as she retrieves her own card, mouthing a thank you in my direction.

After stripping the bed back down to the bare mattress, Miss Smythe and I retreat to the far end of the hall, where the laundry chute hides behind a decorative panel. We toss the sheets down the chute, and Miss Smythe delivers me a bashful look before apologizing. "I am sorry you were present during that mess back there."

"I don't think you have any reason to apologize, though it appears things are not going quite as smoothly as Ms. Thompson would like regarding Miss Roberts."

Her exasperation does not escape my notice. "Miss Roberts . . . Well, she isn't what I would call a typical maid." Miss Smythe directs me through a corridor and around a corner to another hall. "Her father is some well-to-do businessman, and this position is more of a favour than anything else, I imagine."

"I understand what you mean. Another Jane Morgan in our midst." A fraught sigh escapes my lips, though I attempt to keep them closed.

Miss Smythe's face lights up in recognition. "You do understand. I wondered, with Miss Morgan asserting airs and acting a little too comfortable in a guest suite."

"I was hoping she had turned a corner, but—" The words hang alongside my growing apprehension about Jane.

"Miss Roberts isn't all bad," Miss Smythe says. Her wobbly opinion of Miss Roberts reminds me of my own toward Jane. "She is a joyful person to be around, but she seems to lack good sense much of the time. She has no awareness of the urgency required with any task, and on the last day of training"—Miss Smythe lowers her voice and leans closer to me—"They found her canoodling with a bellboy in the linen cupboard."

"What?" I cannot hide my shock at the news but lower my voice so as not to cause a scene. "How on earth?"

Miss Smythe inclines her head toward two narrow doors at the opposite end of the long corridor. "They fired the boy at once but gave Miss Roberts a final warning. Apparently, Miss Roberts' father has sufficient pull to ensure his daughter's name was not tarnished in the incident." Miss Smythe pulls on both handles, revealing the eighth floor's expansive linen closet.

I find myself in awe as I step into a well-organized room

as big as a fifth-floor guest room. "You would think with
only twenty-six suites, fewer linens would be required."

Miss Smythe chuckles under her breath before giving
me a quick tour, pointing out speciality soaps infused with
lavender, embroidered hand towels, and pillows ranging in
thickness to suit the most discerning guest. "Fewer suites,
yes, but they come with more demands, I can assure you."

I cradle the silky-smooth bedding against my torso,
relishing its exquisite nature as we make our way back to
the suite. With a fresh set of linens, I offer Miss Smythe a
few key tips. "If you pull the bench seat away from the foot
of the bed, you will have greater access and will spread a
much more even bottom sheet. As an added benefit, this
also makes vacuuming around the bed much simpler."

I watch Miss Smythe, providing a comment here and
there. Behind me, the suite buzzes with the activity of Miss
Roberts and the other fifth-floor girls. Miss Smythe is
tucking her last hospital corner in place when Jane's voice
lifts in volume, filtering into the bedroom. "I think I will ask
my uncle to inquire about a position on the eighth floor
with you. It might be fun."

My eyes dart toward the living area, and I push down
the urge to state the obvious. The eighth-floor maids are
already in place, and the only position that appears to be in
any sort of jeopardy is that of Miss Roberts. My irritation
with Jane simmers and coaxes me back to my curated list of
ways to put Jane off-kilter.

Hazel asks Jane to wipe the counter and fix the towels in
the suite's bathroom. I seize the opportunity before I lose
my nerve. Stepping away from the bed, I put one foot
outside the bedroom and reach for a stack of towels, in neat
piles on top of the cleaning cart. A quick glance around
ensures nobody is paying me any attention. With a deft

hand, I reposition the towels to the bottom shelf of the cart and place them out of sight. Jane will have to either visit the linen closet or look further than her own nose, which I am doubtful she is capable of doing.

I slip back into the bedroom to find Miss Smythe's eyes on me, her expression unreadable. We remain there, looking at one another for what feels like an eternity. I scour my brain for words to explain my actions but come up empty.

Sounds of rummaging through the cart outside the bedroom door accompany Jane's voice. "Where the devil are the towels?" Her annoyance is hard to miss, and I clamp my lips closed.

"Hazel, where did you— Oh, never mind. I found them." I glimpse Jane as she turns toward the bathroom, her arms loaded with towels.

Miss Smythe raises a palm, pressing it to her mouth to stifle a giggle. Her eyes sparkle with amusement. "Well, I suppose you can't win them all."

"I suppose you cannot." A hiccup of laughter accompanies my agreement. "I swear, I've done nothing like that before."

"Only dreamed about it?" Miss Smythe tosses a knowing look in my direction as she plumps a pillow before lining it up against the headboard.

"Well, perhaps." I walk around the bed, covering my laughter by noting the tight fit of the bedsheets. "Well done. You've got it."

"Really? Oh, thank heavens. I was worried I'd be sacked because of my fumbling fingers."

"I don't suspect Ms. Thompson has any inclination to let you go. In fact, I'd bet she has bigger things in mind for you." I tilt my head to meet Miss Smythe's downcast eyes.

She is visibly uncomfortable at being complimented. "She may have assigned Miss Roberts a slew of help as a last resort, but I suspect she sees all that you offer."

"You are kind, Miss Wilson. Thank you for your help. I promise to remember both your generosity and your tips for hospital corners."

"Clara, please. Call me Clara."

"I will be happy to call you Clara outside of the eighth floor, Miss Wilson, if you will call me Rebecca. On the eighth floor, however, we must address one another by our family names in order to maintain the propriety our esteemed guests will expect."

"I understand, Miss Smythe, but I do hope we can see one another away from the eighth floor, or perhaps even outside of the hotel."

"I would like that very much. Very much indeed." Miss Smythe beams and I am buoyed by the beginnings of a new friendship.

"Shall we give it another go?" I reach for the top sheet and pull it free from the mattress.

Miss Smythe works her way around the bed again, practising the technique I've shared with her. As she works, I step into the suite's main living area, allowing her some time to think through the process on her own, without my watchful eyes.

I almost trip on the vacuum's cord, plugged into a wall socket and strewn across the path that all those in the suite will have to cross. I hear Ms. Thompson's reprimanding voice in my head and bend over, unplugging the cord to avoid a preventable accident before stepping away to examine one of the room's gold-framed paintings.

"Why do I have to vacuum? I already cleaned the bathroom." Jane's pout lines her statement. My tolerance for Miss Morgan's spoiled attitude has reached its limit, and I grimace at her self-absorption.

"I would hardly call wiping a counter and hanging towels cleaning." Hazel's own frustration seems ready to boil over, and I consider retreating to the bedroom to avoid the confrontation.

"Well, I don't like that enormous machine. It's a beast." Jane's high-pitched shriek underlines her unease with the vacuum.

To my surprise, Miss Roberts inserts herself into the discussion. "Miss Morgan, luxury may surround us, but the responsibility of cleaning the suite remains with us." She lowers her voice, stepping closer to Jane. "Please. You heard Ms. Thompson. This is my last chance, and I need your help."

"Well, I suppose I can, to help a new friend," Jane concedes, her agreement iced with sweetness.

Hazel's sigh is audible as she returns to polishing the desk. I step back into the bedroom, wondering how long it will be before Jane's poor disposition regarding any actual work causes someone else to put her in her place. I am considering how such a situation might unfold when Jane announces with a bucketful of drama, "The vacuum is broken."

Stepping into the suite, I pick up the plug and insert it into the socket. "Just needs to be plugged in is all."

A few girls stop what they are doing and look my way. Hazel snickers from the other side of the room. Though I hadn't intended to sound smug, Jane reacts with a fury I have not yet been on the receiving end of.

"You don't always have to be right about everything, Clara." Jane crosses her arms over her chest. "You are such a goody two-shoes. I would have figured it out myself, you know."

"I—I was only trying to help." My confidence sinks as anger over her accusation rises, flushing my cheeks with the heat of embarrassment.

"Next time, don't bother." Jane turns her back on me, switching on the vacuum and drowning any chance of further discussion in the loud vacuum motor.

I return to the bedroom, convincing myself it's to check on Miss Smythe's progress, rather than to escape humiliation.

"Don't let her get you down, Miss Wilson." Miss Smythe, finished with the bed, walks toward me. "She isn't worth getting upset over."

"I unplugged the cord. It was a tripping hazard." My shoulders inch toward my ears. "I was trying to remedy the situation is all. I wasn't purposely trying to make her appear bad."

As the words leave my lips, I see the untruth for what it is. I *was* trying to make Jane look bad. That was the plan I created and was to put into action if Jane got out of hand. Only this time I let my guard down. I forgot to be a devious version of myself and instead plugged in the cord to be helpful.

Chastising myself, I force my shoulders down and decide to do as I planned. If Jane is going to attack me for trying to be helpful, then I will show her how it feels to be on the receiving end of such fury.

Ms. Thompson peeks into the bedroom, breaking my thoughts. "Well done, Miss Smythe. It appears Miss Wilson was correct and you have located the knack for the hospital corner."

"Thank you, ma'am." Miss Smythe beams. "I couldn't have done it without Miss Wilson's help."

"Very nice job, both of you." Ms. Thompson looks at her pocket watch. "There is less than twenty minutes left in the day, ladies. Why don't you head out early? A reward for such accomplished work."

"Thank you, ma'am," we respond in unison.

By the time Miss Smythe and I reposition the bench and run our hands along the length of the duvet, although there are no wrinkles to smooth, the other girls are also leaving early. Jane is the last in the suite, wrapping up the vacuum cord. She fires an angry glare my way as I move to exit.

I step through the open door but stop just in the hallway. I pivot toward the suite as Jane, her back to me, manhandles the cord into place. Without hesitating, I pull the cleaning cart toward the open door, blocking the threshold. I duck low and click the front wheels to the locked position. A pang of guilt stabs me, sending a sharp pain into my chest. I ignore the sensation, stand, and walk away.

With a pleased expression on her face, Louisa greets me as I near the corner of the hallway. I hear the crash of the cart before Jane's cries. We turn together and see Jane sprawled partway over top of the upturned cart, cleaning supplies spilling onto the carpet.

My first inclination is to run, but before I can move, Louisa grabs my wrist and dashes toward Jane, ready to help.

"What happened? Are you hurt?" Louisa reaches her hands toward Jane, helping her to untangle herself from the upturned cart.

I busy myself with lifting the cart upright and unlocking

the wheels. My fingers are all but useless as they pick up
and drop one thing after another in an effort to clean up
the mess before Ms. Thompson discovers us. Thankful
nothing of the liquid variety has soiled the carpet, I scoop
and toss everything I can onto the cart's shelves.

Louisa is examining Jane for bruises and cuts, turning
her arms this way and that. "How did that happen?"

Jane's eyes fill with tears, and for the first time, I
consider her feelings and how scared she might have been
when the cart shifted. My involvement in the accident
burns, feeling as though it's broadcast across my skin like
ink on newsprint.

"I was lifting the vacuum onto the back of the cart like
Ms. Thompson taught us to do when the cart became
unsteady and toppled forward. It took all of my strength to
heave the thing, so I suppose the weight of the machine and
momentum got the better of me. Everything pitched
toward the hall, taking me with it."

"Miss Morgan, Miss Wilson, is there a problem here?"
Ms. Thompson moves with speed in our direction, the fast-
paced swish of her skirt signalling her concern. "Is anyone
hurt?"

"Just a few scrapes, ma'am. I'll be okay." Jane swipes at
her damp face, and I feel my own fill with shame.

Louisa looks from me to the cart to Jane. Switching
gears from her initial concern for Jane, understanding
registers on Louisa's face. "Clara," she whispers with a sad
shake of her head.

Ms. Thompson's relief that all is well restores her
matronly demeanour. I instinctively shrink as a perplexed
assessment of the situation crosses her features.

"Well, that is more than enough excitement for one day.
You ladies head on home now." Ms. Thompson examines

the cart, swivelling it back and forth. "I will take care of the cart. In fact, I will take it down for maintenance, just to be sure there isn't something that needs fixing."

The walk home is quiet. Louisa's silence holds space between us. My shoes shuffle over the sidewalk, regret weighing down each step. I admonish myself with voiceless accusations. I'm a despicable example of humankind. Untrustworthy and out of my mind.

Worst of all, I have somehow sunk far lower than Jane and anything she may have done. I thought I'd feel vindicated and free, righteous and glorified. Instead, an unfamiliar hollowness takes up residence within me, spreading shame and defeat. I harbour an all-encompassing fear of my world spinning out of control.

CHAPTER 27

*T*uesday, May 24, 1927

The front door of The Newbury closes behind me. Louisa makes a beeline for the stairs, but I decide to check the mail slot. Mail isn't a frequent arrival at the Wilson home, but something pokes at me to look. Perhaps hoping to put off the inevitable lashing from Louisa, I slide the key into the slim box's brass plate.

My heart skips a beat at the sight of a small square package in the shadowy slot. I pull the parcel free and flip it over to read the sender's address. "It's from Aunt Vivian. She's written me back." I attempt to keep the delight from my words, not eager to appear anything other than downtrodden to Louisa. "Remember, I told you I was going to write to her?"

"How nice," Louisa says from the third stair, her tone confirming that her disappointment with me has not improved during our walk home.

I follow Louisa up the stairs, my slow stride climbing one for every two she ascends. "No dawdling, Clara. You've got the key. Remember?" Louisa's impatience with me coats every syllable.

"Yes. I remember." I push my own emotions down with a large swallow, unsure what to do with my mixed-up feelings. Distraught mingles with excitement over the package, its weight pressing against my palm.

Inside the apartment, Louisa removes her jacket before moving to stand in front of a kitchen chair. "Sit."

I do as I am told, eyes downcast and feet tripping over each other as I make my way to the table.

"Would you like to tell me what happened?" Louisa pulls out another chair and sits with a purposeful harrumph.

I shake my head no, but the single raised eyebrow she trains on me like a dagger informs me that "no" is not an option. "Jane was being all, well, Jane-like. She was talking boastfully about the certainty of her getting a position."

"Clara, I thought we agreed you wouldn't get involved with any schemes. You said you wouldn't." Louisa taps a fingernail on the table, its repetitive click triggering my nerves to twitch to its unsettling rhythm.

"I said nothing." My fingers play with the string tied around the brown paper-wrapped package. "You understood what you wanted to. And besides, Jane really gave me no choice. I decided to use my plan only if necessary." My feeble attempt to explain myself does little to defend my actions to Louisa, or even myself.

"And what exactly did Jane do that made you think it absolutely necessary to topple a full cleaning cart, with her on top of it? You realize she could have been seriously hurt?"

"I do now, yes. I am sorry. Really, I am." My feeble apology seems too little too late. "It doesn't matter what

Jane did or didn't do. I was wrong to scheme against her. I realize that now."

"Clara, I wish you would believe me. Being yourself is the surest path to becoming a Hotel Hamilton maid. Today, you were not the sister I know and admire." Louisa's anger thaws a fraction as she takes my hands. "I love you, Clara, and I want us both to succeed. I understand the strain you've been under." Reaching a hand toward my face, she lifts my chin with one finger. "But if I see you pull another stunt like the one you pulled today, I will turn you in to Ms. Thompson myself. Am I clear?"

My lip trembles and tears flow freely down my cheeks. Louisa's disappointment in me is worse than any disappointment I could feel in myself. What was I thinking? A gulp of emotion strangles my words.

"That is enough for now. Wipe your tears. Tomorrow is a new day with a fresh start." Louisa stands and a realization hits me. Even though I've always fought to be seen as her equal, demanded it at times, I've never truly valued her role as my older sister.

I search her eyes for more wisdom, more guidance, but all I see there is love. Perhaps that is all I ever really needed for everything to be okay.

"We all stumble from time to time." Louisa lifts me to my feet and wraps me in a tight embrace. "Those times when we fall and scrape ourselves up are the times to remember."

Louisa pulls me back, holding me at arm's length as she peers into my eyes, intent on making her point. "That is where we learn the most about ourselves. You are on the cusp of a great opportunity, Clara. How you go forward is up to you."

"But what if I choose wrong?" The pressure of knowing

what is best, which path will provide a favourable outcome, is immense upon my shoulders. My teeth imprison my bottom lip with childlike nerves, all too aware that saying the words out loud will colour me with a selfish hue. "How do I make certain I get what I want?" My eyes dart to the floor.

"Oh, Clara. Life isn't about getting what you want. Really, it is more about getting what you need and learning to be happy with that."

I want to interrupt her with a reminder of the lack of food lining our cupboards, but my thoughts turn inward. I've always presumed my wants and needs were the same thing. Mama seemed to make them so. As a small child, what I wanted and needed were wrapped up together: the warm scent of freshly baked bread, the comfort of a handmade quilt, or the timely gesture of a mother's kiss on a wound. I fidget in response to a niggling thought. What if this is where I went wrong?

I thought I knew who Mama was. All these years, I have remembered her as perfect in everything she said and did, but in this moment, I question my memory. Mama's way is all I've ever known, all I've ever thought to mimic.

What if I was wrong? What if Mama's way isn't my way? My mind spins with thoughts and questions, grasping an idea for a mere second before it slides through my fingers and disappears. An immense desire presses me to hide under the covers and forget the day. If only my bruised ego and overwrought mind could be eased by Mama's kiss. If only . . .

Louisa nudges my arm, inclining her head toward the package and waiting for my attention. "Well, go on and open it, then." My rollercoaster of emotions has stolen my joy of the parcel's arrival. A dimple emerges on her cheek as she winks, encouraging me to indulge. "You know you want to."

I reach for the parcel, plucking the string free and unwrapping the paper. The dark blue cover of a small book appears as the brown paper slides away. "*Good Housekeeping's Book on the Business of Housekeeping: New Ways of Handling the Familiar Routine of Housework* by Mildred Maddocks Bentley." The book's title is embossed in faded gold. A letter slides out as I open the front cover.

DEAREST CLARA,

I can't begin to tell you how pleased I was to receive your letter. Oh, how I have missed such correspondence from across the pond since your mother's passing. You may not be aware, but I wrote to you, Louisa, and your father. With no response after several months of weekly letters, I must admit, I assumed the ties between us had been irrevocably broken.

Needless to say, I am thrilled to learn you are well and striving to advance yourself with employment. Your mother would be so very proud of you, dear girl, for stepping outside of what is comfortable. She always told me how pleased she was that I endeavoured to do the same. Perhaps we have more in common than I knew. From your letter, I sense she told you a few tales of me and my work here in London.

To answer your question, being a hotel maid has been a wonderful experience for me. I will speak frankly with you, as I wouldn't wish to paint a rosy picture that will do little to prepare you for the task you are seeking. The work is challenging and constant. The wage, though, gave me a freedom early in my life. I take pride in knowing that I can take care of myself if need be. The job provided an opportunity to know myself deeply, teaching me what I am capable of while allowing me to learn what I will and will not accept from others' behaviour.

I was fortunate to be married to a man who understood my desire to be something more than a wife and mother, even if my own well-meaning parents couldn't come to terms with the idea. In the end, when dear Paul didn't return from the war, my employment put food on the table for my daughter and me. Truth be told, my elderly parents grew quiet about my working life, as their own existence depended on my income in their final years.

You might not be aware, but my daughter, Josephine, your cousin, is also a maid at The Grosvenor Hotel. She, too, is quite pleased with the work. The book was her idea, by the way. She suggested we include a copy for your perusal. I find being a maid is about both hard work and ingenuity. If you are anything like your mother, I am quite confident a strong work ethic courses through your veins as sure as blood. The book is where the ingenuity comes in. I hope you find it helpful.

I wish you all the luck with your goal of securing employment as a hotel maid, and I do hope you will continue to write to us. We would both love to get to know you and Louisa better. Please send our love to your father, if you think he might welcome the sentiment.

Oodles of love and best wishes,
Aunt Vivian and Cousin Josephine

I CHECK MY WRISTWATCH FOR THE TIME BEFORE EYEING THE book. I'd like nothing more than to slip beneath the covers and read my new book, but Papa will be home soon and with a grumbling stomach, no doubt.

"What were you planning for dinner?" Louisa asks as she follows my gaze to the book and letter.

"Cottage pie. I've been saving a small mound of cooked beef, since it's one of Papa's favourites."

"Papa doesn't like cottage pie." Louisa's comment feels like a slap to the face.

"Of course he does." My voice lifts toward indignation,

despite my intention to curb it. "Mama used to make it for him every Wednesday night. It's the reason I've continued to cook the dish all these years."

"Trust me. He isn't a fan of cottage pie." Louisa wags a slender finger at me. "He is partial to shepherd's pie, the one with lamb. But to be honest, I am not certain he would call that his favourite either."

"But—how do you know this?" My surprise at this revelation disables any decorum I have been able to muster.

"I've watched him eat it." Louisa's eyes grow wide in disbelief. "Seriously, Clara, I can't believe you've never noticed." Louisa pauses a moment, mulling over her words, I presume. "Maybe you've been seeing what you wanted to see. And maybe Papa has been allowing you to do that as well."

"I—I just don't understand why he wouldn't have told me." Incredulity pours out of me. "Do you know how much beef costs? I have been scrimping and saving for months to afford cottage pie as a weekly meal."

Louisa shrugs and offers an empathetic smile. "I didn't know you did that. I figured you must like the dish." Louisa waits a beat, watching me as I digest the news. "So, what's for dinner now?"

"I don't have a clue, but I best come up with something." My mood sours at the thought of creating an entirely new meal from what little remains as I stalk into the kitchen.

Before Papa arrives, I put the book and letter away. Given Aunt Vivian's mention of previous letters, I am uncertain of how he would respond. I couldn't explain the contents of such a letter anyway. If we find ourselves employed— I mentally correct myself, infusing a certainty into my thoughts. *Until* we have secured employment, there is little I can divulge to Papa. As of now, the letter would lead to more questions than I could reasonably answer. I cringe at the thought of keeping secrets from him, but then the truth about cottage pie rears its head, reminding me that things aren't quite as I presumed. Perhaps this makes things even between us after all.

WITH DINNER DISHES WASHED AND PUT AWAY, I SAY AN EARLY good night, feigning tiredness, though it is not a stretch. I prepare for bed and slide between the cool sheets before extracting the book and letter from under my pillow. I read into the wee hours of the morning, barely mumbling a good night to Lou as she nestles herself into bed a few hours after me.

The manual is rich with not only how-tos but also what-tos. The little blue book is a gem. Though most of the book's topics are matters concerning the household maid, I pluck tidbits of pure genius that I am sure will be useful in the role of hotel maid.

A long yawn convinces me to close the book with only a few chapters left to read. As my head sinks into the pillow and I draw the sheets up to my chin, my mind whirls, mixing the disasters of the day with the information Aunt Vivian's book provides. The sensation of a new path forward lulls me into what I hope will be a deep sleep.

I wake to the sun filtering through a billowing curtain. Occasional breezes through the window's scant opening create a game of peekaboo with the blue sky. Louisa is ready and sitting on the edge of her bed, reading the book I put down a few short hours ago.

Stretching, I lift myself from my bed with a renewed

eagerness to take on the day. The light has dawned beyond my window and inside of me.

"Good morning," Louisa says without looking up from the page. "I expected to have to wake you with a shove this morning."

"Morning." I busy myself with making my bed, humming a joyful melody.

"You seem more chipper than I expected you to be. You were still reading when I woke to open the window around midnight." Her raised eyebrow appears above the top of the book. "You didn't even notice."

"I didn't?" Surprise lifts my words into a question.

"Nope." Lou closes the book, giving me her full attention.

I sit opposite her on my bed, and the words tumble out like they've been building for months instead of hours. "I have figured out a way forward. You were right. I am sorry. I was dreadful yesterday." A firm shake of my head dislodges the memory of Jane sprawled over the cleaning cart. "I have found a way to be true to myself while putting my best foot forward as a maid."

"Would it have anything at all to do with this?" Louisa waves the book in the air. "I certainly hope so. I am shocked to admit it, but even I found the information useful."

"Did you read about the baking soda? I can't wait to give it a go." A rush of enthusiasm fills me as I consider the knowledge I now have, which the other maids-in-training might not possess. "Of course, we will have to wait for an especially stained bathtub or sink to try it out, but we can ask Cookie—you know, the assistant pastry chef I told you about—for a small amount of soda to have on hand, just in case."

"And the vacuum attachments." Louisa's voice climbs to match my own. "I didn't notice any attachments before."

"I was thinking about that," I say. "It might be best to ask Ms. Thompson about them this morning, as they will come in handy for all that trim work. Perhaps our asking will give her reason to notice our dedication to learning."

"Now you're thinking, Clara." Louisa moves to sit beside me. "This is how to be both authentic and skilled."

"You are right, Lou. I can become an accomplished maid and never lose sight of who I am."

Louisa's arm wraps around my shoulders, pulling me toward her in a sideways hug. "That's the spirit, Clara. I hope this means you will stop trying to control everything."

"I will try." Louisa shoots me a questioning look. "I said I will try. Water doesn't smooth a stone overnight, you know. Some things take time." I hesitate. "I realized a few things while I was reading last night." The impending confession takes hold and constricts my throat.

"Oh?" Louisa draws her arm from my shoulders while pivoting her body toward me.

"In the beginning, I went to the hotel for the sake of our family. Of course I felt compelled to do whatever I could to ensure we were safe and had a roof over our heads. But if I am being completely honest, I also wanted to feel steady again. I wanted to have command over something. I hate feeling as though the earth is quaking under my feet. I—I've felt that way since Mama left us."

"I know." Louisa whispers, her understanding well embedded in her own experience. "Did I ever tell you what Mama told me the first time I didn't get the lead role in a play?"

I shake my head.

Louisa clears her throat and faces me straight on. "She

said, 'Control is an illusion. We find stability when we switch the focus of that which we rely on. If you require others to provide stability, they will disappoint you more times than not. Instead, focus on your own reactions. Those are the places you can assert your will to fix, change, or embrace how you see the world. That is all we ever have control over.' "

"Control is an illusion," I whisper. "Yes, I think I understand." I feel my cheeks flush with embarrassment at my thoughts. "Even though I was convinced I needed to do everything on my own to locate security, I would never have come this far if you hadn't insisted on coming along with me."

Louisa's deep-throated laugh tips her head backwards. "Am I hearing you right? Are you admitting that I am less of an imposition than you imagined I would be?"

"Let's just say that, for all the times I resented your amiable nature and ability to fit in wherever you go, I am more aware than ever that such is your nature, and I love you for it."

Louisa beams at me, her eyelashes batting with joy. "Not to press my luck, but I am going to suggest you expand your awareness to include others in your new-found perspective."

"What are you saying?" A bubble of trepidation forms in the pit of my stomach as I sense she is coercing me in a direction I may not wish to travel.

"I won't argue the fact that Jane's actions are questionable. But we don't know why she behaves the way she does. Maybe you could give her the benefit of the doubt. Jealousy makes people do dreadful things, Clara. I think you know this by now." Louisa's arched eyebrow asserts her point.

"Jane, jealous? Of me?" Before the question has even left my lips, I am considering life from Jane's perspective. "I suppose she could have other worries. Different worries than us."

"Something to be aware of is all." Louisa stands, smoothing out the skirt of her dress. "Now, let's get a move on or we'll be late."

As I ready myself for the day, Louisa's words linger in my mind. I pack our lunch and brush my hair, and as I do, I acknowledge Jane might be quite lonesome. She doesn't have a sister rooting for her. She may have financial stability, but perhaps her life at home is unhappy. This could be the reason for her drive to succeed, however misguided. By the time we walk out the door, I am wondering whether Jane even knows what it is to have a genuine friend.

CHAPTER 28

Friday, May 27, 1927

My apron tightens around my waist as I wrestle it into place. I feel pride flood through me as though a river's dam has broken free. The last few days have flown by, with my time spent ensuring the fifth floor is pristine and ready to receive guests, along with helping throughout the hotel wherever an extra hand is needed. Our group of maids-in-training has again dwindled by four, leaving us who remain hopeful that we will receive an offer of employment by Monday.

Though our group is smaller in number, my interactions with Jane have been few. I've occasionally seen her watching me, and I wonder what is going on in that head of hers. Despite my misgivings regarding Jane's intentions, I paste a delighted expression on my face and warm my features with a friendly smile, determined to not let her get the better of me, as that is all I can hold myself responsible for.

"Ladies—ladies?" Ms. Thompson's voice rings above the hum of the busy lobby. "I wanted to bring you here one last time as a group before the hotel opens so you could take in how far we have come." She gestures around the expansive space with a sweeping arm movement. Fresh floral arrangements top every table surface, the biggest one atop the round table set centre stage, close to the front entrance. "Our opening date is set, and we are expecting quite the hullabaloo, if I do say so myself."

I see Miss Smythe in the crowd and offer a quick wave in her direction as our fifth-floor group joins the eighth-floor maids.

"Everyone at the hotel has worked hard to prepare for the grand opening, and Mr. Olson wanted you to be included in the event updates." Ms. Thompson looks over our heads as she gestures behind us, toward a crowd gathering in the lobby.

A round of applause begins as a slow rumble, gaining enthusiasm and speed when Mr. Olson climbs onto an elevated box. He stands tall above the crowd's heads, many of them clad in service hats, their style and shape depicting at a moment's glance the wearer's role in the hotel.

"Thank you." Mr. Olson's handsome features light up in an elated expression as the applause echoes around the room. "Thank you all. I have gathered you together this afternoon to inform you that The Hotel Hamilton will welcome guests with a grand opening celebration on Saturday, June eighteenth."

After attempting to continue, Mr. Olson gives way to the crowd, allowing them to hoot and holler at the news. He stands with patience, a sincere look of satisfaction spread across his features. He waits several minutes for the cheers and applause from the hotel staff to die down. "I am pleased to hear your enthusiasm not only for the celebration yet to come but also for a job well done. You should be proud of yourselves." Mr. Olson extends his arms as if to gather each of us into his warm regard. "There is still plenty of work yet to be done, but we have come further than I imagined possible in a short amount of time. It is because of each of you that we have arrived here."

Another burst of applause reverberates around the room, and I am once again caught up in the excitement. I catch Louisa's attention and stifle a giggle behind my palm as she struts her own glee with a quick little two-step, then sends me a confident wink.

Mr. Olson's voice cracks a fraction as he shouts his departing message. "Thank you again for all that you have done. We look forward to working with each of you to make the hotel a memorable experience for all of our guests."

"Did you hear that?" I lean close to Lou and whisper in her ear. "They look forward to working with each of us. Do you think perhaps they have already decided? Do we actually have jobs?" Relief courses through me, and I feel as though my knees might buckle at any moment. What if all my prayers are to be answered?

"Ladies." Yanking me from my dreamlike state, Ms. Thompson's voice commandeers my attention. "We will meet on the fifth floor."

Louisa joins me for the trip up the stairs. "Don't jump to conclusions, Clara. I am sure all is well, but Ms. Thompson said we were to return Monday for the news." Louisa lets a couple of girls pass us on the landing. "I don't want you to lose your head over this. Not now. We still have the afternoon's tasks to complete, okay?"

"I promise." I wrap Lou's hand in mine, giving it a tight

squeeze. "You have to admit, though, we stand a good chance now."

Louisa looks over her shoulder at me, a glint in her eye. "We've always stood a good chance, Clara. You just needed to believe in yourself in order to see it."

We are full of lighthearted laughter as we reach the fifth floor, quietening our voices and our mood as we gather with the others.

Ms. Thompson appraises the group, counting us off to ensure we've all returned and are ready to proceed. "This afternoon, all that remains to do is one final timed test. Just as before, I will assign you a partner and a guest room to clean."

Ms. Thompson paces the width of the hall, which I recognize as a signal that she is about to present a challenge. I inhale sharply, feeling anticipation build within me.

"The catch is, ladies"— Ms. Thompson looks up from her pacing—"we have left each room rather in shambles."

We look to one another with a chorus of gasps, with both shock at the thought of our beautiful rooms being ransacked and immense concern over having to return such a guest room to its previous stately presentation.

"It is true. While we were enjoying the levity of Mr. Olson's announcement, the rooms were"—Ms. Thompson's lips twist as she restrains her words—"visited by the unruliest of guests."

Another gasp punctuates the fifth-floor hall.

"You will have one hour." Ms. Thompson's words are curt. "All items on your notecard must be checked off for you to pass the test. You are responsible only for your guest room. Together, we have more than covered the duties outside of the rooms, so they will not require your attention today."

Ms. Thompson grips her clipboard with both hands and narrows her eyes, striking a shard of fear into my heart as she speaks. "One hour may just be enough for two well-trained maids to accomplish this task. I wish you all luck and Godspeed."

With that, Ms. Thompson reads from her list, partnering each of us and assigning each pair a room. She instructs us to wait outside the door with the room key at the ready until she gives the "go" command.

The matron pairs Louisa with the capable Hazel, each of whom seems delighted to be in the other's company. "Miss Morgan?" Ms. Thompson seems to ask instead of direct.

"Yes, ma'am." Jane steps forward to await her instruction.

"You will join Miss Wilson in room 512." I sense Ms. Thompson's eyes wash over me, and I suspect she has paired us together on purpose.

"Yes, ma'am." Jane catches my eye and motions for me to join her outside guest room 512.

Passing Louisa and Hazel on the way to our assigned room, I feel the encompassing sympathy Lou exudes toward me. She would switch places with me in a heartbeat. This I know.

I am responsible for myself and my reactions. I recite the words in my head, desperate to embed them into my soul and praying they will be at the ready when I need to follow their instructions.

We stand in front of room 512, Jane fiddling with the key. I decide I have nothing to lose by trying to set some ground rules. "It will be better for both of us if we can work together on this test."

"Better for you maybe," Jane says with an audible huff. "I know it was you who caused my cart to tip over the other day."

"I was sorry the moment it happened." I meet Jane's eyes with a sincere apology. "Truly, I am sorry."

"You hurt me, Clara." Jane's eyes moisten, and I reprimand myself again for my poor behaviour. "You hurt my feelings."

"I was angry with you. It is no excuse, I realize." Searching my brain for words that could make things right, I wrench forward a feeble reply. "I helped you straight away with tidying the cart."

"True. You did," Jane concedes, her hand swiping at a tear about to escape.

Ms. Thompson interrupts our conversation. "Ladies, on your mark. Three. Two. One. Go!"

Jane steps forward, sliding the key into the lock and turning it with a quick flick of her wrist. The door swings open, and both of us gape at the disarray of the room before us. Never have I seen a room in such a mess—chair cushions on the floor, a lampshade askew. My worry leans toward the state of the washroom, and I cringe at the thought of what might await us there.

Fear takes hold of my stomach and squeezes. As I survey the room, a nervous bubble of laughter bursts from my lips. "I wonder who got to mess up the place for us. That is one job I might enjoy."

Jane erupts into a fit of giggles. Though our task is heavy, I feel a sliver of goodwill grow between us. Together, we have a mutual goal, and together is how we will tackle it.

We call out tasks from our notecards, dividing them up

as we go, and set straight to work. Jane's honesty surprises me as she admits where her weaknesses lie, preferring to take on jobs that she feels confident completing. Given our lack of time to discuss her concerns, I decide we are both best served by Jane handling the tasks she can succeed at while I take care of the rest. A sliver of pride rises within me as I spot my willingness to let Jane be responsible for her own actions.

The clock is ticking, and I feel every minute as the small hand scuttles around the face of Ms. Thompson's pocket watch.

With the cushions in their proper homes atop the chairs and the lampshade and other out-of-sort items back in their rightful places, I turn to find Jane struggling with making the bed.

"Let me give you a hand with that. A large bed, such as this is easier to make with two." Louisa flits across my mind, and I consider how pleased she will be with me. The upward quirk of my lip prods me to recognize my satisfaction. I am working alongside Jane while remaining true to myself. I will not deny that I desperately need this job. However, I am far happier succeeding as the real me, and I suspect I always will be.

I head to the bathroom. One glance at the filth-lined tub has me reaching for the small bag of baking soda tucked into my apron pocket. Cookie was kind enough to share the soda with us when Louisa and I asked earlier in the week, giving us each a small amount to test in cleaning. As Jane brings the vacuum to life, I say a silent thank you to Aunt Vivian and Cousin Josephine, grateful for their knowledge and experience and the little blue book they sent.

After several rinses, I am pleased with the tub's

outcome. I move on to the sink, using the soda and scrubbing the porcelain to a shine. I've just completed a final wipe down of the sink and counter when I hear the vacuum chortle to a ragged stop, followed displeased murmurs from Jane.

I poke my head out of bathroom, wet rag still in hand. "You okay out there?"

Jane pivots in one motion, turning her back on the long curtains and the vacuum. "Yes, of course. Why wouldn't I be?"

I am about to ask Jane what the sound was when Ms. Thompson strolls by our guest room door, calling out from the hallway, "Five minutes, ladies."

"Oh my, the time has flown. I am almost done in here." Ducking back into the bathroom, I ensure the counter is dry before I set to straightening the towels. I clutch the few bottles of cleaning products to my chest and move toward the cleaning cart positioned inside the open guest room door.

With Jane turning off the vacuum and wrapping the cord, all tasks listed on our notecards are complete. I am pleased with myself and with Jane. Together, we overcame our challenges, each of us using our strengths and proving we can work together after all. Jane may need a little more time and perhaps more prodding, but she will come along, and I will be there to help her along the way.

My back is to Jane as I check the cart, ensuring I have returned all supplies to their shelves. "I am going to push this into the hall. We can load the vacuum out there. It will be easier to move the cart without the heft of the vacuum weighing down the back end."

With no response from Jane, I try again. "Everything good, then?"

Jane catches up to me and pushes the vacuum into the hall. "Everything is done," she says as we heave the machine onto the ledge of the cart together.

Jane closes the room's door behind us, signalling we have completed our tasks.

To the left of the guest room, we stand side by side, our backs inches away from resting on the wall. "I knew we could do it if we worked together." Filled with the satisfaction of a job well done, I can hardly wait to tell Lou how I stayed true to my considerate self while maintaining my diligent work ethic. I am enough, just as I am, and I couldn't be happier with the realization.

Jane's eyes fall to her shoes, her only reply a subtle dip of her head.

"Time. That is time, ladies." Ms. Thompson passes us as she makes her rounds, ensuring all maids have cleared out of their assigned rooms.

Ms. Thompson's return is far quicker than I expect, but I suppose that inspecting a room occurs at a much greater speed than cleaning one does. I stifle a chuckle at my gaiety. This kind of joy has eluded me for months, or perhaps even years.

Ms. Thompson uses her master key and steps inside. Jane and I pivot, rotating our view past the open guest room door. We remain in the hall and wait for Ms. Thompson's evaluation.

She opens the closet, ensuring it has seen the vacuum and that all hangers are on the designated side, neatly placed in a row. Ms. Thompson thoroughly inspects the bed, lifting the top cover to ensure the corners are precise. She opens the bedside table, finding the Bible in its rightful place.

Ms. Thompson pops out of sight as she moves around

the space. I imagine her running a finger along the windowsill, checking for a speck of dust, when Ms. Thompson startles me with a gasp.

CHAPTER 29

*F*riday, May 27, 1927

I bolt into the room, Jane following close on my heels. "What is it, ma'am?"

"Who is responsible for this?" I crane my neck but cannot see past Ms. Thompson's tall frame. Only when she turns do I spot a torn drape panel in her hands.

I am trying to make sense of what I am seeing when Jane clears her throat and steps forward. "Clara, ma'am. But it wasn't her fault. The vacuum got out of control, and before she could do anything, it sucked up the end bit of curtain."

I gasp, unable to believe my ears. "Jane."

"It is no use, Clara. We must be honest. I imagine the cost of the repair will need to come from the wages we've earned. I am happy to share the cost, as this room was my responsibility as well."

Ms. Thompson looks from me to Jane before she yanks the curtain from its rod in dramatic fashion and marches past us, calling all the girls together. "Ladies, I must show you what can happen when you are not paying all of your attention to the task at hand. We went over the care required when using the vacuum." Ms. Thompson's downturned mouth fumes with displeasure. "But we have first-hand evidence of the true nature and strength of those machines."

Ms. Thompson holds up the damaged drape for all to see. An eruption of distressed gasps shivers through the girls, pierced by the occasional "oh no." They step closer, out of curiosity or worry. Louisa's concern catches my eye, tears burning beneath my downcast lids. Stepping through the crowd, Lou reaches for me, clasping my hand in hers. "What happened?" she whispers.

All I can do is shake my head in disbelief. "Jane."

Ms. Thompson turns, directing her full attention toward me, given Jane has remained in the guest room. Her face is shadowed by the room's entrance. "I will speak with both of you privately, but I must say, Miss Wilson, I am a bit surprised."

I raise my head, meeting the matron's eyes. Louisa's advice remains fresh in my memory. I ball up my courage in the fist of my free hand, determined to view the situation as an opportunity to choose my reaction. I will not overreact or slink away from the shock and pain of Jane's accusations but will stand tall, with pride in who I am and what I have worked for. "Actually, ma'am, I would like to clear this up right now."

Ms. Thompson cocks her head to one side, a questioning expression lining her forehead. "Here? Well, go on."

I clear my throat and release my hand from Louisa's

grip, choosing to stand on my own to defend myself. "I did not damage the curtain. In fact, I did not use the vacuum in this room today." I pivot, stealing a sideways glance in Jane's direction, unsurprised by her look of disdain. "I took on the job of scrubbing the bathroom." My eyes drop to the floor with a far too practised motion, and I yank them back up, reminding myself I have no reason to feel shame. "To be honest, ma'am, I chose the washroom, thinking it the most difficult task."

A murmur from the onlookers rises and falls, and Ms. Thompson's eyes dart toward Jane as I continue.

"I—I will not take the blame for something I had no part in, ma'am. I am a good worker. My apologies if speaking out in such a forward way is viewed as ill-mannered. I realize this may very well cost me the opportunity to become a Hotel Hamilton maid."

Louisa moves closer to my side, squeezing my hand again. I imagine her gesture to be threaded with an abundance of sisterly pride. A boost of strength lengthens my spine. "But it would be dishonest and disloyal to myself and every other girl here if I did not speak the truth."

I look away from Ms. Thompson and pull Louisa close, embracing her in a sideways hug. "Someone wise recently told me I cannot control the actions of others. I am only responsible for my reaction to them."

With one arm around Louisa's waist, I return my attention to Ms. Thompson. "My apologies if I have spoken out of turn, ma'am. I understand if you wish for me to go at once."

The hall goes silent as every head swivels toward Ms. Thompson, waiting with held breaths for her reply. Behind me, I hear quiet sniffles emerge from the guest room. My heart instinctively lurches for Jane and the pain she is experiencing in this moment. She has brought this pain on herself, but no matter the circumstance, I find myself unable to close my heart off to her completely. That wouldn't be like me at all, I think as my lips tug upward.

"If you will allow me, Ms. Thompson, I would be remiss if I didn't add that Miss Morgan was of great help today. She showed a true ability to work as part of a team. I know from experience how menacing those vacuums can be, and I am inclined to believe Miss Morgan's actions regarding the drapery were nothing more than an accident." I nibble around the edges of the situation, letting Jane's decision to blame someone else remain unspoken. Her lie will be dealt with, I am sure.

"Well then." Ms. Thompson smooths her skirt before looking up to address the group as one. "It seems Miss Wilson has found honour, courage, and honesty in her experiences today. This is an excellent opportunity to remind you all that being a maid has many humbling opportunities. Miss Wilson has shown herself to be an excellent judge of moral character while immersed in a challenging situation. Though this was not today's intended test, it is certainly a lesson worth learning." Ms. Thompson takes a step toward me, placing a light hand on my shoulder. "I commend you, Miss Wilson. Your strength of character has shone bright this afternoon."

Louisa's hand wraps tighter around my own, and I wonder how long it will be before there is no feeling left in my fingers. Ms. Thompson pivots to address the group. "Ladies, I will ask each of you to return to your guest room and wait outside the door. I will be with you in a few minutes. We still have several rooms to inspect before I can release you for the day."

As the girls move about the hall, a few of them offer me a smile or a low wave. Hazel is bold enough to step toward us and wrap Louisa and me in a fierce hug of support. "I'm so pleased to have gotten the chance to know you, Clara," she says. Louisa acknowledges her words with a quick smile before accompanying Hazel around the hall corner, toward their assigned guest room.

With the hall vacant, Ms. Thompson returns her attention to me, stepping closer to include Jane, still hidden in the shadows of the guest room. With a look toward Jane, Ms. Thompson drops her chin to her chest, a small smile turning the corners of her mouth.

"Miss Wilson, it may surprise you, but I have been aware of Miss Morgan's antics for quite some time now. There is little that gets by me in this hotel, and anything that does, I allow to do so." Ms. Thompson wears a mischievous expression. My mouth opens in a soundless O shape. "In all honesty, Miss Wilson, I have been waiting for you to locate the gumption within yourself to say as much."

Ms. Thompson gestures for Jane to step forward, and Jane does so with small hesitating steps. "You see, girls, being a maid is as much about knowing who you are as a young woman as it is about presenting a clean and hospitable room. You must clearly understand what you will and will not do." Ms. Thompson's gaze sails over my head, landing squarely on Jane. "What you will and will not put up with. I have found that when you know who you are and what you stand for, you become strong in your conviction to be fully yourself."

Ms. Thompson wags a finger in the air. "Be under no illusion, ladies, The Hamilton will have its share of challenging guests. We will be under demands that might not seem congruent with the real world. This hotel will serve as the meeting place for those in high society, and I have no doubt that our world and theirs will clash from time to time. It is imperative that each of you understand that our guests' comings and goings are out of our control. The one thing we must have a handle on, like Miss Wilson so eloquently pointed out, is our reaction to those challenges.

"The best way to assert yourselves in a polite but confident manner is to acknowledge and accept your own nature. You have what it takes to be proficient maids in this hotel. However, I cannot force upon you the necessary belief in yourself. I can train you regarding a maid's duties, but the rest is up to you. You, Miss Morgan, appear to have some work to do in that regard." Though not directed toward me, Ms. Thompson's pointed stare still elicits a shiver down my spine.

"Well, that was quite an afternoon. I am sure you are eager to be on your way." Ms. Thompson appears a tad worn out herself, and I feel an appreciation for the matron and her deep, though often hidden, care of those under her command. "I will evaluate the other Miss Wilson's room next and release you for the weekend. I ask that you report back on Monday morning at nine o'clock sharp." Ms. Thompson hesitates, moving a hand to her stomach. "You have all done exceptionally well. You have made my job of deciding whom to hire a difficult one. Be proud of yourselves, and know that you are capable of great things."

"Thank you, ma'am," I reply, while Jane remains silent behind me.

A rush of air whooshes past as Jane strides from the room, in a hurry to disappear, I imagine.

Ms. Thompson calls after her as Jane all but sprints toward the back stairs and out of sight. "Oh, and Miss

Morgan, I have put you on notice. If you truly want to be an employee of the hotel, then you had best start acting like one."

Ms. Thompson winks at me. "Miss Wilson." She pivots toward the next guest room waiting for her inspection.

CHAPTER 30

Friday, May 27, 1927
I catch sight of Papa's jacket hanging on
the hook as Louisa and I step into the apartment. "Clara,
what the—" Louisa collides into me, my abrupt stop
disrupting her forward momentum.

I turn my head and see him sitting at the kitchen table,
a less than delighted expression shadowing his face.

"Papa, you are home early." I smooth the surprise from
my greeting and place my bag on the kitchen counter. "You
must be thirsty. I'll fetch you a glass of water."

"I don't want water, Clara." My world tilts at an angle,
and I do my best to ignore his tone, choosing instead to
focus on filling a glass from the tap. "What I want is to
know precisely where you girls have been all week?"

My hand shakes, spilling droplets of water across the
table as I place the glass before him. "What—what do you
mean?"

"Fool me once, Clara." Papa's eyebrows lift, and for the
first time, I see the similarity between Louisa's signature

expression and Papa's. "Sit. Both of you. We are not leaving this table until you tell me the truth."

We settle ourselves, Louisa pulling a chair closer to my own. I cannot tell whether she does so out of solidarity or pure stubbornness. Louisa rarely backs down from an argument. I stifle nervous laughter as she lifts her head and squares her shoulders, ready to commence the battle of words. Watching my sister from the corner of my eye, I marvel at her assuredness.

"We finished early this afternoon." Papa folds his hands atop the table, ignoring the glass of water I brought him. "Mr. Murray paid me my wages and sent us on our way."

My spirits lift at the mention of wages paid, and I find myself desperate to learn more. I bite the inside of my cheek to remain silent, not wishing to receive a verbal lashing for interrupting.

"I thought to myself, what a grand day it is to take my girls out to the ballpark for an ice cream and an afternoon." Papa's love of baseball is hard to tame, even when he is upset. "First year for the Asahi in the Senior League. I thought what a treat it would be to catch a few tosses before the season really gets going."

Papa's disappointment in an afternoon of entertainment missed is the least of my worries. The shame of having lied to him sits like a rock in the pit of my stomach. I glance at Louisa, wondering if we should save ourselves the angst and come clean. Louisa's determined expression has not shifted in the slightest, so I follow her lead, feeling as though I am a lamb being led to slaughter.

"Off I went, to the theatre house." His eyebrows inch further upward, and I wince at the realization of what is coming. "Imagine my surprise when I not only find you missing but learn that the management hasn't seen you in months."

"Papa, I can explain," I blurt out, earning a sharp look from Louisa.

"What Clara was going to say is"—Louisa narrows her eyes at me—"we have an excellent reason for not being where you expected."

Panic grips my chest. Louisa is about to weave another web of lies, and we are already in such a muddle. I can't imagine telling another untruth. I plead with her in my mind, willing her to explain our whereabouts in a manner he will understand—though I do worry there may be no such explanation that Papa will accept.

"I am waiting." Papa leans back in his chair, arms folded across his chest.

Louisa mimics Papa and crosses her own arms. "This all began when Clara, who has no reason to find herself in such a situation, was left scraping together meals with so few dollars that tough decisions had to be made. Did you know she has been covering for your lack of income by scrimping and saving, always giving you and me the best of every meal?

"She serves us the first steeping of tea, strong and sweetened with cream and sugar. Then she takes the remnants, barely coloured boiled water, to spread what little we have for as long as possible. Never once complaining. Never once sharing the burden." I am taken aback by Louisa's words, ignorant to the fact that she was even aware of the sacrifices I have been making. She certainly hid it well, I think to myself as I recall a rather recent comment regarding her preference for one sandwich over another.

"I know things have been tight, but—" Papa's eyes shift between Louisa and me.

Louisa's hand goes up to stop him. "You wanted the truth." A tilt of her head probes Papa into agreement. He gives a single nod. "When Clara found the eviction notice, she took things into her hands and sought employment at a new hotel that is due to open next month."

"How do you know about the notice?" Papa's shame spreads like a wildfire through his body, ravaging his resolute posture and crumpling his face into one of a weary old man.

"I found the letter in your coat pocket the night I helped you to bed." My words are sombre. There is no joy in pointing out another's flaws. "I wasn't being a snoop, Papa. I promise you I wasn't. You said the grocery money was there, and I was only looking for it."

"I was too late." Papa's chin falls to his chest, defeat written all over posture. "When I came home, after not finding you at the theatre, I went to Mr. Watkins and paid him the back rent for March. I figured with my news . . . Well, I figured I might be able to put us back in good standing before either of you could learn of our situation."

"News? What news?" I ask, eager for something good to hang my hat on while easing the conversation away from the less comfortable.

"I heard news today." Papa's face brightens a touch. "Mr. Murray put in a good word for me, and well, I start at the Parks Board on Monday. I will work with the landscape and such around the city."

"Papa, this is great news." The weight of my burdens lifts as they unfurl from my shoulders.

Louisa, unmoved by Papa's announcement, offers no congratulations. "Yes, but will he be able to keep a job?" Her tone is accusatory and unveiled. "We know about your trips to the liquor establishments." She waits a beat, watching his expression. "Both the legal and the illegal ones."

"Louisa!" I shriek.

"This is no time to beat about the bush." Louisa inclines her head toward Papa. "A part of the reason we are in the precarious situation with the rent is because of his imbibing. If he can't control his liquor habit, then we can't count on him to provide for us."

"He is still our father and for that reason alone is due a little respect." I usher the sentiment in a hushed tone, stunned by the path Lou has taken this conversation.

"Girls, please. Don't turn this into a disagreement between the two of you." Papa looks at Louisa with nothing but love in his eyes. "Clara, your sister is right. My drinking has caused much discomfort for our family. I will admit I faltered. I sank very low, especially over the past several months.

"When your mama died, the drink helped me to forget. Helped me to escape the pain." His voice cracks with anguish. "A sip of whiskey here and there to soothe my nerves made each day bearable. Then, as it became a regular indulgence, I found the liquor working to help me remember her.

"Mr. Murray found me in a heap in the garden shed, barely able to stand and not at all fit for work." Papa pauses, his gaze focused on his folded hands. "I lost my job that day and our cottage along with it."

Tears stream down my face, following my jawline before disappearing into the fabric of my dress.

Papa lets out a deep exhale, one I fear might crumple him. "When we moved to the apartment, it became even easier to find reasons and ways to escape. The money we had saved disappeared so quickly, and it wasn't long before I was falling behind with the rent."

Washing a hand over his face, Papa continues, his voice sombre and heavy with regret. "I hope you can forgive me. I am doing all I can to make things right again."

Papa takes a sip of water as his words hang in the air between us. "All I can say is that I will try. I am trying for you, Louisa, and for you, Clara. For the memory of your mama, I promise you I am trying."

Louisa's demeanour thaws at his words, her posture relaxing into a less confrontational stance. "I suppose that is all we can ask of you."

Papa offers her a weak smile.

We sit in silence for several minutes, the three of us digesting all that has been said.

Louisa shifts in her seat. "I suppose we owe you an explanation as well." Her acquiescence of our untruths feels as though she is a castle letting down her drawbridge, and I release a sigh of relief.

Papa meets her eyes, inclining his head. "Tell me about this hotel. I assume this is the actual location where you have been spending your days."

I jump at the chance to steer the conversation, cutting off Louisa before she can utter a word. "Yes, The Hotel Hamilton will open on June eighteenth." I link my arm with Louisa's. "Both of us applied and were accepted into the training program. We have been going through the process for the past two weeks. If things go as we hope, we will officially be hotel maids come Monday morning."

I can't hide my excitement. "We hope you are proud of us, whatever the outcome. Our training wage will help bring the rent up to date. Ms. Thompson, the hotel's matron, will pay us the salary we have earned through our two weeks of training on Monday too. We are to be at the hotel by nine o'clock, as that is when she will announce who has been hired on."

I tap a finger to my lip, straining to remember the math Louisa and I worked out regarding the overdue rent. "With your payment of March's rent and Louisa's and my wages from the past two weeks, we can cover April. We will still be behind, but if all three of us continue to earn going forward, there is a chance we will make it up in time."

Papa looks at me with a question forming on his lips. "In time?"

"Oh, I forgot to tell you." I smother a nervous smile as I consider how Papa might take the news of my going behind his back to the building manager. "Mr. Watkins has negotiated an extension for us to the end of June."

"You spoke with Mr. Watkins?" Papa's surprise is painted across his face.

"Yes—yes, I did. When I saw the eviction letter. I—I realize it may not have been my place to do so, but—" I stammer over my words like a child with their hand caught in the cookie tin.

"Well, Clara, I am surprised. Impressed, but also surprised." Papa's soft chuckle grows into a roaring laugh. "It is just the sort of thing your mother would have done."

"Oh, Papa." I am standing and moving toward him in one fluid motion, eager to hug the father I have been missing since he disappeared into his grief. I wrap my arms around his neck and squeeze as every emotion, every disappointment, and every fresh joy rushes to the surface.

Seconds later, I feel the crush of Louisa's body as she cloaks us with her own fierce embrace. Together, we are a family, and though we may have a few bruises and even a crack or two, we are beautiful because of who we are and what we've experienced together.

Late afternoon turns into evening, and as the moon rises over the Vancouver skyline, we share our lives and our stories with one another. Louisa and I tell Papa about the hotel and our training. We entertain him with details of the luxurious guest rooms and the ornate features of the eighth floor. We shake our heads as we relate Jane's misguided antics and laugh over stories of the friends we've gained along the way.

As I collapse into bed, I can feel the floor beneath me is sturdy and sure once more. I may not have all the answers, and the future remains a mystery to me, but I now know what I am made of. Louisa is right. If you know who you are, you have all you'll ever need. The only thing you can control in this world is your reaction to it. Nothing more. Nothing less.

EPILOGUE

Saturday, June 18, 1927

The air inside the hotel feels electric. Every single staff member is in attendance for the grand opening of Vancouver's newest hotel.

The catering staff bustles from the kitchen to the banquet rooms, whooshing past to prepare for this evening's gala event. Cookie has put together several towering trays of delicate sweets, their exquisite detail making them far too pretty to eat, though she argues otherwise as she slides Louisa and me each a treat to taste.

"Try them for quality's sake." She chuckles. "Somebody's got to taste them before the highfalutin have at them."

With the sweet treats lingering on our tongues, we set about arranging large bouquets for each guest floor's main hallway table. When that task is complete, Louisa and I arrive on the eighth floor with a cart full of smaller spring bundles, each with a personalized card signed by Mr. Olson. There is one bunch of flowers in each room expecting a guest for the evening. Miss Smythe greets us at the service lift with a quick embrace, the excitement of the day raising all spirits. We pass the flowers to her and return the empty cart to the kitchen.

As we round the corner, the cart clattering through the corridor, a flash of movement catches my eye. I see him before he slips out of sight around a bend. The little boy, the one I shared my apple with several weeks back, is roaming the hotel. With a tinge of worry for him, I contemplate the outcome should he be discovered. Today is not the day to set Chef's nerves on edge. His shouts and hollers have already been soaring about the halls for the past several hours.

I send Louisa to return the cart to the kitchen while I track the boy's trajectory. A wall of noise greets me as bellboys, maids, and porters bustle in the chaos of the hotel lobby. I spot his dark mop of hair under an oversized hall table, his eyes wide as he takes in the surrounding commotion. I kneel with care, I pretend to retrieve an item from the floor. Meeting his eyes, I jerk my head to the side, indicating his time to vacate has arrived. Hiding his slight body with the wide folds of my skirt, I usher him toward the safety of Cookie's pastry kitchen.

One look at the lad and Cookie melts into the mothering sort I know her to be. She places a finger sandwich in each of his hands and prods him out the door. "Off with you now. We can't have you underfoot today. Bigger things going on today. Yes, indeed, bigger things going on."

I watch as the boy skips down the alleyway, with both hands, a sandwich in each, raised above his head like a champion. I can't help but notice his ever-present joy. His appreciation for the smallest gifts radiates from his shy smile. He has little, yet he chooses joy. He turns one last time to wave at me, and I am struck by the realization that gratitude's true worth shows itself during challenging times. I lift my arm over my head and wave back to him, wishing him well as he scampers through the lane.

Cookie stands beside me, a soft sigh upon her lips. I place a hand on her arm, thankful for the friend and kindred spirit I've found in her.

Re-entering the lobby, I stop short and almost collide with Jane, her arms full of pillows to stock the linen cupboard. "Oh, Jane, pardon me." I move to the side, allowing her to pass.

Jane walks forward, then pivots to face me. "You know, Clara . . . Well, I just wanted to say I'm sorry. I didn't set out to make you look bad." Jane's usual confidence is missing, along with a full-time position on the fifth floor. Hired as a part-time employee and branded as the "socialite maid," by the other hotel staff, Jane appears to be feeling the repercussions of her actions. "I suppose—I . . ."

"We've both done things we are not proud of. I am pleased, truly, that you can remain in Vancouver." I don't have the time or the inclination to watch the poor girl squirm. "Let's just try to stay on the right side of one another from now on. Shall we?"

"Yes. That sounds like an excellent idea." Jane searches the floor over the heap of pillows in her arms. "Maybe one day we can be friends."

"Maybe one day," I add, before hearing my name being called from across the lobby.

Ms. Thompson waves me over, ticking off her list as she fires questions at me about what has been done. "Very well, Miss Wilson." The matron checks her pocket watch and contains a surprised exclamation. "It's nearly four. Gather everyone. It's time to find our positions."

A few moments later, we are standing in a long V-shaped line, ready to welcome the crowd bustling on the sidewalk. The jubilant voices outside filter past the glass doors, sending a shiver of excitement the length of my spine. The reminder of Mama's words makes me smile. *Everyone is on the outside of something at one time or another.*

Yes, Mama, but this time I am on the inside.

Mr. Olson takes a deep breath before signalling to the doorman. The doorman double-checks the straightness of our line and inclines his head toward Mr. Hamilton. The hotel's owner waits with an impatient expression creasing the lines of his wide forehead, his back to the hotel's front doors. His excitement matches that of a child about to visit the fair, and I can't blame him. Today is an exceptional day indeed.

The doors open with a whoosh of air and cheers from those waiting for the festivities to begin. Mr. Hamilton steps forward onto the plush red carpet beyond the hotel's entrance. He spreads his arms wide, and his voice booms out, amplified by the thrill of the day. "Ladies and gentlemen, Welcome to The Hamilton."

AUTHOR NOTES

~

I would be remiss if I didn't first let you know that The Hotel Hamilton is a fictional hotel, one I created as I began the deep dive into Vancouver's history. There was indeed a hotel situated at the same location as the Hamilton's fictional presence but until recently, I wasn't able to determine further details about the real hotel. I chose the location due to its proximity to both The Hotel Georgia and the courthouse when I spotted a "hotel" marked on a 1926 Vancouver map. It was months later when I learned that the real hotel was called The York and was used primarily as staff quarters for The Hotel Vancouver. Despite being a fictional hotel, the geographic region the novel takes place in is located on the traditional, ancestral, and unceded territories of the xʷməθkʷəẏəm (Musqueam), Sḵwx̱wú7mesh (Squamish), and Səlilwətaɬ (Tsleil-Waututh) nations in Vancouver, British Columbia.

You may have noticed several Canadianisms among the

pages. Given the novel's Canadian location, spelling, along with the imperial system (Canada used the imperial system until 1975 before switching to metric), the British use of Ms. instead of Miss or Mrs. for *Ms. Thompson*, and more were inserted purposefully as a nod to my homeland. That being said, learning Canadian English is not for the faint of heart given that we have borrowed from both the British and American languages while adding a few humdingers ourselves.

As with all fiction, dates and facts don't always line up the way a story demands. The package Clara receives from her aunt and cousin in the United Kingdom would not have arrived as quickly as the story indicates given that Royal Airmail did not exist in Canada until mid 1939. The package would have taken a full two to three weeks traveling first by steamer ship and then by rail car to the depot in Vancouver. Canada retained the British mail delivery system name until the 1960s and then officially became the Canada Post Corporation in 1981.

In addition, the news of Lindbergh's successful transatlantic flight was actually announced on May 21, 1927 but in order to have it line up with the story, I pushed the date ahead two days so it could be a topic of conversation for the girls.

I have listed the UK hotel Aunt Vivian and cousin Josephine are employed at as The Grosvenor, Victoria Station. After hours of rabbit hole research regarding the hotel's name in 1927, I contacted the hotel for verification. Unfortunately, this remains a piece of historical fact I am unable to confirm. If you happen to know the hotel's name throughout history, please reach out to me. I would be extremely grateful.

Sad as it is, the *White Lunch Cafeteria* was in existence in

Vancouver in 1927. The chain of restaurants opened its doors in 1913 and made it a mission to hire and serve only "white" workers and patrons. Though the company's blatant and distasteful operating procedures eventually phased out, the stigma associated with the restaurant remained until the last restaurant closed in the early 1980s.

You may be wondering about prohibition in British Columbia as the United States remained dry from 1920 to 1933. BC however, repealed prohibition very early on and was actually known as the "wettest province" in Canada. Prohibition came into effect in BC on October 1, 1917. On June 15, 1921, after a referendum was voted on, the BC government introduced legislation that gave them complete control over all liquor sales and liquor sales tax throughout the province.

Calling themselves the *Liquor Control Board of British Columbia*, they established a few interesting rules some of which included alcohol sales being legal on specific days and hours of the week. If a bar sold liquor by the glass, the bar was not permitted to play music in the establishment. Then there was the rule that women were required to enter all drinking establishments through a separate entrance from the men and were not allowed in the male drinking areas of the establishment.

I haven't even delved into the stories surrounding the rum running that took place off the shores of British Columbia, but if you ever wondered where some of that prohibition alcohol in the United States came from, you need not look any further than the BC coastline. Several BC men made a small fortune doing legal business in international waters. It was only those who traveled into US waters who were at risk of being arrested and prosecuted.

The Newbury Apartment building where Clara, Louisa,

and their father live is based on a real building. The Manhattan Apartments were built in 1907 and had easy access to Vancouver's streetcar system. You can catch a glimpse of the inside of the apartments in the movie *Look Who's Talking*. The building was threatened with demolition but was saved and turned into Co-op housing for those needing a less expensive option in a very expensive city.

One of my favourite historical finds was the horse drawn milk delivery system. Horse drawn deliveries really did take place throughout the city and even continued well into the 1950s. The streets were often bustling with cars, jitneys, horse drawn carriages, bicycles and pedestrians. The major intersections employed officers to direct traffic with stop/go paddles, before the emergence of traffic lights came into existence in 1928.

If you'd like to know more about the fun and factual aspects of my research, be sure to subscribe to my newsletter via my website at www.tanyacwilliams.com to receive the newsletter exclusive eBook, *At the Corner of Fiction & History* which details the facts and follies that presented themselves to me as dug into the history of Vancouver in the 1920s.

ACKNOWLEDGMENTS

~

This novel would not have made it into your hands had it not been for several amazing people. To Justin, who this book is dedicated to, thank you for pausing at a moment's notice to listen to me ramble. Thank you for your insight, and for your quick and blessedly easy fixes when the story was getting away from me.

I am immensely grateful to have writer friends with exceptional senses of both story and humour, who in addition to this, never fail to tell me when I am overthinking things. Thank you to Diana, Kelsey, and Carla.

To my HNS After Party friends. Our monthly writerly chats keep me thinking, inspired, and entertained. I consider myself fortunate to know each of you.

To my editor, Victoria Griffin, thank you for making the story shine and for taking on the challenge when I decided to use Canadian English for this series. You are a wizard with words and I am inspired by your talent and grateful for your friendship.

The stunning cover for Welcome To The Hamilton is a result of some of my favourite people, all of whom I owe a debt of gratitude to. Thank you to Donna for conversations that lead to solutions. Thank you to Emily for being a spectacular person and a dream model. Thank you to Kari for always having my back, no matter what that job entails. Thank you to Dave for being ever so patient with both me and the camera. These four dear people made the photo shoot a huge success and I am not kidding when I say, I would keep writing novels, just so we could do it all over again.

Thank you to my cover designer Ana Grigoriu-Voicu for taking the above-mentioned photograph to the next level and making it a dream come true cover. I am in awe of your creativity and I can't wait to see what you design next.

I would also like to thank the theatre department at Earl Marriott Secondary School and most especially Linda for their generous loan of clothing, props, and more. You helped make our cover shoot fun and successful.

I was fortunate to work with several historical professionals while researching for this novel. Thank you to John Atkin for your insightful and enjoyable tour around the city. Huge thanks go out to the research librarians at the Vancouver Public Library, you are rockstars and so very appreciated. Thank you to Kira Baker at the City of Vancouver Archives. Thank you to Stacey N. Gilkinson at the City of Surrey Archives.

A special thanks to my Dad for being a far better

"Googler" than me. I was able to watch hours of historic Vancouver footage because he located them on my behalf.

Thank you to my very large extended family for your interest in what I do. Your support, stories of days gone by, and circle of laughter and love always lets me know exactly where I came from.

To my newsletter readers, you are the fuel that kicked off how Clara and Louisa would interact. Thank you for replying to my survey questions about sisters. Your comments were immensely helpful and were responsible for shaping the sisters into who they were meant to be. Thanks also to my own sister, without whom, I would have only half a memory of childhood, for she is the other half.

I consider myself exceptionally lucky to have beta and advanced readers who make my world a better place. Thank you for reading, reviewing, finding the typos, and more. Your support and enthusiasm is what I reach for when I am lost in the words. You are the flashlight that guides me through the mist. Hugs to every one of you.

Thank you to you, dear reader, for taking time out of your day to read Welcome To The Hamilton. I hope the story made you laugh, cry, and feel while exploring your own thoughts on family, challenging times, and our human desire to control the world around us.

ABOUT THE AUTHOR

~

A writer from a young age, Tanya E Williams loves to help a reader get lost in another time, another place through the magic of books. History continues to inspire her stories and her insightful view into the human condition deepens her character's experiences and propels them on their journey. Ms. Williams' favourite tales speak to the reader's heart, making them smile, laugh, cry, and think.

ALSO BY TANYA E WILLIAMS

Becoming Mrs. Smith

Stealing Mr. Smith

A Man Called Smith

All That Was

Printed in Great Britain
by Amazon

27269497R00172